"Winsome and sweetly haunting, *Letters from My Sister* brims with family love, humor, romance, and mysterious insights into the meaning of memories. But Valerie Fraser Luesse also delves into power dynamics and explores the prejudices that can lurk inside people with the best of intentions. Callie is a delightful heroine, challenging the way things have always been done but bounded by love of family and community. A thoroughly engaging novel that probes deep."

Sarah Sundin, bestselling and Christy Award–winning author of *The Sound of Light* and *Until Leaves Fall in Paris*

"*Letters from My Sister* drew me in on the first page with the delightful Callie Bullock, and Luesse's lyrical style and wonderful characters kept me glued to the story. Meals, shopping . . . everything waited until the last page."

Patricia Bradley, *USA Today* bestselling author of the Natchez Trace Park Rangers series and the Pearl River series

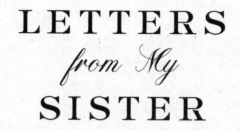

LETTERS
from My
SISTER

Books by Valerie Fraser Luesse

Missing Isaac
Almost Home
The Key to Everything
Under the Bayou Moon
Letters from My Sister

LETTERS
from My
SISTER

A Novel

VALERIE FRASER LUESSE

Revell

a division of Baker Publishing Group
Grand Rapids, Michigan

© 2023 by Valerie Fraser Luesse

Published by Revell
a division of Baker Publishing Group
Grand Rapids, Michigan
www.revellbooks.com

Printed in the United States of America

Library of Congress Cataloging-in-Publication Data
Names: Luesse, Valerie Fraser, author.
Title: Letters from my sister / Valerie Fraser Luesse.
Description: Grand Rapids, Michigan : Revell, a division of Baker Publishing Group, [2023]
Identifiers: LCCN 2022060127 | ISBN 9780800741600 (paperback) | ISBN 9780800742690 (casebound) | ISBN 9781493439744 (ebook)
Subjects: LCGFT: Christian fiction. | Novels.
Classification: LCC PS3612.U375 L48 2023 | DDC 813/.6—dc23/eng/20230105
LC record available at https://lccn.loc.gov/2022060127

Scripture used in this book, whether quoted or paraphrased by the characters, is from the King James Version of the Bible.

Sacred Harp hymns quoted in this book are from *The Sacred Harp 1991 Edition* (Carrollton, GA: Sacred Harp Publishing Company, Inc., 1991).

The author is represented by the literary agency of Stoker Literary.

Baker Publishing Group publications use paper produced from sustainable forestry practices and post-consumer waste whenever possible.

23 24 25 26 27 28 29   7 6 5 4 3 2 1

In loving memory of two sisters—
my maternal grandmother, Icie Wyatt McCranie,
and my great-aunt, Effie Jane Wyatt

ONE

allie Bullock traced an imaginary circle on the windowpane, framing a cluster of ladies in their picnic dresses—swirls of fine cotton in shades of spring. Like pastel swans, they glided across the lawn, gathering in flocks of three or four to preen, pose, and cast an inquisitive eye on their surroundings.

"Deliver me from the company of women," Callie said as she completed the circle.

Her older sister, Emmy, came to stand behind her and followed her gaze. "I hope you'll make an exception for me, Callie, or I'll have to sleep upstairs with the boys. Sometimes they smell."

They laughed as they looked out the window at all the neighbors who had come to enjoy the annual fish fry and picnic their parents hosted on May Day, after the men seined the creek.

"I'll bet you those women spend the whole day lamenting the scandalous rise of hemlines in ladies' magazines," Callie said.

"Could you endure the horror more easily if I let you wear my new blue and tan?" Emmy nodded toward their shared dressing table.

"Might ease the pain." Callie sat down and stared into the mirror as her sister placed the wide-brimmed, tan linen hat on her head and carefully adjusted its band of pale blue raw silk, which was tied into a bow in back.

There stood Emmy with a shiny cloud of golden hair swept up into a perfect pompadour under her Gainsborough—Emmy with eyes the color of aquamarines and flawless ivory skin. She looked nothing like Callie, with her ebony eyes and thick, curly cascade of deep chestnut hair, now subdued into an elaborate French braid—Emmy's handiwork. No one would guess they were even related, but they were sisters and soul mates, just two years apart—Emmy twenty and Callie eighteen.

Callie heard a knock at the door just before Hepsy stepped in. Hepzibah Jordan worked as the Bullocks' cook and housekeeper, but she was far more than an employee. Hepsy kept the entire household running smoothly and was a trusted counselor and confidante to all the women in the family, as well as to Callie's brother George, who was her favorite. She was slim but strong, her eyes a pale amber against bronze skin. She wore her hair braided and neatly gathered into a dignified upsweep.

"Girls, your mama's lookin' for you," she said. "Best get on out there."

"On our way, Hepsy," Emmy said. "How are you holding up?"

"Considerin' I'm 'bout to feed half the county, I reckon I'm alright. Your mama got me some good help for today, so we gon' make it."

Callie and Emmy followed her out, abandoning the refuge of their room to join the crowd. They were standing together on the lower porch of their parents' house when they spotted Ryder Montgomery. Callie rolled her eyes at the sight of him approaching in his pinstriped seersucker suit and perfectly matching boater hat. "Probably spent more time choosing his outfit than any woman here," she whispered to Emmy.

Ryder climbed the front steps, bowed, and kissed each of them on the hand. "If it isn't the fair Bullock maidens, looking lovely as two summer roses."

Emmy all but recoiled, discreetly wiping her hand against the back of her dress. Something about Ryder "brought out the Mama" in Emmy, their brother Sam always said. She offered him a starched greeting. "I trust you and Lucinda are well."

"Good as gold." He grinned and winked at her, tipping his hat as he made a beeline for Minnie Weeden, the voluptuous daughter of a scrappy couple who had just moved into the community to run the cotton gin. Minnie, Hepsy said, was "common as a house cat and not as particular."

"Do you think he's sincere about *anything?*" Callie asked.

Emmy shook her head. "The only thing Ryder's sincere about is getting what he wants, no matter who he hurts in the process."

"Why do you let him get to you, Em? He's so predictable— not worth worrying about, if you ask me."

Emmy rubbed the hand Ryder had kissed. "I'm not sure that's true. Look, there's Lucinda."

Ryder's wife was refined and striking, with deep auburn hair and smoky gray eyes. Emmy and Callie watched her move as far away from Ryder as she could, distancing herself from the humiliating stares as her philandering husband made a spectacle of himself chasing after the ginner's daughter.

"No woman deserves to be treated like that," Emmy said. "And to think she could've had George."

As the musicians began to play, all the children at the picnic gathered around the maypole, its long multicolored ribbons streaming down from the top. They chose their colors and began a circuitous dance around the tall pole, plaiting the ribbons over and under each other.

An army of kitchen help, discreetly and efficiently directed by Hepsy, filed toward the long, rectangular tables laid end to end at the front edge of the lawn, each one covered with a crisply ironed white tablecloth. One after another, Hepsy's crew streamed out of the kitchen and around the house, carrying mounded bowls of coleslaw and potato salad made with Hepsy's homemade mayonnaise; cast-iron pots of long-simmered collard greens seasoned with ham hocks; cut-glass plates of sliced onions and last summer's canned bread-and-butter pickles and dills; and finally, platter after platter of golden-fried bass, bream, and catfish. Off to the side, a single table, probably ten feet long, was overladen with layer cakes, cobblers, and pies, seven wooden freezers of hand-turned ice cream lined up like soldiers in front of it. Some of the servers placed baskets of Hepsy's homemade dinner rolls on every table and quilt on the grounds while others poured and refreshed glasses of sweet tea and lemonade.

As Emmy joined the throng of guests, Callie drifted, looking for a quiet spot where she could observe the whole to-do at a distance. She paid her respects to the women gathered around her mother and then slipped through the crowd to a solitary rope swing hanging from a centuries-old oak near a rear corner of the house. Giving a light push with her foot, she leaned back so she could look up into the branches as she glided back and forth, stirring a gentle breeze.

The white oak was at least eighty feet tall, its trunk so big that Callie's two oldest brothers, James and George, could stand on either side of the trunk, reach their arms around it, and never touch fingers.

From the swing, she watched George dip ice cream for some of the senior ladies. As he set the serving spoon on a white napkin, someone across the lawn caught his eye—Lucinda.

Callie watched Ryder's long-suffering wife, wondering what George was thinking as he looked at her. She jumped at the unexpected voice behind her. "Sooner or later, Miss Bullock, you'll have to talk to *somebody*."

She turned to see Knox Montgomery, Ryder's twin brother, standing behind her. Dragging her foot to stop the swing, she smiled up at him. "I guess you'll have to do."

Such a strange thing about the Montgomery brothers—if you didn't know them, you probably couldn't tell them apart, but once you did know them, they barely resembled each other. The twins had the same dark hair, but Knox kept his neatly combed while his gadabout brother always looked like he'd just stepped off a sailboat. Their eyes were the same shade of ice-blue but looked at the world through completely different lenses. Ryder's indifferent stare reflected his selfish nature but could turn deceitfully charming, should it suit his purpose. Knox viewed everything and everybody through the constant and true filter of his innate kindness and compassion, which you sensed when he looked at you. Ryder was a shallow mud puddle, his brother a deep, deep well.

Knox sat down on the grass beside the swing. "Give me the lay o' the land?"

"Well, let's see." Callie surveyed the lawn. "The Bartell sisters are actively—and obviously—trolling for husbands."

"All five of them?"

"All five. Be glad you're taken. Up on the porch, Miss Nicey Malone is leading a shocking discussion about the raising of hemlines in ladies' magazines. Miss Nicey is an anti-ankle-ist."

"As well she should be." Knox stretched out his legs and leaned back on one elbow. "I don't suppose you'd take pity and share Emmy's whereabouts to spare me the ordeal of trying to find her in this hungry mob?"

Callie watched as he searched the crowd for her sister, his eyes wide and hopeful, his lips slightly parted as if he were holding his breath until he found her. The expression on his face flooded Callie with a peculiar fear that had long plagued her. Perfection made her uneasy. The most pristine lawn was the very one that fire ants would tear into if somebody didn't look out. The prettiest Lady Baltimore cake at the church fellowship was the one most likely to get knocked off the table and ruined if everybody wasn't careful. And the love that Knox and Emmy felt for each other—something anybody could see the moment they were together—was as perfect as anything could be, like a pearl of great price, sure to attract thieves and marauders.

Callie scanned the crowd and spotted Emmy, as she always could in any situation. "There she is."

Knox hurried to his fiancée, and they took each other by the hands—the only public show of affection Aurelia Bullock allowed her daughters—then returned to the swing together.

"Shouldn't you two kiss or something?" Callie teased Knox and Emmy to chase away her own misgivings.

"I'm going to smother you with a pillow the minute you fall asleep tonight," Emmy said.

Knox offered an arm to each sister. "Ladies, it would be my honor to escort you to the feed trough."

The three of them worked their way through the crowd to the food tables, then found a shaded quilt to settle on. Soon a parade of young men made their pilgrimage to Callie, as they always did. She was polite—or tried to be—but quickly tired of them all.

"I'm going for a walk," she said as one of Hepsy's helpers came around to collect her empty plate.

"Better to be a moving target?" Knox asked.

"Exactly." Callie dusted a few cake crumbs from her dress and strolled around the edge of the gathering, stopping here and there to greet her parents' friends and neighbors, as was expected of her. Just beyond the far reaches of the crowd, which covered the front yard and wrapped halfway around one side of the house, Callie saw a stranger standing a few rows into her father's field.

Ordinarily, she would never approach a man she didn't know, but he was openly examining her father's cotton and wasn't dressed in work clothes, so he must be a guest of her parents. Moving closer, she could see that he looked to be about George's age, late twenties or so. He was probably six feet tall. His beard and mustache were neatly trimmed, cut close to his face, and his tousled hair—longer than most men wore theirs—was a golden brown with honey-colored sun streaks. He wore gray trousers, a white shirt with the sleeves rolled up to his elbows, and no tie.

Kneeling to study a cotton plant, he picked up a handful of field dirt and was sifting it through his fingers when he looked up and caught Callie staring at him.

Smiling, he stood and lifted his hand in a half wave. She waved back and walked to the edge of the field. "Good afternoon," she said.

He dusted his hands together to knock off the dirt. "Afternoon."

"Are you lost or hiding from the crowd?"

Again he smiled. It was a nice one, honest and sincere. "Maybe a little of both. How about you?"

"Well, I live here, so I'm definitely not lost. I guess that makes me a fugitive from the party."

"I'm Solomon Beckett," he said.

"Callie Bullock."

"Mr. Ira Bullock's daughter?"

"Yes. Are you new to our community, Mr. Beckett?"

"I am." He stepped out of the cotton field and came to stand beside her. Up close, Callie could see that he had unusual hazel eyes, their golden center melding into a soft bluish gray. "I met your father at the feed store last week," he was saying, "and he invited me to your picnic. I just bought the Cruz farm."

Callie frowned as she remembered it. "The old Cruz place is . . ."

"A challenge," he finished for her. "But most of the soil is good, and the land was cheap. I'm afraid I'm not as prosperous as your father."

"Nothing wrong with that. Daddy started with forty acres and two ornery mules that cussed each other all the way to the field. At least that's the way he tells it."

"Then maybe there's hope for me?"

Callie shrugged and grinned. "Maybe. Is the old house still there?"

"Such as it is. Needs a lot of work I don't have much time for."

"Oh, but it'll be worth it!" Callie forgot her usual reserve with people she barely knew. "The corner porches and the beautiful staircase—did you know Mr. Cruz carved the leaf pattern on the newels himself?"

"No, I didn't," Solomon said.

"Miss Katherine—that's what everybody called Mrs. Cruz—she must've told us about those carvings a million times. Before she got sick, she used to host Christmas tea parties for all the girls in her Sunday school class. My sister, Emmy, and I never missed one."

"You've convinced me." Solomon raised his right hand. "I solemnly swear that I'll make the house tea-party worthy again. Just as soon as I get the farm going so I don't lose it all."

"How do you mean to go about building your farm?" Callie asked. "Will you raise cotton or corn or cows . . . ?"

"Too expensive to jump into cotton right away—and I don't know enough about it yet—so I'll start with cattle."

"Beef, I imagine?"

"Black Angus, most likely."

She bent down, pulled a dandelion from the grass, and absently twirled it as she tried to imagine the overrun Cruz farm in lush pastureland and beef cattle. "I've heard Daddy talk about some of the new grasses they're trying over in Georgia. Do you think you might plant some of those?"

"First I have to clear the land and let it tell me what it's good for, then I can— What? You're looking at me like I'm crazy."

Callie was frowning, her head tilted to one side. "Where exactly did you learn to speak with dirt?"

Solomon put his hands in his pockets. "I read a lot, especially

The Progressive Farmer, but I learned most of what I know on a small farm in Missouri."

"And does it say different things—the dirt in Missouri and the fields here in Alabama?"

"It does." Solomon nodded toward the field, and Callie followed him a few rows into it. He bent down and scooped up a handful of red dirt to show her. "Where I grew up, the soil is loamy and brown, best suited to grains. Alabama dirt has iron and oxygen in it—that's what makes it red—and the oxygen helps it drain. Plus it gets hot summers and mild winters. So it loves cotton—soybeans and lots of produce crops too, but maybe cotton best of all."

Callie knelt down and scooped up a handful of rust-red earth, then let it fall through her fingers. "It's amazing, isn't it?" she said as much to herself as her new acquaintance. "Something we can't even see makes these fields want to grow cotton."

"You won't get any argument from me." Solomon stood and offered Callie his hand to help her up. He pulled a handkerchief out of his pocket and gave it to her to wipe her hands.

"Have you always farmed?" she asked.

"No, I spent quite a few years working sawmills and riverboats on the Mississippi. But I got tired of it—never being still. Farming's more—I don't know—solid, I guess."

She looked at the red dust now covering his white handkerchief. "I should wash this."

"No need." He took it from her and shook it before putting it back in his pocket. "Have you always been interested in science?" They walked through the tall cotton plants back to the edge of the field.

"I'm very interested in nature," she said after thinking about it. "The phases of the moon and the rise and fall of the rivers and the weather and wildlife and the cotton crops—would you call that science?"

"I would."

"Then I guess I'm interested in science." She reached down and plucked another dandelion, held it to her mouth, and blew, sending its miniature feathers into the air. "Hepsy—she runs our house—she says it's good luck if you blow a dandelion and all its feathers fly."

Solomon looked at the bare stem. "Looks like you've conjured yourself some luck then."

"We'll see." Callie scanned the crowd in her parents' front yard and sighed. "Maybe I'll make it back to my sister without having to endure any wearisome conversations."

"Can't be all that bad," Solomon said.

"Then what were you doing alone in Daddy's cotton field instead of squiring some female to the dessert table?"

He raised an eyebrow. "How do you know I'm not married?"

Callie pointed to his left hand and then his neck. "No ring, no tie, no wife."

Solomon laughed and nodded. "Maybe I need a missus. She'd know how to behave at big to-dos like this."

"Not to worry," Callie assured him. "I'll introduce you to my sister. Emmy's engaged, so she's out of the running for your missus, but she's very good at making people feel at home. You've got to meet your neighbors sometime. Might as well get it over with since they're all here. Give me your arm so we look respectable."

Solomon sighed and extended his elbow. Callie took it and led him toward the house.

"Just remember," she said, "if we should encounter any girl by the name of Bartell, you should act completely smitten with me or she'll have you at the altar before sundown. No one will be able to save you then."

When they reached the edge of the Bullocks' lawn, Solomon stopped at the massive white oak that held the rope swing. "Now that's impressive."

Callie waved her arm at the trunk like a magician presenting her next trick. "Behold the fabled Lookout Tree—that's what we call it anyway."

Solomon stared up at the towering oak. "Why 'Lookout'?"

"Well," Callie said, "about twenty feet up there's a big U-shaped fork where the original owner of our house, a Captain Brooks Calhoun, hid from the Home Guards who came for him during the Civil War."

"He deserted?" Solomon studied the tree, trying to see the fork.

"He made it through Chickamauga alive, but then I guess he decided he'd done his part. Rode his horse home to Alabama in the middle of the night. The guards who came for him must have looked everywhere but up because they never found him."

"What happened to him?"

"He lived to be an old man but eventually lost his mind and spent his last few years wandering the fields, looking for his regiment. My uncle Wally likes to tease Daddy about it—tells him he spent a fortune on a coward's manse. Are you contemplating desertion this very second?"

Solomon ran his free hand over the rough bark of the tree and groaned.

Callie laughed and tugged at his arm. "Come on. It won't be so bad."

She guided him through picnic tables, clusters of couples on quilts, and children racing each other to the ice cream freezers, introducing him along the way as "Daddy's friend, our new neighbor, Mr. Beckett." After navigating him to at least one member of all the families in the community, Callie led him to Emmy and Knox's quilt.

"Solomon, hello!" Knox stood and shook his hand.

"You know each other?" Callie asked.

"I handled the sale of the Cruz place," Knox explained. "Solomon Beckett, may I present Miss Emeline Bullock."

"Otherwise known as my sister, Emmy," Callie added.

Solomon made a slight bow to Emmy. "Pleased to meet you, Miss Bullock."

Emmy smiled up at him. "You're our neighbor, so 'Emmy,' 'Knox,' and 'Callie' will do. We'll skip past 'Mr. Beckett' and call you our new friend Solomon if that's alright. Won't you join us?"

"Thank you." He waited for Callie to sit down and then took a seat.

"Tell me, is the old house still there?" Emmy asked him.

"Your sister asked me the same thing. You'll be happy to hear it's still standing, hidden behind a tangle of overgrown azalea bushes and crepe myrtles that are being strangled by ivy as we speak."

"I'm so happy to hear it!" Emmy clapped her hands together. "Not the crepe myrtle strangulation, of course, but I'm delighted the house is still with us. I expect it needs lots of work, but believe me, it's a diamond in the rough."

Solomon shook his head. "Emphasis on 'rough.' You're right, though—there's something about the old house that I took to right away."

Callie made a sweeping gesture with her hands. "It's the curved porches on each side of the front door. They're like outdoor parlors."

"She's right," Emmy said. "They give the house such a graceful air. Are you living in it?"

"Camping in it might be more accurate." Solomon tasted his ice cream. "That's about the best I ever had. Who made it?"

"Hepsy," Callie answered. "She says the trick is milking the cow under a full moon. And if you ask her for the recipe, she'll leave out an ingredient. Nobody makes Hepsy's ice cream but Hepsy."

"Callie at least tried a few times," Emmy added. "I never even made the attempt. Is there anything we can do to help you settle in, Solomon? Anything you need for the house?"

"Right now, it's still in need of nails and lumber, but once I get it repaired, I'd sure appreciate some advice. Men don't know much about making a house a home."

"We'd be happy to help," Emmy said.

"Emmy's better at the domestic arts than I am," Callie told Solomon.

"That's not true," her sister countered. "You can cook circles around me. And your handwriting's prettier." She turned to Solomon. "I loop my *i*'s."

Callie bowed her head. "It's the family shame, Solomon. Emmy loops her *i*'s."

Emmy laughed and threw a napkin at her sister.

"I should have all your copies of the title and deed back from the courthouse next week," Knox told their new friend.

"I appreciate your help," Solomon said. "But I'll bet you've got more interesting cases than my farm."

Knox shooed a dragonfly fluttering close to Emmy. "The biggest one I have right now is not so much interesting as sad. It's a class action suit against a small factory that wouldn't allow sick employees any time off or take precautions after one of the workers contracted tuberculosis. Now twenty former employees have it—all of them fired as soon as they got sick. They need expensive treatment if they're to have any chance of surviving. The owner's out of state and doesn't care at all about the people here."

"It's just awful," Emmy said, her eyes misting.

"Think you'll win?" Solomon asked.

Knox shooed the persistent dragonfly again. "Hard to say. I think our case is solid, but the owner has deep pockets, and time is on his side. Once we're in front of a jury, though, I think I can persuade them to do the right thing. Hope so anyway."

Emmy clasped his hand. "You'll win the day for those poor sick people. I know you will."

As Emmy asked Solomon about his journey to Alabama,

Callie noticed a strange drift among the crowd. It began with one or two, then four or five, until almost half her parents' guests were moving to the backyard, where Hepsy and her help would be having their lunch in between refilling tea glasses and replenishing the serving tables. Callie's mother would not be happy about guests wandering into the backyard where they had no business.

"Emmy, look," she said, nodding toward the flow of humanity.

"What on earth?" Emmy followed Callie's direction as two or three small clusters of their neighbors joined the crowd.

"Nobody ever goes back there during a gathering," Callie said. "They know Hepsy and her help are either working or having their dinner. What's going on?"

Knox stood and offered Emmy his hand. "Only one way to find out. Shall we, everybody?"

Solomon helped Callie up, and they all started to follow another group around back.

Callie abruptly stopped. "Wait—let's go to the upstairs porch so we can see over everybody."

She noticed Solomon carefully wipe his shoes on a rug just outside the front door. Upstairs, Knox led the way to the upper porch overlooking the crowd. Emmy and Callie stood together, the men flanking them.

A few yards from the house stood an old well, where George had helped Hepsy pump water before the kitchen was outfitted with a working sink. Now the well was used primarily for wash days. But Hepsy hadn't come to the well for water today. She was watching what had attracted everyone else to it—a girl who looked about Callie's age, maybe a little younger. She was singing. And she was mesmerizing.

Callie could see that she was neither colored nor white, occupying an indefinable space somewhere in between. Her fair skin was like porcelain, only warmer, kissed with gold. She had fine features—high cheekbones and a full mouth. Black hair, held back with combs on either side of her face, fell in shiny curls below her shoulders. Her dress, a delicate rose print, had an empire waist and lace trim.

The girl's voice reminded Callie of a soprano she and Emmy had once heard at the opera house in Talladega, where their father took the family to see *H.M.S. Pinafore*. She was singing an old spiritual Callie had heard the field hands sing as they plowed her father's cotton with his many teams of mules, but the girl's version sounded more like the jubilee quartets that sometimes played local fairs and picnics, its upbeat rhythm contradicting the minor key and eerie lyrics. The girl held one hand about waist high and softly snapped her fingers to keep time.

> *"Wade in the water,*
> *Wade in the water, children.*
> *Wade in the water,*
> *God's gonna trouble the water."*

Hepsy's mother, Tirzah, always said "Wade in the Water" was "both a promise and a warnin' from Almighty."

Callie looked at the crowd encircling the singer, all captivated as much by her beauty as her voice. But there was something else—a disturbance among the women, who kept tilting their heads to one side, whispering to each other even as they kept their eyes on the girl. Callie could see colored frowns of concern and white ones of disapproval. It was strange how easily she could tell the difference, even from the height of the porch.

Hepsy stood directly behind the singer. She was composed as always but clasped her hands tightly together the way she did when she was anxious. Looking around the crowd, Callie found the primary source of Hepsy's discomfort. She nudged her sister and nodded toward a mulberry tree just beyond the crowd. Standing in its low fork, elevated and partially hidden from everybody, was Ryder Montgomery. Something about his stance and his unwavering focus on the girl at the well—like a cat waiting to pounce on a bird—made Callie want to leap off the porch, jerk him out of that tree, and shake some sense into him. Emmy shuddered and silently squeezed her hand.

As the song ended, Hepsy suddenly looked up, not at Callie and Emmy but at a spot to their far left. She nodded, relaxed her hands, and went to the singer, then put an arm around her and led her into the house. Callie and Emmy turned just in time to see their mother leave the end of the porch, where she had been silently observing.

"Well, I guess the show's over," Knox said, still looking down at the crowd before turning to Emmy. "Shall we go back outside with the masses?" Emmy smiled at him and took his arm.

Solomon said his goodbyes before Knox and Emmy rejoined the picnic guests.

"I hope it wasn't too brutal," Callie told him.

"Not at all. You were a fine guide, and I thank you. I hope you and your sister will come and see the house when it's no longer a danger to your safety."

"We'd love to see it." Callie smiled at him. "Just don't expect me to carry on about draperies and settees."

"Wouldn't dream of it." Solomon turned to go but then stopped and faced Callie again. "One of these days, you'll have to help me understand what just happened on that porch."

TWO

allie awoke to distant thunder, one of her favorite sounds. Thunder brought rain and lightning and wind, changing the world in unpredictable ways. Farm work would cease, and a sudden stillness would fall, as if the storm required the whole earth's full attention.

She looked across the room at Emmy's bed, watching the slow rise and fall of her sister's shoulder as she lay on her side, fast asleep. Emmy didn't share her fascination with storms. She didn't seem to need them the way Callie did.

The fragrance of gardenias drifted from Emmy's side of the room. This time of year, she clipped a few every day and kept them in a vase on her nightstand. Sometimes she'd pin one in her hair when Knox took her to a house dance or some other evening entertainment.

Slipping quietly out of bed, Callie put on her robe and stood by the open window. Her parents' lawn, covered with neighbors just yesterday, lay empty now. In the early dawn, she could see wind stirring the rope swing that hung from the Lookout Tree as its heavy limbs began to undulate, their leaves sighing at the disturbance in the air. It seemed that the tree had been holding its breath and could now exhale in the release of an approaching storm, which was coming from the west. It would be a strong one. In the distance, lightning flashed.

A window's worth of dramatic weather wasn't nearly enough for Callie. On tiptoe, she crept up the staircase. Not a sound came from her brothers' rooms as she stepped onto the upper porch and immediately felt the wind on her face. She embraced the turbulence of the storm as it purpled the sky, blowing her hair back and lifting her robe like angel wings behind her. For a split second, she thought she might fly, no longer earthbound but ascending into the heavens to float among the clouds and dance with the lightning.

Strangely, Solomon Beckett flashed in her mind—Solomon and his parting words to her: *One of these days, you'll have to help me understand what just happened on that porch.* A lot had happened on the porches of this old house—including things Callie knew nothing about but could feel, just as Solomon sensed something happening beneath the surface as the girl at the well sang her song and Callie's mother silently summoned Hepsy.

Once Solomon left and the other guests began drifting back to the front yard, Callie had wandered among them, listening to their whispered comments about the girl. *Likely loose as a goose . . . Better watch your men . . .*

The girl had done nothing more than sing an old spiritual—music she'd probably learned in church—but all the Miss Niceys of the community acted as though she aimed to wreck every home in ten states. Pure jealousy, Callie decided. Those women conjured faults for the beguiling singer so they wouldn't have to feel guilty about envying her.

Now the rains were coming hard and fast. Callie knew she should hurry back inside, but she didn't want to. What she wanted was to run through the rain barefoot, to splash in every puddle and let the water soak her to the bone, then come inside, shed her wet clothes, and wrap up in a warm robe to have a cup of hot tea. That would never happen. Her mother would allow no such "public cavorting" in one's nightgown in the pouring rain.

Callie watched as the lightning changed from distant flashes to bright bolts in the sky. Reluctantly, she went back inside. By now, Hepsy would be busy in the kitchen, preparing breakfast. Callie decided to pop in and see if she might sneak a slice of bread covered with butter and sugar before the family came down for breakfast.

She was quietly descending the back stairs when she heard voices in the kitchen—unusual for this time of morning, as Hepsy was too busy making biscuits to visit with anyone. A few steps above the kitchen door, Callie realized it was her mother who had interrupted Hepsy's breakfast preparations.

"Do you mean to tell me he showed up at your *house?*" her mother asked, keeping her voice low.

"Yes, Miss 'Relia, he did." Hepsy, too, spoke in a hushed tone.

"And what on earth did you do?"

Callie could hear the clink of coffee cups on saucers. She pictured her mother and Hepsy sitting together at the kitchen table as they so often did, discussing anything in the Bullock household—or the community, for that matter—that needed seeing about.

"I knew he was comin'," Hepsy explained. "My nephews seen him a-headin' this way, and they cut across the creek to gimme warnin'. I hid Lily in my root cellar and told him she done gone off with her cousins and I don't know where."

Another clink. "And then what happened?"

"He left. But ain't no doubt he'll be back. I seen the look in his eye, plain as day."

The kitchen was quiet for a moment before Callie's mother spoke again. "Lily must come here and work at the house with you, Hepsy. It's the best way to keep her safe until we can come up with a better situation for her. I know she's not accustomed to domestic work, but it's only for a little while. That'll take care of the daytime."

"My grandbaby can make herself useful. Lily knows how to work—'specially since her man died."

This time the clink of the coffee cup was loud, as if the news of Lily's man had stunned not just Callie's mother but the very china itself. "Lily was married? So young?"

Callie heard a chair scuff across the floor and then the sound of the oven door opening. Hepsy must be sliding the biscuit pan inside. The oven door closed, and the chair moved again as Hepsy spoke. "Lily was fifteen when she become a wife, Miss 'Relia. She's goin' on eighteen now. Still got a little bit o' the fin'ry he bought her when he got him a good job on the railroad up there in Chicago—same job that killed him a few months ago. But Lily got sense enough to know when it's time to pack away her city clothes and go to work. And I want you to know, Lily ain't one to go 'round callin' 'tention to herself. People notice her on accounta how she looks. Ain't nothin' she can do 'bout that. One o' my helpers heard her hummin' to herself yestiddy and asked her to sing for ev'body. That's the only reason she done it—thought she was bein' a help to us. But it sure caused a stir."

"It needn't have," Callie's mother said, "if certain men didn't behave like the hound dogs they hunt with. I've seen plenty of blueticks with more sense than Ryder Montgomery—and they're much better company."

Callie could hear the concern in Hepsy's voice. "Lot o' them white women looked at Lily mighty funny."

"Well, they had no business being back there," Callie's mother insisted. "Lily was singing for the workers, not our guests. If everybody had stayed where they were supposed to, none of this would've happened. From what I understand, that witless Milligan boy came back there to see if you knew where Callie was, and when he heard Lily singing he proceeded to tell everybody else to come and listen. How ill-mannered! I intend to have a word with his mother. From now on, we'll just keep Lily away from any situations that might cause her trouble."

"I 'preciate your help, Miss 'Relia. And I know Mama does too. I 'spect she can figure out somewhere to put Lily at night."

"Yes, we need Tirzah's advice. Please let her know I'll be coming to see her tomorrow afternoon. She can send word by you in the morning if there's anything she'd like me to bring her when I come."

The kitchen was quiet for a moment before Callie's mother said, "How do you think Lily will handle living here after all that time up north?"

"She's spent a lot o' summers with us. Came down on holidays sometimes too. Her and her husband was here just this past Christmas. I believe Lily knows what's what, Miss 'Relia. But it'll be hard, I won't lie. Me and Mama tries to comfort her and tell her it's only for a little while till she . . ." There was a long pause before Hepsy spoke again. "Miss 'Relia, they's something else I need to tell you . . ."

Callie heard voices coming from the direction of her brothers' rooms. Any minute now they would come barreling down the back stairs to snatch a hot biscuit from the pan on their way to the dining room. They would give her away before she could shush them all, and the mere thought of what would follow trumped her desire for information. She scurried back upstairs, crossed the upper floor, and ran down the main staircase, then ducked back into her bedroom. Sitting on the floor next to an open window, she watched the rain pouring down, splashing into puddles.

"How long have you been up and what have you found out?" Emmy sat on the edge of her bed, yawning.

"A long time and plenty." Callie nodded toward the window. "Come and watch the storm with me while I tell you about it."

Emmy put on a light cotton robe and grabbed two pillows

off the bed. She handed one to Callie. "At least sit on something besides the bare floor." Emmy took a seat on the other pillow and looked out the window. A streak of lightning made her jump. "I'll never understand why you love these things so much, Callie. And before we get to your latest news, what did you think of Solomon?"

"He was nice." Callie kept her eyes on the window.

Emmy gave her a playful nudge. "He was a lot more than nice! *Very* handsome, if you ask me. And smart. And interesting. And taken with you."

Callie caught the curtain as it billowed in the wind, then let it slip through her fingers to fly free again. "He was not *taken* with me. He just didn't know anybody."

"Not true."

"Back to Hepsy's granddaughter."

"Don't change the subject."

"Her name is Lily," Callie pressed on. "Her husband died not long ago. Something about his job on the railroad killed him, but I didn't hear what."

"*Husband?*" Emmy's eyes opened wide. "But she couldn't be more than—"

"Seventeen. Going on eighteen. Married at fifteen."

Lightning flashed three times, followed by a big roll of thunder.

"Goodness." Emmy tentatively peered out the window at the Lookout Tree, its branches in constant motion from the stormy winds.

"Lily came here to stay with Hepsy after her husband died," Callie went on. "Yesterday one of Hepsy's helpers heard Lily humming as she worked and asked her to sing something for everybody. That's what got all the commotion started. That pest Buck Milligan went into the backyard looking for me, heard Lily sing, and invited everybody else to come and hear it! Can you even imagine something so stupid? The very idea—interfering with Hepsy's help and then inviting other guests to join in. What right did he have? Mama's not done with him—you can be sure of that."

Emmy jumped slightly as a gust of wind blew the curtains back and a big roll of thunder made the floor vibrate. "Married at fifteen and widowed at seventeen. I can't fathom it."

That was so like Emmy, ignoring all the backyard drama and focusing only on Lily and her loss. No one felt for other people the way Emmy did. It was one of many things Callie admired about her sister.

She paused to watch an impressive bolt of lightning before telling Emmy the rest. "There's more, Em. Ryder went to Hepsy's looking for Lily last night, but Hepsy got tipped off and hid her in the root cellar before he could find her. Mama thinks Lily should come here to work with Hepsy to keep her away from Ryder."

"He's a jackal—an absolute *jackal*!" Emmy's jaw clenched in anger.

"Mama and Hepsy are going to talk to Tirzah to figure out where Lily should stay at night."

Emmy pulled her robe tight against her. "To think, all these women having to go to such lengths to protect a girl who shouldn't *need* protection. Ryder Montgomery belongs at home with his wife instead of chasing every young woman in the county. It's disgusting."

"And it's not fair," Callie said, lifting her face to the cool wind blowing in. "What use is Ryder to anybody? None. And yet here we all are, arranging ourselves around him. Makes me want to scream. How he and Knox came from the same family, I'll never know."

"Cain and Abel," Emmy said, looking out at the rain now pelting the roof of the house.

Callie saw the sadness in her sister's eyes and regretted being the cause of it. "I'm sorry, Em. Don't pay me any mind. Hepsy would say I'm just spoutin' off."

Emmy smiled and laid her hand over Callie's. "You're not the cause of my worry. It just makes me sad to think of Knox—and Lucinda—living under the same roof as Ryder and his parents."

"I was only eleven or so when George brought her here," Callie said. "Do you think she loved him?"

"Very much."

"Still does?"

"Yes," Emmy said with a sigh.

"And George loves her."

"Dearly."

Emmy looked as sad as Callie felt. More than sadness, what suddenly washed over her was something worse—more like despair—at the thought of her brother longing for Lucinda. George, who could take his pick of all the marriageable young women in the whole county, was denied the only one he truly wanted and so chose none of them.

"All the meanness and spite in the Montgomery house," Emmy went on. "I can't wait to carry Knox away from it."

Callie's spirits took a dive. "What will Knox carry *you* away from, Emmy? You said he's talked about setting up a law office someplace away from his family."

"Yes, he has." She squeezed Callie's shoulder. "But don't you worry. A few miles can't separate you and me—not really. Even Knox can't do that."

Callie forced a smile. But she couldn't shake the terrible vision of a flawless Lady Baltimore cake tumbling off the fellowship table—the innocent victim of carelessness. She prayed Emmy never would be.

THREE

*T*he Bullock house held a relic from its original owner, who'd had his grand home outfitted with an elaborate system of bells hidden behind panels in the walls. The kitchen could be rung from just about every room in the house, including the bedrooms, should a family member sleep in and require breakfast in bed or stay out late and call for a midnight cordial. Any room in the house could be rung from the study.

Aurelia Bullock had long disdained the bells, which she declared "the height of decadent sloth." Any of her children who couldn't appear at the table with the rest of the family, she said, could fend for themselves. She would not have Hepsy bothered with the "whims and fancies of privilege," nor would she raise children too lazy to get out of bed.

Contempt for the bells was among the many contradictions Callie saw in her mother. Unlike Ira Bullock, who had grown up on a small family farm that barely kept food on the table, Aurelia came from wealth, yet she maintained the air of someone who had worked for everything she owned and expected her children to do likewise.

Aurelia believed in utility, and she had at last found an acceptable use for the decadent bells. The women of the house turned them into a warning system, the perfect means for alerting each other to any possible trouble for Lily. They could easily see it coming, given the tall windows that wrapped the house.

The kitchen bell had sounded late on a Thursday morning a few days after Lily came to work for the Bullocks. From the upper porch, standing far enough back so they wouldn't be noticed, Callie and Emmy watched as Ryder Montgomery tied his chestnut horse—likely the only Thoroughbred in the whole county—to the mulberry tree in the Bullocks' backyard. The basket of tomatoes he carried was, no doubt, a contrivance to get himself inside the house.

Callie could hear the shock in his voice when her mother answered. "Why—why, Miss Aurelia, I expected a servant at the kitchen door. What a—what a pleasant surprise!"

Callie elbowed Emmy as Ryder tried to charm his way into the house.

"We just had a visit from family who brought Mama some fresh tomatoes from their farm in Florida. She insisted I deliver you some in person. Shall I set them on the kitchen table?"

"No need to trouble yourself," Callie's mother said. "One of the porch rockers should serve the purpose."

"Mama just dropped the temperature forty degrees," Emmy whispered to Callie.

"Why, it would be no trouble at all to bring them in." Ryder was nothing if not persistent, but he had met a brick wall in Aurelia Bullock.

"The rocker, please."

"Well—alright then," Ryder said. "I suppose I should be going—unless there's anything else I might do for you, Miss Aurelia?"

Her voice was pure ice. "How kind of you to sacrifice your morning in service to women, Ryder. Rest assured you're finished here. Enjoy the rest of your day, and do express my thanks to dear Camile."

"She'd better check those tomatoes for worms," Callie whispered, giggling with Emmy as they both struggled to keep quiet.

Ryder hurried back to his horse and rode away at a swift gallop.

"He has to know everybody sees right through him," Callie said.

Emmy shook her head. "That's where you're wrong. Men always see through him. But most women don't—not until it's too late anyway. Look at Lucinda. If her father had still been alive when Ryder came calling, things might've turned out differently. But her mother pushed her into marrying him. Ryder fooled her with all his big talk of running for the state senate."

"Ryder Montgomery couldn't get elected to the church hostess committee if they were shorthanded on homecoming day," Callie said, making her sister laugh.

They went downstairs to help Hepsy and Lily pack lunches for their father and brothers working in the fields. Their mother said every young woman "*should* know her way around a kitchen and garden, whether she *needs* to or not." Emmy and Callie had been helping Hepsy since they were children. When they were little, of course, they were more of a hindrance than a help, but Hepsy had "the patience of Job," as their mother said. Over the years, she taught them both how to tend a garden, to cook, and to bake, though Callie was always much more at home in the kitchen than Emmy.

Callie carefully wrapped slices of caramel cake and handed them to her sister to put into each lunch pail, glancing up now and again to see Lily quietly slicing roast beef for sandwiches on the opposite side of the table. It was hard not to stare at her even now, without the city clothes she had worn as she sang by the well. She was clad instead in a plain cotton dress with a white bib apron, just like Hepsy. Her hands were graceful, with lithesome fingers that would look more at home playing a spinet than clutching a butcher knife. Her eyes were not amber like Hepsy's but a deep brown, arresting against her flawless skin.

What was Lily thinking about, Callie wondered, as she stood in a house where she didn't belong, making lunches for people she didn't know? Was she wondering whether any of the Bullock men were turned like the one who had leered at her from the mulberry tree? Did she fear for her safety in this house?

Emmy finally broke the silence. "Well, aren't we a bunch of quiet mice, working away without making a peep. Lily, I've been meaning to ask you, where did you learn to sing so well?"

Lily smiled at her but kept slicing. "I've been singing all my life, mostly in church. I learned a lot about it at the college."

Emmy and Callie stopped packing cake and looked at each other. "You—you went to college in Chicago?" Emmy asked.

Lily handed Hepsy a stack of sliced beef. "Oh, no. I worked there—typing and filing and running errands for the professors in the music school. My desk was right in the same hallway with the little rooms where they gave the students their voice lessons. I expect I picked up a few things—tried to anyway."

"You must've picked up quite a lot." Emmy resumed her packing duties. "I think you sing as well as anybody I ever heard, Lily. I really do."

For a moment, Lily stopped slicing and smiled at Emmy. "Thank you, miss. I appreciate that."

"A voice like yours is such a blessing," Emmy said.

Just then a bell sounded in the kitchen. All the women froze.

"I'm not so sure about that." Lily went back to work, staring down at the cutting board. "Brought those bells on us—might be a curse."

Callie left the table to look out one of the kitchen windows.

"Who is it?" Emmy asked.

"Camile Montgomery, of all people," Callie said.

"Knox and Ryder's mother coming here this early?" Emmy followed Callie to the window.

"Have I got to hide in the broom closet, Grandmama?" Lily kept staring down as she chopped the roast beef faster and faster.

"Doesn't look like she's coming in," Callie reported, peering out the window with Emmy.

Hepsy put her hands on her hips. "You mean that woman done come all the way over here and then she ain't gonna come in?"

Callie and Emmy watched Camile ride away before they returned to the table and began sealing the filled lunch pails.

"She just slowed the buggy down." Callie finished with a pail smaller than the others—her baby brother Theo's. "Probably checking to see if Ryder's horse was anywhere in sight."

Emmy slammed one of the lids onto the table. "I wish every Montgomery by name would get shipped across the ocean to cook for the missionaries, as Mama says—all of them except Knox, of course."

"I'm sorry," Lily said.

"What for?" Emmy asked her. "You haven't done anything wrong. Not a thing in this world. It's that despicable man and his selfishness ruining everything."

Callie hadn't seen her sister this worked up in a long time. In her anger, Emmy kept packing food, even though they had already made enough lunches for the Bullock men.

"And I'll tell you something else, Lily," Emmy fumed. "From now on, there'll be no broom closet for you. The sewing room would be much more comfortable, and it's completely out of the way."

"Now, Miss Emmy—" Hepsy started to protest, but Emmy put up her hands.

"I'll speak with Mama, Hepsy, and I know she'll agree. Why should Lily endure dust and spiders when Ryder's the one who deserves to be squashed like a bug? We'll have no more of that."

Lily looked up at Emmy but said nothing.

"We best get to the washin'," Hepsy told Lily.

Callie felt a sudden dip in her stomach, as if she had been galloping too fast on her horse and barely missed a spill. Troubled by the thought of Lily's delicate hands on a scrub board, she suddenly realized that she had never considered Hepsy's hands at all. They always seemed so at home rolling biscuit dough or dusting banisters or washing clothes. Were Hepsy's hands really meant for that? For that and nothing more?

Callie busied herself helping Emmy gather the sealed pails to load into a buckboard. A trip to the fields would lift her spirits, especially today, since her father and brothers were working her favorite spot—two hundred acres skirting the Coosa River.

Emmy drove the buckboard, pulled by a mare named Daisy Bell. The sisters followed a narrow dirt road that led from the Bullock home and its tenant houses to a larger one that ran north and south, connecting a string of small communities—the kind that dotted the Appalachian foothills of Alabama. In between a scattering of farmhouses and the occasional clapboard church were red-clay fields, the cotton plants growing tall and green in the springtime sun. By late October, they would be snow white, with fluffy clouds spilling out of the prickly bolls that studded their stalks.

"Penny for your thoughts," Emmy said as she guided Daisy Bell onto a narrow bridge across a branch of Yellowleaf Creek, the mare's hooves clip-clopping against the wood.

Callie started to tell Emmy what she'd been thinking about, but it would only make her sad. Instead, she smiled and said, "I'd be glad to get a penny because they aren't worth a plug nickel." She spotted a welcome distraction. "Oh, look, we're passing Solomon's farm. Looks like he's started clearing the old split-rail fence and front gate so you can tell it leads to something."

"Maybe soon we'll be able to see the house from the road," Emmy said. "It's a shame to have it hidden away by all that overgrowth."

As they journeyed along, Emmy began to sing Callie's favorite hymn but in a peculiar way she had—skipping words here and there, sometimes because she forgot them and sometimes just because she felt like it.

> "*For the beauty of the earth,*
> *La-ti-da-ti of the skies.*
> *For the love which hm-hm-hm,*
> *La-ti-da around us lies.*
> *Christ, our Lord, to thee we raise*
> *Hm-hm-hm of grateful praise.*"

Callie put her hands lightly around Emmy's neck and pretended to choke her. "For heaven's sake, learn the words, woman!"

"For heaven's sake, I know the words, woman!" Emmy replied, giggling.

Still laughing with her sister, Emmy guided Daisy Bell off the main road and onto a much rougher one that led through their father's cotton all the way to Shay's Bend, an especially deep curve in the river for which the nearest town was named. Here floodwaters had created some of the richest farmland in the county—probably the whole state.

Emmy drove the buckboard into the shade of a sprawling oak just a few yards from the riverbank and locked the brake. Callie could see the rolling store—a covered wagon loaded with food for sale from her father's commissary—parked a little farther down. Already a long line of field hands had formed, waiting to buy bologna and crackers, tins of sardines, sharp cheese, homemade cookies, small bottles of milk, and thick slices of smoked ham with white bread.

Off in the distance, Callie saw a cloud of red dust just before her father and brothers appeared over a small rise in the cotton field. As was their custom this time of year, they had unhitched

the mule teams that pulled their plows and were riding them
to the riverbank for lunch. First came two black mules named
Rogue and Buster, carrying Callie's father and oldest brother,
James. George rode Star, a silver-gray. Trailing those three was
a roan called Dusty, with Sam, born two years after Callie,
holding the reins, and five-year-old Theo, baby of the family,
riding behind him and holding on to his waist. Theo was too
young to work the fields, but he so wanted to be with his father
and brothers that they brought him every morning and let him
ride one of the mules as it plowed. The girls would take him
home at lunchtime.

As her sister climbed down and began arranging quilts under
the tree so the men would have a proper place to sit, Callie carried a bucket to the river and dipped up a cool drink for Daisy
Bell. Then she unhitched the horse and removed her bridle,
replacing it with a simple harness attached to a long coil of
rope. She tied the free end of the rope to the oak tree so Daisy
Bell could meander and graze, but the horse didn't budge until
Callie had fetched a bucket of apples from the buckboard and
fed her two of them—their daily ritual. Daisy Bell would take
a bite of apple, then dip her mouth into the bucket of water.
Callie's father said she spoiled the animals, but she thought it
only fair that Daisy Bell have a rest and a reward after pulling
the buckboard all the way to the field.

"How are my best girls?" her father said as he climbed off
Rogue and kissed his daughters on the cheek.

"Tip-top," Emmy said. "How's our favorite fella?"

"Fine and dandy."

Callie and Emmy brought the men their lunch and poured
them tin cups of coffee—milk for Theo—before taking their
own pails to the quilts and joining the daily lunch banter.

"Callie, my sandwich is too big," Theo said.

"Oh dear, we can't have that." She took the sandwich from
her little brother and broke it in two.

"Callie, *my* sandwich is too big," Sam said, batting his eyes at her.

She laughed and tossed an apple at him. "Then go graze with Daisy Bell. Only Theo gets butler service."

Callie looked around at her brothers having their lunch—Theo sharing her quilt, Sam sharing Emmy's, George sitting between the two pairs, and James beside their father. That was the order of their family. Emmy had always mothered Sam, while Callie was fiercely protective of little Theo, teaching him his lessons and doctoring his skinned knees. George fell somewhere in the middle—the most charming and easygoing of all the Bullock boys, the one with the best sense of humor and the best shoulder to cry on. No wonder he was Hepsy's favorite. There was nothing they wouldn't do for each other.

James, the eldest, was something of a mystery to Callie. Maybe it was just the age difference, but maybe not. Serious and guarded, James kept his feelings to himself. Hepsy said he came into the world an adult. After Callie's mother delivered James, she had miscarried a baby and then given birth to twin girls who lived only a few days. Sorrow and loss, it seemed, stood between James and the other Bullock siblings.

Callie took a napkin and blotted Theo's mouth. "What do you think of the cotton so far, Daddy?"

"We're trying a new variety here by the river, so we'll have to see how it fares against the others. I expect we'll have a good crop if we get rain when we need it and sun when we don't."

"And no hailstorms," George said.

"Don't forget frogs and locusts," Sam added with a grin.

Their father took a sip of his coffee. "Yes, Sam, barring any plagues of biblical proportions, we ought to do alright."

Emmy slipped Sam an extra piece of cake from her pail. He grinned and winked at her as he took a bite.

"Have any of y'all been to Solomon Beckett's farm?" she asked.

"We have." George nodded to James. "Daddy sent us over there yesterday to see if he needed anything."

"What did you think?" Emmy asked.

"Definitely has his hands full, but he seems to know what he's doing," James answered.

"Most of that land is a tangled-up mess," George said. "I don't know how he'll ever make heads or tails of it. But James is right. If anybody's up to it, Solomon is. Got a good head on his shoulders, and he's not afraid of hard work."

"I'd like to go by there and see it myself," their father said.

"Did y'all know he used to work on riverboats traveling the Mississippi?" George asked.

Callie reached over to shoo a fly away from Theo's cake. "I did. He told me the day of the fish fry. He said he eventually got tired of never being still—all that traveling up and down the river."

"Well, I'd *never* get tired of it," Sam said. "I think it'd be a real adventure to live on a boat, never knowing what you might see next." He grinned at Callie. "But back to the fish fry—how about those suitors of yours?"

Callie rolled her eyes. "Bradford Tillis thought I'd be fascinated with his *endless* account of a trip to Selma to visit his cousin. In the time it took him to tell me about it, I could have ridden Daisy Bell down there to see Selma for myself."

"Well, what about good ole Denny?" Sam asked.

Callie swatted at another fly buzzing around Theo. "Good ole Denny bored me to tears bragging about how much land his granddaddy has. If you're going to annoy everyone by bragging, you should at least have something of your own to crow about."

Her family laughed at how quickly she'd sized up the boastful Denny.

"Buck Milligan?" Sam suggested.

Callie shuddered. "You mean Buck *You*-Again?"

"I don't blame you for passing on them, Callie," said James, who didn't always engage in the family banter. "None of those boys sounds up to snuff."

"The key word is 'boys,'" Emmy spoke up. "Callie needs someone more mature, someone who can challenge her mind."

"Old man Chester's available," Sam said. "He's got one foot in the grave and the other on a banana peel, but he's available."

Everybody laughed, including Callie. "I'd rather dance with old man Chester than waste five minutes on the others."

"Say, how's Lily making out?" George asked.

Callie glanced at Emmy. "Fine. I'm sure she must feel like a fish out of water, but she's settling in. She's got Hepsy to show her the ropes."

Sam glanced at George. "Fisher's glad she's here."

"What do you mean?" Emmy asked.

Sam took a swig of coffee to wash down an enormous bite of cake. "He's all moony-eyed over Lily. I was helping George get an upstairs window unstuck when we saw Fisher carry water to the washpot for her."

"Who are Lily's parents?" George asked.

Their father took out his pocketknife and began peeling an apple. "Lily belongs to Hepsy's middle boy, Omie. His first wife got killed just a year or so after they married—ferry got loose and she drowned. Omie took off up north somewhere. Seems like it was Baltimore. Next I heard, he'd married and they had a little girl. That was Lily, I believe."

"Fisher might not be a bad match for her," George said. "He's smart and works hard."

"And he's kindhearted," Emmy added. "That's important too."

"Now might be a good time to remind y'all that it's none of our business," their father said.

Lunch continued with the usual talk of crops and cotton

prices, weather and boll weevils. Callie could happily have stayed all day. She felt sure she was strong enough to handle a plow and a team of mules, though her father would never allow it—not as long as there was any chance her mother would find out.

As they began clearing away the lunch pails, Emmy said, "Daddy, why don't you ask Mama if we might have Solomon over to supper or maybe Sunday dinner sometime soon? He has no family here, and he's just getting to know his neighbors. I'll bet it gets lonesome on that farm."

"I'll see to it," he said. "Theo, are you 'bout ready to head home with your sisters? Thought I saw you yawning on that last row."

"Yes, sir." Theo rubbed his eyes.

Callie kissed him on top of his head and packed up his lunch pail.

"How come there's an extra pail?" George called from the buckboard, where he was hitching up Daisy Bell.

"Emmy had a lot on her mind and forgot how many brothers she had," Callie called back.

"You girls pass by Solomon's place on the way home," their father said. "Till I can ask your mother about a supper invitation, why don't you carry him that lunch. Theo can be your chaperone. I'll bet Solomon hasn't had anything as good as Hepsy's roast beef and caramel cake lately."

"Consider it done," Emmy said as she and Callie hugged their father goodbye.

"If you get tired of Sam's nonsense, just say the word," George told Callie as he helped her climb onto the buckboard. "He's not too big for me to whip—not for another year or two anyway."

She settled into her seat, waiting for Emmy. "Maybe it'll shut him up if I can reel in old man Chester before that banana peel puts an end to him."

"There's something to be said for a merry widow," George replied, making Callie laugh.

He helped Emmy up and lifted their baby brother into the back of the buckboard. Callie used one of the quilts to make a pallet for Theo and another to fashion a little shade tent for him. By the time she and Emmy made it to the main road, their chaperone was snoring.

FOUR

here do you suppose Solomon might be?"
Emmy was guiding Daisy Bell up a gently winding road—more of a wide path, really—which had been cleared about three feet on either side. Beyond that, the landscape was completely overgrown.

"Let's look at the house first," Callie suggested. "Even if he's not there, we'll get to see it up close."

"Good idea." Emmy followed a sharp curve to the left before the path opened onto a small, cleared patch of lawn and an old house long hidden.

Callie gasped when she saw it. "Just like I remembered—a little worse for wear, but still."

"It's not as grand as our house, but it sure is something special," Emmy said.

"You're right, Em. It's not imposing, but it's impressive."

Solomon's house had three front gables arranged in a triangle of sorts. The center and highest one, which came off the roof, sheltered an upstairs porch. The left and right gables dropped down and covered two rounded, ground-level porches with bay windows flanking the main entrance. Though it sorely needed paint, traces of the original white managed to hold on.

Solomon gave them a start when he stepped from behind the house, blotting his face with a towel. "I thought I heard voices. To what do I owe the honor?" His hair was wet, but his clothes looked dry and clean.

"Hello there!" Emmy called to him. "We come bearing a lunch pail with Hepsy's roast beef and caramel cake. Will you have it?"

Solomon rubbed his stomach. "With gratitude. I just had a good dousing in the creek, so maybe I won't smell to high heaven."

"As it happens," Emmy said, "that's our one and only standard for male companionship: Must not smell to high heaven."

"Allow me, ladies." Solomon helped Emmy and Callie down from the buckboard. "What's under the quilt?"

"Not what—who," Callie said. "Our little brother Theo. He was supposed to be our chaperone, but he's sleeping on the job."

Emmy grabbed the lunch pail from the buckboard and handed it to Solomon. "Will you think us loose women if we sneak a peek inside your house unchaperoned?"

"Your reputation's safe with me." Solomon led them to the front steps.

Emmy and Callie followed him onto the porch, where the floor of heart pine felt as solid and steady underfoot as ever. The front door, which Solomon held open for them, had also remained intact except for its two large glass panes, both broken. He had tacked a piece of heavy canvas over them.

"The upstairs is too wrecked for visitors, but the ground floor's fairly passable," he said. "Not clean but passable."

Just inside was the staircase. Unlike the Bullock stairs, which rose from the first floor to the second in one grand sweep, these hugged the right-hand wall and turned like a backward L.

"Oh my goodness!" Callie couldn't contain her excitement at seeing the staircase again for the first time in years. As Emmy drifted down the central hall, Callie stopped to marvel at the wide oak railing and beautifully carved newels, though they were covered with dust and badly scratched. Climbing the few steps to the landing, she remembered all the times she'd sat here as a child, waiting for her mother to deliver a gift basket to an ailing Miss Katherine.

"I know what you must think," Solomon said. "It's a mess."

"Not in my mind." She slowly ran her hand along the railing as she looked up toward the second floor. "I can see it the way it wants to be."

"And how is that, Callie?" The softened tone of his voice made her turn around. He had one hand on the railing, the other on his hip. His eyes were riveted on her, not the staircase.

Her heart pounded so hard that she feared he might hear it, and her knees turned to water, but she managed to answer. "Freed. It wants to be freed of all the layers covering it up and holding it down. It wants to soar."

Solomon slowly nodded, never taking his eyes off her. He stepped onto the bottom stair. For a second, she thought he might join her on the landing. And then what?

"Callie, come in here!" Emmy called from the old dining room. Solomon and Callie followed and found her pointing to a massive china cabinet that filled an end wall. "Can you believe it's still here? And not one pane of glass is broken."

"I can't imagine ever owning enough dishes to fill that thing," Solomon said.

"Mrs. Cruz had a sister who lived in England," Emmy explained. "The sister would send her china, and Mrs. Cruz would reciprocate with Alabama pottery. They did that swap for every occasion, including some that the sisters made up, according to Mama. When we were little, this cabinet was overflowing. Some of it was really beautiful, but some of it was . . ."

"Heinous!" Callie said.

Emmy laughed with her sister. "She's right, Solomon. If you ever take to collecting pink china elephants, we'll have to disown you."

"Callie! Callie, where are you?" Theo was at the front door, shouting for her.

"Our chaperone awakes," Callie said. She stepped out of the dining room, back into the main hall. "In here, sweetie."

He came inside and put his arms around her waist. "Where are we?" he asked, looking around.

"You remember Mr. Beckett from the fish fry." Callie led her brother into the dining room with Solomon and Emmy.

Theo looked at Solomon and crinkled his nose.

"It's alright, Theo," Solomon said. "I'm pretty forgettable."

"Mr. Beckett was just showing us his house," Callie explained. "When he's done with all the work, it'll be even more beautiful than it used to be."

"I don't remember how it used to be," Theo said.

Callie tried to comb his hair with her fingers. "That's because you weren't born yet. But trust me. It was lovely."

Solomon led them into a large kitchen on the back of the ground floor. The old woodstove and icebox were still there, as well as a sink with no faucets or pump. A back door opened onto a tattered screened porch that ran the length of the house.

"I'm afraid to try the stove till I have time to give it a good going-over," he said. "Might burn the whole place down. So I cook on a campfire out back. The old icebox still does the job, though."

"Do you need help?" Emmy asked. "We could ask Daddy to send over Fisher Dobbs. He can repair anything, and he's a good carpenter too. Mama and Daddy keep him so busy with projects that he doesn't work in the fields at all anymore."

"I appreciate that," Solomon said. "But I'll get to it soon enough. Besides, the few things I can cook are probably better suited to a campfire."

"Alright then." Emmy smiled. "I'll stop meddling. But just let us know if you change your mind."

They followed Solomon out of the kitchen and circled back around to the front parlor. Callie stood before a bay window that overlooked one of the two deep porches flanking the entry. "Can't you just imagine sitting out there during a summer rain?"

"I can now."

Callie heard that same soft tone in Solomon's voice and swore she could feel him looking at her.

"My sister loves storms as much as sunny weather," Emmy said as Callie turned around to see that she had been right. "I could be hiding under the bed to escape the lightning, and Callie would be slipping out onto the porch to get a closer look."

"We might be kindred spirits," Solomon said, smiling at Callie. "First sound of thunder and I want to feel the power of that wind."

Theo pulled at Callie's skirt, breaking her gaze with Solomon. "I suppose you're ready to go," she said. He nodded. "Alright then. Thank Mr. Beckett for showing us his house."

Theo extended his hand to Solomon. "Thank you for showing us your house, Mr. Beckett."

Solomon shook his hand. "You're quite welcome, Theo. You come back anytime. And bring your sisters with you. They just might inspire me to get this old house up and going again— even if it kills me."

FIVE

Girls, is that you?" their mother called.

"Yes, Mama!" Callie answered as she, Emmy, and Theo followed their mother's voice to the front parlor, where she was having a glass of iced tea with Camile and Lucinda Montgomery.

Lucinda, looking painfully self-conscious, fidgeted with her wedding ring and kept her eyes lowered. It was George who had first brought her into this parlor years ago—George, who loved her. Now here she sat with his family, who knew what a horrible choice she had made—in fairness, surrendered to—after Ryder successfully boondoggled her mother.

"I was about to send out a search party," their mother said once they had greeted her guests.

"We delivered lunch and then Daddy had an errand for us," Emmy explained.

Her mother nodded. "I suspected as much. You girls come and join us. Callie, would you put Theo down for his nap first?"

"Yes, ma'am." Callie took Theo upstairs, led him to his bed, and pulled off his shoes. Then she pushed back the drapes so the air could blow through. He was asleep before she could get out of the room.

Rejoining the women, Callie took a seat next to Emmy on a settee by the side windows.

"Surely you agree with me, Aurelia," Camile was saying.

"I can't imagine why you think I would," Callie's mother answered. "Hepsy has been a trusted member of this household for years, just as her mother was. Now a member of her family needs our help. I cannot imagine turning Lily away."

"Lucinda, speak up," Camile said. "Tell her how that girl is leading Ryder astray."

"I believe Miss Aurelia knows all she needs to," Lucinda said.

As close as they were sitting, Callie could hear the slow, deep breaths Emmy was taking, something Hepsy had taught her to do when she felt overwrought. "You too kind to handle mean-ness," Hepsy had told her, "so you got to learn how to soothe y'self when it comes along."

Camile set her tea glass on a silver tray and crossed her arms over her chest. "That girl is creating an unwelcome distraction. You've seen how all the men gawk at her. And it's hardly their fault, the way she sashays about, throwing herself at them. Especially a man like Ryder, who's been given no children to distract him from temptation."

Lucinda's cheeks flushed—from anger or embarrassment, Callie couldn't say.

"Not *all* the men are leering at Lily," Callie's mother argued. "And I don't believe I have ever seen her sashay. As for Ryder, if he's having difficulties, perhaps he should see Dr. Embry."

Callie thought she saw the quickest, faintest smile cross Lu-cinda's lips before she suppressed it.

"There is *nothing* wrong with Ryder!" Camile stood up and whirled to face Emmy. "I'm surprised you'd have such a floozy right here under Knox's nose. He's not a saint, you know."

Emmy stopped taking deep breaths and became as rigid as a fence post. Camile had just "brought out the Mama."

"Lily is *not* a floozy." Emmy's tone was icy, her speech slow and measured. "She is a lovely girl in a terrible situation. And Knox does not need to be kept away from her or any other woman in order to behave like a gentleman. Knox has *character* to guide him. Knox has *honor.* Knox has *love* and *compassion* and *decency.*"

Camile waved a dismissive hand in the air. "He never was as red-blooded as Ryder. But even so, why fling a temptress in his face? A woman with no morals is a danger to every Christian home."

Callie's mother gave Camile a glare so fiery Callie feared it might set the whole room ablaze. "And why do you think Lily has no morals?"

"Common sense," Camile answered.

Callie's mother had heard enough. She stood up and folded her hands in front of her. "Camile, in the very near future, Knox will become part of our family, and Emmy will become part of yours. I would like to keep the peace, for our children's sakes. However, my decision where Lily is concerned—and I have Ira's full support—is that anyone who trespasses on our farm with intent to molest one of our workers can expect a load of buckshot in his pants."

Camile stared at her adversary, who clearly wasn't backing down. "Lucinda, we're leaving." Snatching her purse off her chair, Camile angrily strode across the room toward the main hall before her daughter-in-law had time to collect herself. "Lucinda! Come along!" Camile demanded at the parlor doorway.

Lucinda followed her mother-in-law out of the parlor. The front door opened and slammed.

Callie peered out the window as the Montgomery women hurried off the porch, just in time to see George ride into the driveway on his horse. Lucinda froze when she saw him, but Camile grabbed her by the arm and urged her toward their buggy. They sped away, Lucinda stealing a glance over her shoulder at George, who watched them till they were out of sight.

As Callie turned away from the window, her mother walked over to Emmy and laid a gentle hand against her cheek. "I'm sorry, my dear."

Emmy covered her mother's hand with her own. "I'm not. I'm so proud of you, Mama. You're the strongest person I know. Don't tell Daddy."

That brought a laugh from the women, even Callie's mother, who was as serious as her husband was jovial.

"Did Daddy really say he'd give Ryder the buckshot?" Callie asked her.

"No," her mother answered, "but I know that's what he *will* say if I feel the need to tell him what's been going on." She sat down next to Emmy and took her hand. "Emeline, you listen to me. When you and Knox marry, you must move far away from his family. It breaks my heart that such distance will take you far from us as well. But I believe he will make you happy. And I am willing to miss you in order to preserve you. His family is poison. Period. Your marriage will not survive proximity to them. *You* will not survive proximity to them. How Lucinda has lasted this long, I'll never know."

Emmy burst into tears, and her mother held her tight.

Callie could hear doves calling out the window. Their peaceful song made her want to cry with Emmy. But she didn't. Callie did her crying alone.

SIX

ome things we simply do not discuss.

Callie had absorbed her mother's mantra at a very young age and heard it invoked many times over the years, usually when a conversation drifted toward anything too painful or personal or disturbing for the family. On the surface, it kept the Bullocks on an even keel, but a host of unresolved questions lurked down below.

George had come into the house right after Camile and Lucinda left. He asked to be excused from the supper table that night and remained uncharacteristically removed for a few days after, keeping to himself and talking mostly with Hepsy in the kitchen.

It was a Sunday afternoon when Callie spotted him in the horse pasture. She had gone there to see two new mares her father bought at auction but instead found George sitting under a tree beside the small pond where the livestock drank. He stared into space, an unopened book in his lap.

"Want me to go away and let you read?" she asked when he looked up.

"No." He set the book on the ground. "I haven't turned the first page. Pull up a seat."

Callie sat down on the grass next to him. A breeze blew

ripples across the pond, where several draft horses had gathered to drink. Callie and George watched them in silence before she said, "I could prattle on about nothing and pretend I don't know how much it hurts you to see Lucinda, or I could ask how you're doing. It's up to you."

George took a deep breath and smiled at her. "God bless you for your candor."

"Are you alright, George?"

"No, but I'll live."

"Do you want to talk about it—any of it?" Callie picked a dandelion and blew it, sending all its feathers into the air.

"Trying to win me some luck?" he asked.

"Can't hurt. I'll blow till I'm winded if it'll help."

George rested his head against the tree and closed his eyes for a moment before turning to Callie. "I could get past it if I thought she was happy—if I'd lost her to a better man. But that's not what happened. She just couldn't stand up to all that pressure from her mother. Now she's miserable. It's like a kick in the gut every time I see her."

Callie took her brother's hand. "She devastated you, but your main concern is *her* misery. You're a much better person than I am."

He gave her a half smile. "No, I'm not."

"Do you ever think about leaving, George? Starting over someplace where you won't have to run into her all the time?"

"Yes, but where would I go? If I traded the pain of seeing Lucinda for the loneliness of being separated from y'all, I'd just be 'swappin' six of one for half a dozen of the other,' as Hepsy says. And then there's Tirzah."

Callie frowned at him. "What does she have to do with it?"

George picked a dandelion and blew it bare. "She had a vision—a mighty strange one—and she saw it three times. Sent word by Hepsy."

"What did she see?"

"She saw me embracing Lucinda—at the cemetery gate."

Callie shuddered. "The *cemetery*?"

"I know," George said. "Tirzah's vision is a touch on the grim side."

"She doesn't think anything's going to happen to you, does she?"

George gave her hand a comforting squeeze. "Don't send for the undertaker just yet. According to Hepsy, Tirzah says I should 'fear not what shall come to pass.' She also says that I 'dare not leave this place,' for my 'balm' lies here."

"Mercy," Callie said. "That's the strangest thing I've ever heard."

"Will you do me a favor, Callie? Will you keep this just between us—well, between us and Hepsy and Tirzah?"

"Of course."

"Will you do me another favor?"

"Yes."

"Never marry somebody you don't love. Ever. Promise?"

"Promise."

SEVEN

On a bright morning in May, Callie stepped outside to discover that a rare gift had been bestowed on Alabama—a blustery day. It wasn't stormy—not a cloud in the sky and no sign of a raindrop—just blustery, filled with the motion and energy of high winds. Lush green leaves danced against a clear blue sky as trees swayed and swirled, celebrating their respite from the heat, which was rising quickly this year.

The men were in the fields, little Theo riding along with them. Her mother and Emmy had gone to church to fulfill their duties on the annual homecoming committee. Hepsy had just left for the Bullocks' commissary to restock the kitchen. The house was completely empty, giving Callie an opportunity.

She hurried upstairs, took off her shoes and stockings, and hid them under the seat cushion of an armchair in case anyone should come home unexpectedly. Then she opened the window by the Lookout Tree and climbed out, holding tighter than usual as even the biggest limbs swayed in the wind. The journey up would be chancy until she got to the fork, which was so massive that nothing short of a tornado could disturb it. Pausing for the big gusts, she climbed up until she reached what had been one of her favorite spots on the entire Bullock farm since she was a child.

It was always magical up here, but today, in the strong winds, the tree was especially exhilarating. Callie wasn't sure what she loved more—the impressive view of her father's sweeping cotton fields, the strength of the tree that held her safe, or the powerful winds that cooled and enthralled her. They would feel even better without the voluminous petticoat underneath her skirt. There was no overstating what trouble she could expect if her mother ever found out, but on a day such as this, she was willing to take that risk. Bracing herself against the tree, she lifted her skirt, unfastened the petticoat, and tugged it down. Then she draped it over a limb and felt the wind blow straight through her cotton skirt. She held her arms wide and laughed out loud. Then she sat down and hugged her knees to her chest, leaning against the boards her brothers had nailed across the back of the fork long ago. They had called it their park bench in the sky, the boards forming a back for the natural seat of the fork.

Closing her eyes, Callie listened to the leaves whispering in the wind. Every few seconds, a gust would set them talking again. She looked out at the fields now blanketed in green as her father's cotton plants grew taller and stronger with every rain. The verdant landscape was enough to take her breath away.

Callie had always felt the most alive outdoors. No house, not even the grandest, could compare to the woods when they were brilliant with fall color, or a creekbank in spring when the water was running fast and high, so clear that you could see all the way to the bottom. The most finely stitched quilt was no match for a properly cultivated cotton field with its perfectly symmetrical rows of clean red earth, or a lush, well-tended garden ripening in the sun.

Just then Callie heard a horse, its hooves thumping against the ground as it trotted into her parents' yard. Looking down, she saw Solomon dismount a handsome dapple gray. Solomon—and here she sat up a tree with her petticoat hanging from a limb.

Fate Barbour, the blacksmith who oversaw her father's stables, came up from the horse barn. Solomon reached out to shake his hand, and they talked for a minute before Fate began leading the horse away. Solomon started to follow when the wind caught Callie's petticoat, tossed it up, and dropped it on a lower limb, where it dangled in midair. The movement must have caught his eye. At first, he stared up at the wayward garment waving like a flag of surrender, as if he couldn't quite put together what it was. But then he walked under the tree and looked up.

"Good morning," Solomon called.

"Good morning," Callie answered.

With one hand propped against the trunk of the tree, his head tilted to one side, he looked up at Callie. "I have so many questions."

"I'll come down."

Before she could start her descent, Solomon stepped onto the swing hanging below and began climbing one of its ropes. Once on a limb, he advanced to the fork, stopping on his way up to grab the free-flying petticoat, which the wind kept lifting and dropping. When he reached Callie, she was standing barefoot, braced against the tree, the wind blowing her skirt against her legs. Emmy had left in such a hurry that Callie hadn't troubled her to braid the long, curly hair that must now look as wild as Medusa's. Under Solomon's gaze, her petticoat in his hand, she felt heat rush to her cheeks.

Clutching the petticoat with one hand while holding on to a limb with the other, he studied her face. "I've never seen quite that shade of red. But it suits you." He handed her the petticoat and bowed slightly. "Your underpinnings, ma'am."

Callie felt another blush. But then, almost against her will, the corners of her mouth began to curl, and she broke into laughter.

"What?" Solomon asked with a smile.

"It's just so ridiculous. 'Good morning, Mr. Beckett—may I offer you an undergarment, and do please join me up a tree.'" Now Solomon was laughing with her, and Callie found his laugh, which was deep and mellow, as appealing as everything else about him. "Can you sit for a moment, or are you off to gather corsets down the road?"

"I can sit," he said. "One petticoat is about all I can handle this early in the day."

They sat down together in the fork, dangling their legs over the giant trunk. "We will never speak of this in front of my mother," she said.

"Secret's safe with me. I'm scared to death of your mother."

"Most people are, so don't feel bad," Callie assured him. "What brings you here this morning?"

"Your father stopped by when I was trying to fix two of Diamond's shoes with none of the right tools. He offered the help of your stable manager."

"Diamond? That's the gray's name?"

"Yes."

Callie smiled. "Suits him. How's your farm?"

"Pretty sure my farm—if you can call it that—is trying to kill me." Solomon pulled a leaf from the tree and tossed it into the wind. He looked discouraged.

"You're completely up to this, Solomon. Daddy and my brothers are very good judges of farmers—and character. They say you can do it."

"And what do you say?" The wind gusted, blowing his unbuttoned collar open so that Callie could see the hollow of his throat. She had to think for a minute to remember what he had asked her.

"I know you can," she said. "You've bought some beautiful property. I wish you could've seen it before it got so run away."

"Why don't you tell me about it? Maybe you'll give me a little hope."

"Well," she began, "what's special about your land is that Mr. Cruz didn't *have* to farm it. He was retired when he bought it. So every improvement he made on your property, everything he planted, says something about how much he loved the farm and enjoyed working the land. Once you uncover the old arbors behind the house, you'll see that they were designed to make it easy to gather the muscadines and blackberries and blueberries. Then he built raised beds around them so he could grow his tomatoes and squash and okra and greens right there close to the kitchen. It was always so pretty in season."

Solomon brushed at his sleeve, dusting off some moss he'd picked up on his climb. "I guess that explains all the odd piles of timber I found in the backyard."

"Yes! They're the remains of those raised beds, and you can build them back—or not. You can do whatever you want—make it your own. That's what's exciting. And then there are orchards that separate the homeplace from the pastureland and all the acreage that was never touched at all—a blank canvas. Is the old barn still there?"

"Yes."

"I'll bet it's solid. Everything on that farm always was."

A gust pressed them against the boards behind the fork. Callie laughed and held her arms out, embracing the wind. "That was a humdinger!"

"Yes, it was," he said, laughing. "A most definite humdinger."

Struggling to keep her hair out of her face in all the wind, Callie pulled it over her shoulder and loosely braided it. "You know, Solomon, you don't have to get your farm ready all by yourself. We'll help you if you'll let us."

"Your father didn't have any help."

"Daddy started with forty acres. You're starting with two hundred. There's a difference. And he didn't have the land that we're on now—not back then. He always says his first farm was 'hardscrabble on a good day.'"

Solomon ran a hand through his hair as Callie went on. "You're looking at Daddy the way he is now, not the way he was when he was just starting out. He didn't buy this farm all at once. Give yourself time."

"I guess I need to climb a tree with you now and then to keep the faith."

Callie smiled at him. "From now on, I'll fly a petticoat when I'm up here so you'll know I'm available for advice and counsel."

"I'd appreciate that. Now, as I said earlier, I have questions for you."

"Be about it then."

"Why exactly are you up this tree?"

"Why are you?"

"I'm up it because you're in it. I asked you first."

"I wanted to feel the wind from up here," Callie explained. "No, wait—that's not quite right. I wanted to feel it and see it all at once—the wind, the tree, the fields. It's like flying." She loved the way he was smiling and looking at her, like someone who not only understood but couldn't agree more.

"Can I ask another question?" he said.

"Yes."

"The first time I saw you in all your party finery, you looked like a rich man's daughter. The second time, coming home from the fields, you looked like a farm girl. Who are you right now, with your long, dark hair *and* your forsaken petticoat flying in the wind?"

Callie tucked a loose strand behind her ear and felt the wind against her bare feet, which dangled next to Solomon's. She looked at him straight on. "I'm myself."

He smiled and nodded. "Good. That's what I was hoping. Can't be easy, though, in a family like yours."

"Like mine?"

"Large. Wealthy. Prominent. Seems like it might be hard to

chart your own course with so many ties binding. Lots of rules and expectations, I'd imagine."

"You're not wrong—not entirely." Callie lifted her face to the sunlight seeping through the green and closed her eyes briefly, then turned to Solomon. "I'm blessed and I know it. But sometimes I can't breathe."

He stared at her, and once again, she found his eyes hypnotic. "Can I ask you something else, Callie?"

"Yes."

"The May Day picnic. Who was that girl singing? And what was all the commotion about?"

Callie sighed and hoped the gust of wind now stirring the tree might blow in an answer. "That's a big, big question, Solomon."

"Figured as much."

She slowly twirled her braid. "Well . . . I guess it goes back to those ties you mentioned. They don't just bind me to my family—they bind our family to Hepsy's. The girl at the well—the one who sang—her name is Lily and she's Hepsy's granddaughter."

He frowned. "Hepsy—she's your housekeeper?"

"Yes," Callie said. "But she's a lot more than that. Her mother, Tirzah, is a midwife and healer. A seer too. Mama's always said that Emmy and I both would've died in childbirth if it weren't for Tirzah. Mama might've died too."

"So it's all about gratitude?"

"Yes, but not *just* that. It's . . . I don't know . . . a special kind of trust between us, I guess. Mama feels a lifelong duty to Tirzah and her family, and Daddy's always made sure the rest of us honored that. Of course, as we've grown older, it's not so much about duty for my brothers and Emmy and me. We were raised with Hepsy and Tirzah always in our lives. We care a lot about them."

"How did all that figure into May Day?"

"One of the workers asked Lily to sing, and she did, never thinking all the picnic guests would show up to listen. Mama could see the same thing I did—talk starting. So she signaled Hepsy to bring Lily in."

Solomon pulled a twig off the tree and twirled it through his fingers as he listened.

"It's so ridiculous," Callie continued. "Those women will sit in church on Sunday with their heads held high but go around spreading lies about Lily just because she's a colored girl who's gifted in ways they aren't. I think they're jealous of her—and that scares the daylights out of them. Lily makes it hard for them to keep believing they're better than she is."

A gust of wind caught her hair and blew a loose tendril across her face. Solomon reached over and brushed it away with his fingertips. Her lips parted, but she couldn't speak.

"Miss Callie! You up that tree again?" Hepsy had come home from the commissary. Callie and Solomon looked down to see her at the hitching post. "Miss Callie?"

"Yes, Hepsy," Callie finally managed to call down.

"Am I gonna find y' shoes and stockin's hid under that seat cushion upstairs?" Hepsy asked.

Callie smiled at Solomon, who put his boot under her bare foot and lifted it up. "I expect so," Callie answered.

"Mr. Solomon s'posed to bring his horse by today," Hepsy called up. Solomon still had his boot under Callie's bare foot, and he was gently swinging it back and forth. "If he's up that tree," Hepsy said, "he better get down 'fore your mama comes home, 'less he's lookin' to die."

This time, it was Solomon who answered. "Yes, Hepsy."

EIGHT

After Solomon left, Callie came into the kitchen, where Hepsy was sitting at the table, snapping green beans for supper. "Want some help?" she asked.

"You know I ain't one to turn it down," Hepsy answered.

Callie took a bowl from a kitchen shelf and filled it with beans from one of Tirzah's handwoven baskets on the floor, then pulled up a chair at the table. She sat quietly working for a minute or two before Hepsy said, "What you got on your mind?"

"What makes you think—" Callie started, but Hepsy gave her a familiar look that told her denial was pointless. Callie sighed and resumed her snapping. "Hepsy . . . what do you think of Solomon?"

Hepsy smiled and raised an eyebrow. "That man brings the heat."

Callie frowned at her. "What do you mean?"

Hepsy threw her head back and laughed. "You gon' know soon enough, 'less I miss my guess. Some men, they got no fire in 'em. They don't know how to make a woman feel like herself. They runnin' cool. But yo' Mr. Solomon—he brings the heat."

Hepsy chuckled and pointed at Callie. "First time he kisses you, you gon' know *exactly* what I'm talkin' about."

"What makes you think he's going to kiss me?"

"Ha!" Hepsy laughed again. "You know well as I do he's goin' to."

Callie couldn't help smiling at the thought of it. "Do you like him, Hepsy? I mean, do you think he's a good man?"

"Yes." Hepsy picked a stray leaf out of her beans. "I think he's a good one. But it ain't my opinion that matters, now, is it?"

"It matters to me," Callie said.

They worked in silence before Hepsy slapped her forehead and got up from the table to grab a box of notepaper and pencils she kept on the shelf with the tea and coffee tins. She sat back down and began making notes, telling Callie, "I was about to forget it's time to polish the silver."

Callie watched Hepsy write her notes in neat, precise cursive letters. "Hepsy, I never thought about this before, but I've heard Daddy say that a lot of the field hands can't read or write. Do you mind if I ask how you learned?"

Hepsy finished her note and looked up at Callie. "It was part o' the promise between my mama and yours."

"What promise?"

"Mama promised to train me to take her place here and run the house if Miss 'Relia would teach me from books. Mama wasn't worried about your folks workin' me to death. Said Mr. Ira and Miss 'Relia was cut outta fine cloth. She knew they'd treat me right and pay me good. But she wanted me to get some education. Y' mama taught me to read and write and cipher. Let me borrow any book in this house I wanted to read."

Callie emptied her beans into a big Dutch oven on the table and reloaded her bowl. "Why do you think Mama and Tirzah are so close, Hepsy? Lots of women hire midwives and never get attached. Grandmother Cleary thinks it's odd. I've heard her tell Mama so."

Hepsy put down her notepad and returned to the beans. "They's the South and then they's the *old* South. Miss 'Relia's mama is *old* South—prob'ly go to her grave hopin' for the war to start up again and put us all back like we was. She ain't never gon' change. Never gon' budge a inch. But Miss 'Relia's differ'nt. I reckon she never come up against anything she couldn't handle till she become a wife and went to havin' her babies. Mama said she never felt a call so strong as the one what pulled her to this house."

"And that happened when James was born?" Callie asked.

"Right when Miss 'Relia first found out she was carryin' him. She had a regular doctor back then—Dr. Embry's daddy—but as it turned out, he was deliverin' another baby when Mr. James come early, so Mama brought him into this world. Later on, after Miss 'Relia miscarried with old Dr. Embry tendin' her, and then he delivered those two little babies that didn't make it— well, after that, she wouldn't listen to nobody but Mama from the time she knew she was carryin' a chile till y'all was safely born an' 'stablished in good health. She ate what Mama told her to, drank what Mama told her to, fed her babies the way Mama told her to. Everything Mama said, she did. And y'all's all here. That's cause o' Mama's gifts. Miss 'Relia knows that."

"It's hard for me to imagine Mama scared or needing help with anything," Callie said.

"Childbirth throws a woman into the storm," Hepsy explained. "They's life at the center o' the birthin' bed but death swirlin' all 'round. Sometimes you got to fight mighty high winds to get y'self and y' chile through it. My mama showed Miss 'Relia the way when she couldn't find it by herself. Mama held the lantern. Miss 'Relia still follows that light 'cause she knows it's gon' lead her and her chil'ren to safety."

"But what about you, Hepsy?" Callie asked. "Did you want to work here like Tirzah? Did you have a choice?"

Hepsy silently stirred the beans with her hand, picking out

a few bad ones that had slipped by. "'Choice' is a funny word. I had one. But I knew I wouldn't get many. My husband was done gone from the cancer. My chil'ren was young. I guess you could say I chose the best situation I was ever likely to get. I was blessed to land here with your family. Saved me from some bad situations. But you got to wonder—would y'all have saved *me* if Mama hadn't saved *y'all*?"

Callie stared at the beans in her bowl. Her hands were still. "Hepsy, I'm sorry."

They looked at each other, Hepsy with a furrowed brow. "What for?"

"For everything," Callie said. "Everything in this world."

NINE

*E*mmy poured water into the washbasin and dampened two cloths. She handed one to her sister. "Here, Callie. Maybe this will help."

They sat on the edge of their beds, blotting their faces and necks. May's milder days had given way to the warm ones of June, and if tonight was any indication, summer would be a scorcher.

Callie fanned the damp cloth in the air to make it cooler, then touched it to the back of her neck. "I might have to move up north before this summer's over. Maybe I can get a job in the coal mines."

Emmy giggled. "You'd probably end up the foreman, bossing all the other miners around."

Callie got up and stood in front of the window, holding her hair up and fanning her face with her hand. "Not a solitary leaf is moving out there. Quiet as a church mouse and twice as still. I wish it would pour rain right this second—buckets and buckets of rain."

"Me too." Emmy pulled the hem of her nightgown up to her knees and blotted her feet and legs. "You know where I wish we were right now?"

"Where?" Callie sat back down on her bed.

"Dewberry's Dip!" Emmy said with a grin.

Callie laughed at the thought of it—the two of them plunging into the blissfully cold, spring-fed swimming hole. It was tucked into the woods that once belonged to a sawyer named Felton Dewberry but had been part of their father's farm for as long as they could remember. Their older brothers had named it Dewberry's Dip.

"Wouldn't that feel like heaven?" Emmy said.

Callie sighed and held the damp cloth against her face. "As opposed to this heat, which feels like Torment?" Their mother found the word "hell" objectionable, as if speaking it might summon it. Never mind that her daughters heard preachers say it every Sunday. She insisted that Callie and Emmy refer to the eternal fire as "Torment" or "Perdition."

"I believe Torment would feel chilly compared to this room right now," Emmy said, dropping her nightgown back down over her legs. "Maybe the sweat on my gown will cool me off."

Callie watched her sister push damp tendrils of blond hair away from her face. "Emmy, why don't we do it?"

"Do what?"

"Go to Dewberry's Dip—right now!" Callie grabbed Emmy's hand and clutched it the way she used to when they would get a running start, jump into the swimming hole together, and come up shivering in the chill of its cold, clear water, even on the hottest day in August.

Emmy laughed and answered with one of Hepsy's favorite expressions. "Are you outside your mind, Callie? We can't go rambling through the woods at night!"

"I disagree. It's the only time we *can* go on a ramble because everybody who would tell us not to is asleep."

"Callie, are you serious?"

"I am. Come on, Emmy. Let's do it. Let's do something girls aren't supposed to. Or we could lie here and sweat till morning."

Slowly, a smile spread across Emmy's face. "If we get caught, you know Mama will never let us leave the house again."

Callie clasped her hands together. "It'll be worth it."

As quietly as they could, the sisters traded their nightgowns for swim dresses, slippers, and a couple of towels from their washstand.

"The doors are too loud," Emmy whispered.

Callie nodded and used a letter opener to unscrew the window screen at the bottom so that she and Emmy could climb out. They tiptoed off the porch, around the house, and into the backyard, then followed a narrow dirt road that led between the horse and mule barns, through a small field, and into the woods beyond. A bright moon lit their way past the shadowy rows of cotton plants growing taller and taller in the summer heat.

"Is this the road to Perdition we've heard so much about?" Callie whispered, which made them both laugh out loud, though they knew they shouldn't.

Eventually, the road made a deep dip so that they could no longer see the Bullock house, and then it curved slightly east, ending in a stand of tall pine trees.

"No turning back?" Callie asked.

"No turning back," Emmy said. "At least the excitement made me forget how hot I was. You lead the way. You've slipped off with Daddy and the boys enough to know the woods better than I do."

"Just don't step on a snake," Callie warned, "or we'll end up in the funeral home instead of the Dip."

She loved the woods at night. She and her father had a long-kept secret, which she'd shared only with Emmy. Now and again, he would allow her to slip out of the house and accompany the Bullock men on a nocturnal hunt. As she soon learned, these hunts had little to do with any serious quest to kill a raccoon and were instead an opportunity for the hunting dogs—and the men—to rip and run, unencumbered, through the night. Her father somehow sensed that Callie, unlike Emmy, also needed to run free.

For those moonlit hunts, Callie kept a pair of Sam's outgrown breeches and boots hidden in a box beneath some blankets in her chifforobe, but tonight, her swim dress and slippers would have to do. The pine straw crunched beneath her feet as the path narrowed and wound its way through towering loblollies and longleafs, which would serenely sigh and sway in the gentlest wind but were silent in the suffocating stillness of this hot night.

Memory took her back to the brisk, cold air of a November hunt with her father and brothers. The sky on that clear night had been a vast black carpet, lit by a crescent moon and dusted with millions of stars. The hounds had led them over one pine-covered hill after another, each one a little taller than the last, until finally, at the highest crest on her father's land, Callie looked down to see what appeared at first to be an open valley below. But as her eyes adjusted to her surroundings and the moonlight did its work, she could see that her valley was in fact the river flowing smooth as a satin ribbon.

A mosquito bite brought Callie back to the heat and sweat of this summertime evening. "I know what you're thinking," she said over her shoulder to Emmy. "You're wondering if I'm lost, but you don't want to say so."

"Am not."

"Are too."

"Well, maybe a little. But you know my sense of direction is terrible, so don't take it personally."

"I knew it!" Callie laughed. "Let me put your mind at ease. See that big white rock at the top of that hill—the one the moon is really lighting up?"

"I do."

"Just past that rock is where the trail turns right and goes downhill before it crosses the creek—remember? And then it's just a short walk a little further down to the Dip."

"I never doubted you for a minute," Emmy said.

"Did too."

"Did not."

They held their towels on one arm and extended the other for balance as they carefully stepped from one slick rock to another—a natural bridge across the shallowest part of the creek, which was one of many local tributaries feeding the Coosa River. Then they made a short downhill trek to the swimming hole and its promise of cold water.

Once, Dewberry's Dip had been a freestanding spring a few hundred yards from a sharp bend in the Coosa. But over the years, the river currents had worn away at the bank until they finally claimed the crystalline pool as a slough that now spilled into the river, bluing its earthy waters with the pristine flow of an underground spring. You had only to stand on the bank to see exactly where the spring gifted the muddy river with a turquoise patch of purity. Locals called it the Bluing, and it became a landmark for hunters, fishermen, and the occasional secret rendezvous: *I'll meet you at the Bluing.* The Bullock boys had felled a cottonwood tree across the mouth of the spring at the very spot where it spilled into the river, so they could easily cross from one side of the Dip to the other. Unlike the shaded swimming hole, the fallen tree lay in full sun, making it a handy spot to sit and dry off without the bother of all the red bugs in the tall grass around the water.

Callie and Emmy stepped cautiously as they made their way downhill and finally arrived at the spring. Under moonlight, Callie could see the water's glimmering surface, smooth as a hand mirror in the still summer night. Without saying a word, she and Emmy dropped their towels, kicked off their slippers, joined hands, and jumped in. They could not contain their squeals as the ice-cold water enveloped them, washing away the heat and the sweat, leaving them to shiver in pure spring water now doused in silvery moonglow. They giggled as they swam over to a flat rock submerged beneath the surface, where they could sit in water up to their shoulders and swirl their feet and legs in the refreshing pool.

"I'd almost forgotten what a great swimmer you are," Callie said. "Remember when we were kids and George bet you that you couldn't swim all the way across the river? You did it, though."

"Well, it's narrow here," Emmy said.

"Yes, but still. That was impressive."

"My twelve-year-old self thanks you for the accolades. But I think *this* is the most wicked thing we've ever done."

"Speak for yourself," Callie answered. "I've gone hunting at night with Daddy and the boys, remember."

"Well, it's definitely the most wicked thing we've ever done together."

"Agreed."

They sat quietly, relaxing as their bodies adjusted to the chilling temperature of the spring.

"Don't you think it's fascinating—this water, I mean?" Callie asked.

"No." Emmy splashed her face with water. "I just think it's blissfully cold."

"But think about its source. The water we're sitting in is bubbling up from underground. Somewhere under the cotton fields, water is flowing—like the river Styx in *Bulfinch's Mythology*."

"I still can't believe Mama allows that book!" Emmy splashed her face again.

While their mother had redone most of the Bullock home to her liking, she had kept the original library intact. All the books left behind by Brooks Calhoun—a collection that included everything from diaries of Confederate wives to poetry by the English Romantics and adventurous tales of the Greek and Roman gods—remained on their shelves, dutifully dusted by Hepsy every week. The library reflected the contradictions in their mother's nature: It held no copy of the wildly popular stories of Jack London because Aurelia considered him a dangerous radical. Yet Callie and Emmy were free to read tales of the sensuous Aphrodite, the huntress Artemis, and poor abducted Persephone because those stories, their mother said, were "classical literature from the historic library of our home."

Callie gently pushed back the spring water with her hands and watched the ripples glide across it. "I guess we're all a bunch of ripples," she said to Emmy, who was cupping water in her hand and spilling it back into the pool.

"What do you mean?"

Callie pushed the water out again. "I mean one person causes something to happen to another. Lily's husband died. That made her come to live with Hepsy. That made Hepsy bring her to the fish fry. That made one of Hepsy's helpers ask Lily to sing. That made Ryder notice Lily. That made Lily go into hiding. See what I mean?"

"I do." Now Emmy pushed the water, sending small waves out in a half circle around them. "The trouble comes when somebody like Ryder doesn't care what he pushes somebody else into."

Callie looked at her sister. "Why does he bother you so much, Em? It's not just what he's doing to Lily, because you couldn't stand the sight of him way before she got here."

Emmy silently ran her palm over the moonlit water as Callie waited for her answer. "You know that thing Hepsy taught us to do if a boy ever got too pushy with us?" she finally asked.

"Yes."

Emmy turned to face her. "Well, it works. And thank goodness." She pulled a cattail from the bank behind them and set it adrift on the spring water. It slowly bobbed and floated, barely leaving a trace of itself as it traveled. "Remember last spring," Emmy went on, "when Aunt Roxie took a fall?"

Callie thought for a minute and nodded. "You went over to stay with her one night."

"That's right. Mama thought it might cheer her up to have some of Tirzah's tea and a chicken casserole—a few other odds and ends. I was going to stay the night with her and make sure she took her medicine right. Well, since the Montgomerys live so close to her, Knox said he'd ask their cook to wrap up some plates for us, and he and I could have a quiet supper together after Aunt Roxie went to bed. But Ryder got wind of it somehow. He actually dressed in Knox's clothes and combed his hair for once, then showed up at Aunt Roxie's early—not long after I'd tucked her in with her pain medication. Ryder fully intended to pass himself off as Knox."

Callie tossed a rock in the water. "That is just like him to think he could fool absolutely anybody."

"I went to greet him—to greet Knox—on the front porch," Emmy continued, "but the minute I looked into his eyes, I knew who it was. Even if I hadn't, Ryder knows so little about his own twin that he had chosen a light blue suit Knox doesn't like. It was a gift from Judge Armbrester, who was his mentor in law school, so he wears it in court but no place else." Emmy paused and threw water over her shoulder, letting it spill down her back. She took a deep breath. "Even though I recognized him, he decided he'd do what he came to do anyway. He grabbed me and started trying to kiss me . . ." Her voice trailed off and she closed her eyes.

Callie laid her hand on her sister's shoulder.

Emmy turned to her. "I'll be forever grateful to Hepsy. I'll bet they could hear Ryder holler all the way to Georgia. I left him writhing on the porch, ran inside, and locked both doors. Then I loaded Aunt Roxie's shotgun and hoped and prayed Knox would get there soon, which he did—right after Ryder left. Or maybe I should say right after Ryder slithered away."

"Does Knox know?" Callie asked.

"Yes." Emmy scooped water and splashed it on her chest and neck. "I wasn't going to tell him at first. I was afraid it would be too hurtful for him to know his own brother cared so little about him. Now, of course, I can see Ryder was counting on that. But I was far too shaken to pretend everything was alright. And I knew I could never hide anything from Knox."

Callie relaxed her legs and watched her feet bob up in front of her. "What did Knox do?"

"It was right around that time when Ryder supposedly took a spill on his horse and broke his jaw—you remember that?"

"Yes."

Emmy smiled. "Knox was the horse."

Callie's mouth flew open, and she pushed her feet back underwater. "Kind and gentle Knox?"

Emmy nodded and laughed. "Yes, kind and gentle Knox broke his sorry brother's jaw—with what I believe they call a right hook."

"What did their parents say?"

"They believed the horse story like everybody else," Emmy said. "Knox thought that would be best for me—you know how people talk and jump to all kinds of conclusions—and Ryder has way too much pride to admit he'd been spurned by a woman *and* whipped by his twin, so he kept his mouth shut."

Callie patted her cheeks with spring water. "There is no end to him—to what he'll do, I mean."

"No, there isn't. And you remember that, Callie. I know you don't take him seriously, but what he intends, should he get the chance, is no joke. Never forget that."

"I won't."

"Remember something else. Men like Ryder depend on your silence. Don't ever let somebody like him convince you that you can't tell anybody what he's done. You shout it from the mountaintops. That's the only thing that's kept him from trying the same thing with me again. He knows now that I won't be silent."

Beneath the water, Callie took her sister's hand and squeezed it tight.

They were sitting together without talking, looking at the moon's reflection on the water, when they heard something in the river. It was coming from the direction of the Bluing, just beyond the Dip.

Emmy put her finger to her lips, then mimed a breaststroke. The sisters silently slipped off their rock and swam to the fallen tree, keeping their kicks and strokes underwater. Callie wasn't as strong or skilled a swimmer as Emmy, but she managed to keep pace with her. Holding on to the cottonwood's low-hanging limbs, they dropped down close to the water so that they could peer beneath the trunk and see what had made the noise in the river beyond.

It was Lily. She had pinned her hair on top of her head and left her clothes on the bank. Standing in water up to her shoulders, she looked up at the moon, extended her arms, and slowly twisted back and forth, trailing her hands and arms in the river. It was a scene both ethereal and sublime, like a piece of music that stirred your soul—deeply felt but impossible to describe.

The music was soon interrupted.

Callie and Emmy heard him before they saw him. Ryder's footsteps tapped across the felled tree, and now he was standing right above their heads. Lily looked sickened at the sight of him but made no sound.

Ryder squatted down on the tree, the way you would lower yourself to calm a cowering dog. Callie was certain he cared no more about Lily than that.

"Just look at you," he said softly. "To think I came all the way down here for a little romp with the ginner's daughter, but I found my prize instead."

Lily didn't move. She was as still as a doe in the woods listening for any hint of a threat.

"I don't know what those women have been telling you,"

Ryder was saying, "but I'd never dream of hurting you, Lily. All I want to do is give you the kind of attention you deserve."

Callie peeked under the tree at Lily. Still she didn't move. But where could she go?

"Come on over here and let me show you how a gentleman can take care of you," he said in a soothing voice. "You and me—we're practically old friends. Didn't you know that?"

Callie could see Lily stripped bare in water up to her shoulders. Just like Emmy, Lily stared straight ahead with a mixture of fear and rage, her eyes hard, her face frozen.

"Why, just last Christmas, I spotted you boarding a train at the station," Ryder went on. "Had no idea who you were or where to find you. But now I know. From now on, I'll make it my business to know."

Callie heard Emmy's breath coming hard and fast and imagined Lily's doing the same. Looking up at Ryder's backside jutting off the fallen tree, Callie's own anger bubbled up until she could no longer stifle it. With a single swift motion, she used one hand to push herself up from the low-hanging tree limb and the other to shove Ryder in the rear as hard as she could, sending him tumbling into the river.

The minute he hit the water, Lily scrambled out of it and grabbed her clothes. She was frantically looking about, trying to pick a direction, when Callie waved to her from the edge of the Dip, where she and Emmy had climbed out. Without hesitating, Lily ran to them, and the threesome sprinted back up the path and through the pines.

A woman's voice called out, "Ryder? Ryder Montgomery, where are you?"

It was surely Minnie, the ginner's daughter, but they never stopped to look back until they had reached the Bullock house. Callie hurried to the loosened window screen and held it up, first for Lily, then Emmy.

Finally safe, the three of them stood in the sisters' bedroom, breathing hard, dripping wet, and shivering in silence. Emmy got them towels from the washstand while Callie tiptoed to her bureau, pulled out two nightgowns, and handed one to Lily. As Lily dropped the clothes she had been clutching and took the towel, Callie caught a glimpse of her rounded belly.

She looked at Emmy. Her sister had seen it too. Lily let the gown fall and smoothed it before she looked up and met the sisters' stunned stares.

"Lily, are you—are you expecting a baby?" Emmy asked her quietly, just above a whisper.

Lily nodded, her eyes wide and anxious.

"You were expecting when you got here?" Callie asked.

Again, Lily only nodded. But then she began to cry, silent tears streaming down her face.

Callie and Emmy rushed to her and put their arms around her. They led her to Callie's bed and sat down on either side of her.

"How far along?" Emmy asked.

"About six and a half months," Lily said, wiping her eyes. "Mama Tirzah says I'm mighty small for my time, but she's sure my baby's alright." She wrapped her arms around her belly and smiled through her tears. "Me and Levi—that was my husband—we dreamed about the babies we'd have, raisin' 'em up in Chicago where they could be anything they wanted to be."

Emmy reached for the nightstand drawer and pulled out a handkerchief for Lily. She blotted her eyes and took a deep breath before telling the rest of her story, smiling at the memory of it. "I was so excited when the doctor told me about the baby. It was nearly quittin' time at the rail yard when my appointment was over, so I didn't even go home after. Went straight over there to meet Levi and tell him so we could go celebrate together." Lily's smile faded. "But the foreman says he's not there. Says there's been an accident and Levi's down at the hospital. I never saw him alive again. Not long after that, I came here."

"Oh, Lily," Emmy said, wiping her own tears with her fingertips, "we're so sorry."

There in the darkness, the bedroom lit only by moonbeams streaming through the window, Callie studied the two figures next to her with a distance that, she hated to admit, came easily to her. Always, she'd had the strange sensation of living her life and observing it at the same time. Part of her never stopped watching, listening, interpreting as best she could—even with Emmy. And when she let her mind float high above that room and look down on the scene below, she couldn't help feeling that she was meant to protect the two women beside her, even though Emmy was older and knew what it was like to fall in love, even though Lily had experienced life more directly and painfully than either of them—was in fact carrying it inside her.

"You can't go back home, Lily," Callie said.

Emmy and Lily both stared at her.

"You can't go home," Callie repeated. "You're not safe anywhere but right here until something's done about Ryder."

"She's right," Emmy said. "You're not."

"Colored girl sleeping in a white house?" Lily objected. "That's not allowed. You'd be in enough trouble just for putting me in your nightgown."

"For tonight, the rules don't matter," Callie said. "We'll figure out the rest tomorrow, but you can't leave this house tonight—not with Ryder out there. I don't know if he saw Emmy and me or not, but even if he did, he'd never come near Daddy's house in the middle of the night. He's a snake, but he's not stupid."

"How should we manage, do you think?" asked Emmy, who usually took the lead but tonight seemed relieved to have her younger sister in charge.

Callie thought about it. "Won't Hepsy be missing you, Lily?"

"No," Lily said. "I was staying with my cousin. Mama Tirzah moves me around to make it harder for anybody to find me. After everybody else went to bed, I was sitting up reading in the loft where I sleep, and it just got so hot. I thought I'd slip down to the river for a minute—doubt my cousin's even missed me."

"You sleep on my trundle tonight," Callie said. "You've got clothes to put on for tomorrow. We'll slip you out in the morning and you can just meet Hepsy in the kitchen for work like nothing happened."

Together, the sisters slid the trundle from underneath Callie's bed. Emmy fetched a pillow and light spread from a trunk at the foot of her bed. "I doubt you'll need any cover, as hot as it is, but just in case." She laid the pillow at the head of the trundle, pulled back the top sheet, and folded the spread at the foot. "We should all get some rest. As late as it is, daybreak will come mighty early."

Soon Emmy and Lily were both fast asleep, their slow, rhythmic breathing almost in sync with each other. But not Callie. She remained vigilant, resecuring the screen over the window and peering out to keep watch until she could no longer hold her eyes open. Hepsy would say this was one of those nights "when you got to do like Paul in the Bible—drop your anchors and pray for daylight."

Callie would be praying that prayer—over and over until sunrise lit the sky and chased away the troubles that hide in the night.

TEN

*Y*ou did *what?*"

Callie knew her mother was waffling somewhere between shock and fury as she tried to take in what her daughters were telling her. The three of them stood around the kitchen table with Hepsy and Lily. The unbearable heat had finally broken with a thunderstorm during the wee hours, and rain was pouring down. There would be no work in the fields today, which meant the men could sleep late. Callie's mother never slept in. She had found Hepsy pacing in the kitchen, frantic with worry, just before Lily arrived. They were both interrogating her when Callie and Emmy came to the kitchen, saw Lily's predicament, and confessed.

"So you see, Lily didn't do anything wrong," Callie said. "She came home from the woods with Emmy and me because we knew it wasn't safe for her anywhere else with Ryder out there—and mad as a hornet most likely. But don't blame Emmy. It was all my idea to go down to the Dip. I talked her into it."

"She didn't have to try very hard at all," Emmy said. "I wanted to go."

"What on earth were you thinking, Callie?" their mother demanded. "Two young women traipsing through the woods at night? Anything could've happened. How did you even know how to *find* that swimming hole in the dark?"

"Well . . . the moon was pretty bright," Callie said. Nothing under heaven could make her betray her father's trust and tell her mother about the night hunts. "And I inherited Daddy's sense of direction. I guess I just remembered from going there with the boys."

"And you, Emeline?" their mother pressed.

"Oh, Mama, I would've been lost as a goose without Callie. She's the reason—the only reason—we got home safely, all three of us."

Their mother rubbed her forehead. "Everybody sit down. This standing around is getting on my nerves."

Everybody took a seat except Hepsy, who poured the coffee first and then joined them. "What 'bout you, Lily?" Hepsy asked. "After all we been doin' for yo' protection, you went wanderin' them woods at night too?"

Lily looked like she might cry any minute. "It was just so hot, Grandmama. I didn't have any idea that man would be there. Thought I could just cool off for a minute and slip right back to bed without worrying anybody. I didn't think cousin Juba would even miss me, let alone tell you I was gone. Last thing I ever want to do is worry you—or you, Miss Aurelia. I know you're right mad at your girls, ma'am. But if they hadn't been there, well . . . I believe we all know what woulda happened to me. I can't swim. Wasn't nowhere for me to go but back to the riverbank, and there he'd be. If I'd defended myself, he could've had me thrown in jail or worse." She looked at Callie and Emmy. "I'll go to my grave thankin' God they were in those woods. They did what I'm not allowed to. That's why they were there. They were sent to fight when it took all I had *not* to. Grandmama taught me a long time ago what to do when men get out o' hand. But if I'd done that on the riverbank, I would've brought down all kinds o' trouble on my family."

Callie's mother leaned back in her chair and sighed. "Of course we're all thankful that you were not harmed, Lily. And if my girls had something to do with keeping you safe, I'm grateful they were there." She looked across the table at Callie and Emmy. "But I am not done with you two. If I *ever* hear of you pulling a stunt like that again, I promise you before all that's holy, you'll regret it. Do I make myself clear?"

"Yes, Mama," Emmy and Callie said together.

"Now," she went on, "to Lily's situation."

"It ain't right y'all so mired up in this," Hepsy said, staring at her coffee. "Something to worry this house just about ever' day. The girls runnin' through the woods at night. Mighta got hurt or worse. It ain't right, Miss 'Relia. This got to end."

"What's not right is letting this get so out of hand because I didn't want to bother Ira with it," Callie's mother said. "We are beyond that now. I'll have him speak in no uncertain terms to Ryder and let him know, face-to-face, that I will not have the workings of my house dictated by a selfish, useless popinjay—and that his unwelcome presence on our farm will henceforth be met with a shotgun. Lily, I think, should stay closer to the house until the baby comes. And then we can find a better situation for her. I just need to determine where she might stay."

"What about the old kitchen, Mama?" Emmy asked. When it was first built, the Bullock house had a separate kitchen in the backyard where all the meals were prepared. It was a measure taken to protect the house from kitchen fires. When Callie's father remodeled the house for his wife, he had a brand-new kitchen built onto the back, leaving the original cookery building empty but still standing. The girls had made it their playhouse when they were little.

"You think it's suitable?" their mother asked.

"Not as it is," Emmy answered. "But I think Fisher could make it work just fine. The old woodstove is still there. It was big enough to feed an army in its day. I'm sure it can keep the building warm when the time comes. Lily can fix herself plates from our kitchen at mealtime, just like Hepsy does, so she needn't worry with cooking out there. It just needs a good cleaning and a few repairs, which Fisher can certainly handle. Then a little furniture, which I'm sure we have in the attic."

Their mother nodded as she listened. "Hepsy, what do you think?"

"Seem like a awful lotta trouble for y'all to go to," Hepsy said.

"Lily needs a safe place to have her child so that she can get on with her life," their mother insisted. "I cannot imagine going through those nine months worrying about my personal safety on top of all the other trials that come with bringing a baby into the world. Lily will not be tormented during this time of preparation. I simply will not have it. I'll speak to Ira this evening so we may get started right away. Girls, I entrust you with selecting furniture from the attic. Fisher and one of the field hands can move it for you. I'll have your father arrange it."

"Yes, Mama," Callie and Emmy said.

Their mother stood up from the table. "That's settled. Now let's be about breakfast for the men."

As she followed her mother and sister out of the kitchen, Callie turned to tell Lily that everything would be alright. But Hepsy was holding her tight. Callie kept silent and let them be.

ELEVEN

Watching the progress on Lily's new home, Callie and Emmy had to agree with their brother Sam—Fisher was most definitely sweet on Lily.

Working day and night, their father's carpenter had cleaned, repaired, and painted the former kitchen, putting the old wood-stove and hand-pump sink into good working order. Fisher asked permission to add a little porch with a swing for Lily. He even made two planters to flank the steps, which, together with the porch and a new door, made the drab old building look more like a cottage than a vacant kitchen. Lily had already sown zinnia seeds in the planters.

Callie and Emmy outfitted Lily's new home with a large rug to warm up the wood floor. At the opposite end from the woodstove and sink, they had Fisher place a simple but pretty walnut spindle bed and bureau, along with a cradle and rocking chair. A small kitchen table with two ladder-back chairs, placed in front of the woodstove, gave Lily a place to sit with Hepsy for a visit. Fisher left enough of the original kitchen shelves to hold a few essentials but replaced the oversized icebox with a small one to give Lily more room inside.

For her part, Callie's mother had the backyard framed with

an iron fence from New Orleans. Its ornate gate had a keyed lock. Never again would her picnic guests wander where they didn't belong. She had it anchored with gas lamps just like the ones she'd seen on Royal Street during her honeymoon.

As requested, her husband and two oldest sons paid a visit to Ryder Montgomery, who ceased his intrusions on their property. The Bullocks considered Ryder handled. But not Hepsy.

"He ain't through," she told Callie and Emmy. "He's just patient."

∽

One night after supper, Callie was walking back from the horse barn, where she had smuggled Daisy Bell some fig preserves, a rare treat the horse loved even more than apples. In summer's lingering twilight, Callie stared up at the Lookout Tree, its massive branches reaching out like open arms to the sky. She had a sudden urge to climb it—something she rarely did at night.

George and Sam had gone to a house dance with Emmy and Knox. They tried to persuade Callie, but she didn't see the point. She already knew everybody who would be there and had no desire to spend the evening with them.

She found her father rocking Theo in the front parlor, reading to him from his new favorite, *The Shepherd of the Hills*. "If you're sorry you stayed home, I can have Fisher drive you over to the Thompson house for the dance," her father said as she bent down to kiss a drowsy Theo good night.

"Thank you, Papa, but I'm not sorry," she said. "I just didn't feel like dancing with the same old partners again tonight."

He squeezed her hand. "You'll find a good one soon enough, my girl. I'm not in any hurry to have you leave my house."

Callie smiled and kissed him on the cheek before telling her mother good night and taking the back stairs to the upper floor. She slipped off her shoes and stockings and tucked them into their hiding place under the seat cushion. Then she opened the window closest to the Lookout Tree and climbed onto a limb, pulling the window down behind her.

Up she climbed until she reached the fork, which held her like a cradle. From here, she could look down at the world below.

The last traces of twilight still lingered when Callie heard voices. In the still quiet, she easily made them out—Fisher and Lily.

"Grandmama says I shouldn't have any menfolk in the house," Lily said, though she sounded regretful.

"That's alright," Fisher said. "Reckon she would mind if we set a spell right here under this tree?"

"I expect that would be fine."

Callie suddenly felt like an intruder in her own yard. Fisher and Lily were sharing a rare private moment, and here she was listening high above. It wasn't right, but she was too afraid of attracting attention to move. Peeking through the branches, she could make out both of them, dimly lit by one of the gas lamps.

"You did a fine job on my little cottage," Lily said. "And my swing is about the prettiest I've ever seen."

"Thank you. I'm real glad you like it." Callie could imagine Fisher smiling. They were quiet for a moment before he asked Lily, "You miss your family?"

"Yes," she answered. "Before me and Levi married, I used to spend lots of summers here. Mama and Daddy and me, we'd always come for Christmas or Thanksgiving—sometimes the Fourth of July. I even talked Levi into coming down last December. But visiting your family's different from living with them."

"I can see that."

"I was really enjoying all the time with my grandmama and Mama Tirzah—getting to know them," Lily said. "The woods where they live—and the river too—they're so peaceful. At least, they *were* till that man started showing up all over the place. I could walk to visit my cousins—Juba and Esther and the rest. It was nice to feel like I was part of a big family, 'specially with a baby coming soon."

"It ain't fair, you havin' to stay here, Lily. It ain't fair a-tall." There was such resignation in Fisher's voice, its rightful anger stifled far too long to make itself heard anymore. Callie felt sick at the sound.

"No, it's not fair," Lily said, "but it could be a lot worse if the Bullocks weren't good people. Not many families would do what they have to keep me safe. And I'm grateful. I am. It's just that—well, I don't think they even realize they're deciding your life for you."

"Mm-hm," Fisher answered. "You speakin' the truth."

"Nobody asked me if I wanted to live in the old kitchen," Lily said. "Doesn't mean I'm not grateful to have it, or that I don't love it since you made it so nice for me. But still—nobody asked me. That's all."

"It's the same with me," Fisher said. "Nobody asked me if I wanted to be a carpenter. I like it—lot better than the fields. And it comes natural to me. But nobody asked me if I wanted to do it. They just said, 'You a carpenter now.'"

Callie felt her eyes sting.

"When I first came down here to stay, Grandmama told me that white folks are like king snakes and coral snakes," Lily said. "They look almost the same, but one'll kill you and the other won't. So you've got to watch your step till you figure out which one's crossing your path."

Fisher chuckled. "She's got that right."

"It's not like this everywhere, Fisher. Did you know there's towns in the South built by freed slaves? Colored folks run everything."

"You pullin' my leg?" Callie could hear the surprise in Fisher's voice.

"No, I'm not kidding you," Lily said. "Down around Mobile, there's one called Africatown. Texas has a whole bunch of them. Florida's got some. They're all over. You just got to know where to find them."

"Do you think—that is—maybe after your baby comes, we could—"

Just then Callie heard a buggy coming down the road. Fisher and Lily must have heard it too. He walked her back to the cottage as Callie scrambled down from the tree and climbed back inside the house. Before her brothers came up the stairs, she had just enough time to duck into the upstairs sitting area, grab a book, and curl up on a settee where she could hide her bare feet under her skirt.

"You should be ashamed of yourself," Sam said to her with a grin. "Ole Denny was heartbroken that you didn't show."

Callie rolled her eyes. "Ole Denny can go fly a kite. Why are y'all back so early?"

"Knox was tired," George said. "He's worn out from the case he's been working on—the one with all the sick cotton mill workers."

"He won it late yesterday," Sam added. "That sorry mill owner is about to pay a heap of doctor bills, among other things."

"And I'll bet Emmy's already planning a celebration," Callie said.

George nodded. "Yep. I would expect a *lot* of silver on that table."

Callie closed her book. "Will I be called into active duty?"

"Absolutely," George said. "Knowing Emmy, she's making a list right now. I'll bet we all have assignments. We're going downstairs to see if we can talk Daddy and Mama into a game of rummy. Want to come?"

"Save me a seat," Callie said. She waited until her brothers had gone downstairs before she reshelved her book, put her shoes on, and made sure her stockings were well hidden under the seat cushion. Then she crept down the back stairs into the darkened, empty kitchen. At the sink, she looked out the windows above it and could see Lily's cottage outlined by the gas lamps and moonlight. As she watched, a familiar figure came from somewhere in the darkness, spread a blanket under one of the front windows, and lay down. Fisher was keeping watch over Lily.

Callie backed away from the windows. And three words echoed like a drumbeat: *Nobody asked me.*

TWELVE

Many white people in the community were afraid of Hepsy's mother because she was beyond their reach, possessing undeniable gifts that were not of this world. Tirzah had saved the lives of birthing mothers, predicted things that came to pass, and discovered what was lost when no one else could. Ninety years old and well over six feet tall, she had a solemn and regal carriage. Tirzah never hurried and rarely smiled. Year-round, she favored long plaid skirts and white cotton blouses, which were covered with thick wool sweaters and shawls in winter. She was never without a long strand of red beads, a gift from Hepsy.

Tirzah had been enslaved until the surrender. Her grandparents survived a horrific journey across the Atlantic in the hull of a ship. "Don't you be foolin' yo'self," Tirzah would say as she finished every story of her family. "Ain't no slave love the master; ain't no master love the slave. Love can't abide no chains."

Callie had never been afraid of Tirzah and happily volunteered for errands to her cabin. Today she had delivered a chocolate cake and was rewarded with an invitation to sit at Tirzah's table and have a cup of her special tea, which no one else but Hepsy knew how to blend.

"Do you expect any of your grandchildren will build houses here on your land, Tirzah?" Callie asked as the old woman rose to her full height and took the kettle from her stove to refill their teacups. Long ago, Tirzah had saved enough money to buy fifteen acres on the river from Callie's father, and all her children raised their families there.

"They will not stay," she said, taking her seat and dripping honey into their cups from a jar on the table.

Callie slowly stirred her tea and watched the honey dissolve. "Why did you, Tirzah—if it's alright to ask? Why did you stay in Alabama after you were free?"

Tirzah took a long sip of her tea before she spoke. "Promised Almighty."

She grew very quiet until Callie couldn't resist urging her on. "You promised God you would stay here?"

"No." Tirzah looked straight at Callie. "Promised Almighty to serve where He led. Almighty led me to the birthin' bed— most 'specially to Young Miss."

"Young Miss" was Tirzah's name for Callie's mother, even now that she was fifty. Tirzah never paid attention to names. She called you what she thought you ought to be called.

Callie wrapped her hands around the warm cup and took a drink. Nothing on earth tasted like Tirzah's tea. "When did you make that promise—your promise to God?"

"Got sold to a Alabama planter—me and me alone—tore from my people in South Carolina. Wasn't but fifteen. Promised Almighty if He give me a balm to soothe my soul, I serve Him all my days. Almighty faithful. He give me a fam'ly o' my own—a husband and chil'ren and generations to come. He give me the sight. He give me healin' power. He know I done see plenty sufferin' bring death. Now He let me see sufferin' bring life. Ever' generation got power to do better. Ever' chile bring hope. That what Almighty showed me. Make me His deliverer. Let me deliver hope."

Callie tried to imagine what it must have been like for a fifteen-year-old girl to be forced away from her family, all alone. It made her feel nauseated, and she wrapped her arms around her stomach.

Tirzah got up and retrieved a small bottle from a shelf above her sink. She sat back down and poured two small drops in Callie's tea. "Stir that. Sip slow. Settle y' stomach."

Tirzah stared at her as she sipped the tea, which now sent a warm trickle down her throat and into her stomach. Tirzah was right. She did feel better.

"Y' sister got a tender heart," Tirzah said. "You got a wonderin' heart." She pointed her finger at Callie and leaned forward in her chair. "You gon' need strength. You gon' need courage. Some questions got hard answers. Bring no comfort. Only pain. But Almighty say truth make you free. You seek truth. That good. But you gon' pay a price for y' freedom."

※

In the early afternoon, Callie said goodbye to Tirzah on her front porch and looked up at a troubled sky, its blue dimmed to gray, the clouds moving faster than before as a cool breeze began to blow. The seer's words echoed in her mind: *"You gon' pay a price for y' freedom."*

Callie was still turning Tirzah's words over in her mind when she and Daisy Bell were about two miles from the Bullock house. The breeze picked up, and she could smell rain coming across the cotton fields, stirring up the red dirt as it struck the ground.

"Callie! We're about to get drenched!" She looked behind her and saw Solomon riding Diamond in her direction, the dapple gray moving at a fast trot.

"Daddy's got a hay barn right up there." Callie pointed to a bend in the road ahead. "Want to try for that?"

Solomon pointed to the sky. "Beats the alternative."

It was already beginning to sprinkle, so they let the horses gallop to a long barn with a wide, open hall and deep sheds on both sides, just a short jaunt off the road. Solomon and Callie dismounted quickly and led both horses inside. Soon the rain was pelting the barn so hard that it sounded like marbles hitting the tin roof.

"Never saw that before." Solomon pointed to the short horizontal hall in the center of the barn. It opened to the sheds on either side.

"Makes it easier to get to everything," Callie said. "There's a trough out there so we can give the horses water. They can pretty much graze in here, with all the loose hay on the ground."

She brought two halters and lead ropes from a tack room so they could take the bridles off and make it easier for the horses to eat and drink. After watering the mare and the stallion in one of the sheds, Callie and Solomon brought them back inside the main barn, a better shelter from the blowing rain.

He pulled two hay bales next to each other. "Our settee," he said.

Callie smiled and nodded as they sat down in the thick, loose hay on the floor of the barn and leaned back against the bales to watch the weather.

Solomon stretched out his legs, which were long and lean. "I don't think we'll get a storm. Looks like it's just a hard rain."

"I don't understand people who hate rain." Callie hugged her knees to her chest. "It's about the most peaceful thing there is—makes you stop whatever you were doing and just be still."

Solomon covered his mouth with his fist as he yawned. "Always makes me sleepy."

"Don't do that." Callie yawned herself. "It's contagious."

"What would you be doing right now if it weren't raining— besides riding the rest of the way home, I mean?" he asked.

"Suffering a fate worse than death." She shuddered at the

thought. "I promised to look at fabric swatches with Emmy. Mama says we need new summer dresses."

"What's so bad about that?"

"You try looking at swatches with Emmy," Callie said. "She has to study each one endlessly, touch the fabric over and over to consider the texture, hold it up to the window so she can see how it might look in sunlight, compare it with her other dresses to ponder whether the color might be too close to something she already has, and on and on and on. I love her dearly, but she could drive a preacher to drink with those swatches."

Solomon laughed. "And what about you?"

Callie mimed pointing at fabrics. "That one, that one, and that one. Takes me less than a minute. You either like yellow or you don't."

"How else are you different from your sister?"

"About every way there is." Callie glanced down at her arms wrapped around her knees. "For one thing, she would never sit like this in front of a man. She'd think it wasn't ladylike. Emmy's . . . kind of perfect, really."

"Sounds tiresome."

Callie laughed at the idea of anyone finding Emmy tiresome. Everybody adored her, including Callie. "I guess she could be aggravating if she were turned differently. But Emmy's not the least bit conceited. She's very humble and generous and tender-hearted. She is who she is, and she wants the same for me—she wants me to be myself, I mean, and ignore anybody who says I need to change. She's beautiful inside and out."

"So are you." He said it so matter-of-factly, without a hint of flirtation.

Callie was too startled to respond. She could only look at Solomon, who seemed as relaxed and self-possessed as she was unsure of herself right now.

"It's just the truth," he said with a shrug.

Callie smiled at him. He had the most handsome face.

"So you're never jealous of each other—you and Emmy?" he asked.

"No. I wish I were more like her sometimes. She never gets impatient or restless the way I do. And her mind is quieter—sleeps like a baby. I wish I could do that instead of tossing and turning with my thoughts in a jumble."

"And what about your brothers? Looks to me like they'd be fighting for position with all this land at stake."

"They don't have to. They're all expected to help work Daddy's farm until they're eighteen, and then they can either become a partner or he'll help set them up to go out on their own—whatever they want to do, even if it's not farming. James is staying. Sam will go. George is kind of in the middle. He doesn't really enjoy growing cotton, but he likes the business side of it, so he's learning that from Daddy while he runs some ventures of his own."

"Doesn't that leave you and Emmy out?"

"No. Daddy will give each of us whatever homeplace we want when we marry, and if we choose somebody who wants to farm, he can become part of the family business. If he doesn't want to, Daddy will give us a cash gift to invest in some other enterprise."

"What if you and Emmy want the same homeplace?"

"Not likely," Callie said, laughing. "Emmy wants to be around people as much as I want to dodge them most of the time. She'll choose a homeplace as close to civilization as she can get. I'll choose one as close to the river as I can get."

"There's more to it than land, though," Solomon said. "I haven't been around your family all that much, but you seem to genuinely like each other—enjoy each other's company."

"We do."

"But real families aren't like that."

"You don't believe we're a real family?"

"I guess anything's possible—even having a family you don't despise."

Callie's eyes narrowed as she stared at him, trying to decide if he was serious. "Surely you don't despise your own family, Solomon."

"I do," he said. "I hope I never see them again."

Her lips parted as she searched for the right thing to say. "Can you tell me why? Or would you rather not talk about it?"

Solomon sighed and ran his hands through his hair—something he did, Callie had noticed, when he was uncomfortable. "It's not a very pleasant story."

"That's alright. You can tell me anyway, if you want to." Callie turned toward him, resting her arm on the bale and bending her legs to one side.

He picked up a short piece of stray baling twine, slowly running it through his fingers. "My father was a taskmaster," he explained. "Pitting my brothers and me against each other was his way of getting us to work harder—for him, not for anything that would ever be ours. He had plenty of money to make his family comfortable but chose not to. My mother died because he sent her to a county free clinic when he should've taken her to a specialist in St. Louis."

"How old were you?"

"Ten. My sisters married the first boys who asked, just to get off that farm. I was the youngest and the last to go, but I got out of there as quick as I could." He tied the baling twine into a slipknot.

"I'm so sorry, Solomon," Callie said. He shrugged off her concern, but when she put her hand on his arm, he stopped staring at the knot and turned to her. "I really am sorry," she repeated.

"Why?" He was looking at her so intently that she could see every fleck of color in his eyes.

"I don't like the thought of you being unhappy."

He tilted his head to one side. "You think everybody needs a family to be happy? Look at how hard you work at pleasing yours. Wouldn't you rather be out on your own sometimes?"

"I guess it's hard for me to imagine being happy without the people who love me."

"You think they'd still love you if you didn't do what they say?" he countered.

"I think a true family loves you no matter what."

"And you want that for me?" He was staring at the twine, untying and retying the slipknot.

"Yes. I want you to have people in your life who'll love you no matter what."

Solomon looked up at her. "You think somebody like me deserves that?"

"I've never met anyone like you. And I think you absolutely deserve it."

Solomon took the piece of twine, wrapped it like a bracelet around Callie's wrist, and tied it into an impressive figure-eight knot, his fingers brushing against her skin as he worked.

When he was finished, he looked at her and slowly traced the line of her cheekbone with his fingertip. Neither of them moved or took their eyes off each other until the sound of a horse and buggy broke the spell. Callie struggled to recover as her brother George approached the barn.

"Solomon!" George exclaimed when he came inside. "Mama sent me to find Callie. If I'd known she was with you, I would've stayed home. I trust you have behaved in a courtly manner?"

"Missouri boys are always courtly," Solomon said, standing and helping Callie up before shaking George's hand. "Especially when we know there's a shotgun waiting for us if we get out of line."

"What brings you out this way?" George asked him.

"The tools I ordered at the feed store finally came in, so I was returning some your father lent me. I spotted Callie just ahead of me right before the bottom fell out."

"Don't look now, but I think your horses are sweet on each other," George said.

Callie and Solomon turned to see Daisy Bell and Diamond nuzzling each other's necks. Solomon rolled his eyes. "Just what I need—a distracted stallion."

George gave him a friendly slap on the back. "Happens to the best of us, my friend. Let's get to the house before Mama comes looking."

"Would she really do that?" Solomon asked as they led the horses out and tied them to the buggy.

"Yep," George said. "And just so you know, Mama's broken more than a few distracted stallions in her time."

THIRTEEN

For a week now, the Bullock house had been a flurry of activity, with Callie and Emmy helping Hepsy and Lily prepare for Knox's celebration supper on the first Friday in July. Solomon was invited.

Callie was setting a tea pitcher on the buffet when Knox came in and greeted them both, kissing Emmy on the cheek. He had been so busy that Callie hadn't seen him in weeks, and his appearance startled her. His face looked gaunt, his eyes shadowed by dark circles. The long court case had taken its toll.

"May I congratulate the guest of honor?" Callie's mother asked as she came into the dining room and held Knox's hand between hers. "We're very proud of you, Knox. You have performed a great service for people in desperate need."

"Thank you, Miss Aurelia. That means a lot to me."

"Callie, I believe Solomon has arrived," her mother said. "Why don't you go and greet him for us. Emmy, take Knox into the parlor and give him a nice glass of sherry while we wait for Hepsy's rolls to come out of the oven."

As with all her evening gatherings, Callie's mother had sent Hepsy home to rest once the cooking was done. "Any household with three women can surely put food on the table," she always said.

Callie stepped onto the front porch just as Solomon, who was carrying a shoebox, shook Fate Barbour's hand and gave him Diamond's reins.

"I brought a small—very small—gift for each of the ladies," he said as he climbed the front steps. He reached into the box and handed Callie a bouquet of three pink roses, their delicate petals almost as densely layered as a peony. Their stems were cut short and tied together with a simple white ribbon.

"The Duchesse is blooming!" she said with a gasp as she took the bouquet. It was the only one of the three tied with the same figure eight as the twine bracelet he had made for her at the barn. "Thank you, Solomon!" Callie breathed in the heady fragrance of the roses.

"Who exactly," he asked, "is the duchess?"

"You're in the presence of royalty," Callie explained. "This is Miss Katherine's Duchesse de Brabant rose. It took the blue ribbon at every county fair of my childhood." She smelled the roses again. "Don't you just love it when beautiful things appear out of nowhere?"

"I do." He smiled down at her. "Especially when they appear in trees and barns."

Callie felt the now familiar hammering in her chest whenever she was alone with him. "We haven't seen you in a while."

"Not my choice," he said with a weary sigh. "There's just so much to do on my farm right now that I'm too tired to do anything else. At least I have some help now that your father connected me with a few good workers."

"It's going to be amazing, Solomon. You'll see."

"I guess I need to come by here and let you tell me that every day," he said. "Is this the part where I give you my arm so we look respectable?"

"It is indeed." Callie took his arm and led him inside to the front parlor, where he was greeted by all the family and offered his congratulations to Knox. Then Callie's mother summoned everyone to the table and dictated the seating order: her husband at the head and she at the foot; to his right, George, Callie, Solomon, and Sam; to his left, Knox, Emmy, James, and his wife, Mary Alice, who was expecting their first child. Callie had already given Theo his supper, and once he had greeted their guests and congratulated Knox, their mother excused the youngest Bullock to go upstairs and play until bedtime. He would summon Callie when he was ready to be tucked in.

Their father offered thanks before Callie and Emmy passed the dishes Hepsy had prepared and then set them on the buffet, beneath a gilded mirror that was a wedding gift to their parents from Grandmother Cleary. Emmy had planned a supper of baked Virginia ham glazed with brown sugar and apple cider, tomato and cucumber salad, candied yams, fresh green beans cooked in bacon drippings, deviled eggs, and yeast rolls. Dessert would be Knox's favorite seven-layer chocolate cake, which Emmy had baked herself with Hepsy's guidance. They toasted him with homemade muscadine wine from the root cellar.

Callie saw Solomon's hand hover over one fork, then another. As the others chattered, she leaned over and whispered, "Emmy went a little overboard with the silver. The short fork is for the salad, the short knife is for buttering your roll, the fork above your plate is for dessert, and everything else is what you think it is."

He gave her a grateful smile and relaxed into his chair.

"Knox, I expect you won't have any trouble attracting clients after winning such a big case," Callie's father was saying.

"I hope not, Mr. Ira," Knox answered. "Maybe the next case won't be as grueling as this one. I feel like I haven't spent five minutes with Emmy since May Day."

"There's no shame in hiring help."

"Especially to plow your cotton," George interjected, which brought a laugh from the table. As all the Bullock siblings knew, their parents believed in the value of hard work and expected them to do their share on the farm.

"I don't have to hire more help," their father said with a grin. "I feed it around my table."

George gave him a conspiratorial wink. "Seriously, Daddy, I don't think it's fair that we have to work when you could pay people to do it for us."

"Oh, is that a fact?" their mother said. "Well, let me set every one of you straight right this minute—"

Callie, Emmy, and their brothers were all stifling laughter. Their mother caught on, rolled her eyes, and shook her finger at her son. "George Bullock, if you bait me one more time . . ." Laughter erupted around the family table, as it so often did.

"Hey, Knox, did that sorry factory owner really threaten you on the courthouse steps?" Sam asked.

"Must we gravitate to the lurid?" their mother interrupted.

"No, ma'am." Sam paused and took a bite of his yams. "But did he, Knox? Because I heard he threatened to kill you right there on the steps, and you pulled a gun out of your coat pocket and pointed it right between his eyes and said, 'Listen, you no-good, greedy so-and-so—'"

"Samuel!" Their mother sat back in her chair and shook her napkin at her son as if she were trying to flag down a speeding train.

Everyone had to laugh at Sam's dramatic account—even Knox, who still seemed too tired to be social.

"Miss Aurelia, if you'll permit me," he said before turning to Sam. "I did not point a gun at Mr. Garrison. I only made him aware that I had one. But maybe I should always let you tell it for me, Sam. I'm much more impressive in your version."

Again, everyone laughed, and then they all quizzed Knox about his final victory in court.

Eventually, the conversation turned, as always, to farming.

"Solomon," Knox said, "you haven't told us about your progress on the farm. How is it going?"

Solomon set down the roll he was buttering. "I expect it'll come along much faster now that I've hired a few workers. Thank you again, Mr. Bullock, for sending them my way."

"Happy to." Callie's father took a bite of ham and nodded approvingly at Emmy. "That's first-rate, Emeline."

"Thank you, Daddy." She was beaming. The whole family knew that Emmy had never been especially confident in her cooking skills.

"I'd do about anything to see that fine old place going again, Solomon," Callie's father said. "Always made me sad to ride by there and see what it had come to since Miss Katherine died."

Callie's mother pointed to the vase on the buffet. "Did you see the roses he brought us, Ira?"

"I did. Miss Katherine always had the touch, didn't she? Nice to see her Duchesse can still shine."

Solomon told them about his efforts to clear the land and repair the house before Emmy spoke up. "If you don't share at least a little something about your riverboating days, Solomon, I believe Sam might explode right here at the table."

"I think it's safe to say my experience was unremarkable," Solomon said. "I guess you're either born for the river or you're not. It didn't take me long to miss all the ordinary things you can't do when you're traveling constantly."

"You must've had *some* adventure on a riverboat." Sam was making an odd sandwich of sorts, stuffing a piece of ham and a yam into his roll and smearing butter on top.

"About the most exciting thing I ever did was jump off of one," Solomon said. "There was an outbreak of smallpox in one of the towns where we docked, so the pilot called us all back to the boat and headed downriver. But by the third night or so, some of the crew were already sick, and I knew it was just a matter of time before we got quarantined. Then we'd *all* get sick, closed in together on that boat. So I jumped off right in the middle of the Mississippi."

"Man alive!" Sam took a big bite of his sandwich, chewing as he talked. "Didn't you think you might dwown?"

"Samuel!" his mother said. "Where are your table manners?"

"Sowwy, Mama," he said through the mouthful of sandwich, making everybody laugh again.

"Solomon, do continue before I strangle my child right here at the table," she said.

"I was pretty *sure* I would drown, Sam. But I was able to ride the current till I could catch onto a tree the river had swallowed up. Then I stayed by myself in the woods for a couple of weeks until I could make sure I wasn't sick. Didn't want to give it to anybody else."

"You were wise," Knox said.

"After that, it seems like I worked just about everywhere you can work along the river."

"Did you ever work for the railroad?" Knox asked.

"No, that's one place I missed."

"I just wondered if you knew how they operate. I've been thinking about Lily and wondering whether there might've been any negligence involved in her husband's accident. If there was, we might be able to get some sort of settlement to help her and the baby. It's unfamiliar territory for me, but I could look into it."

"I think that would be mighty kind of you, Knox, and we're happy to pay for your time," Callie's father said.

"Oh, no, sir. It would be my pleasure."

When everyone finished with supper, Callie's mother signaled for her daughters to clear plates and begin serving dessert. Solomon stood and helped Callie with her chair.

"I'd like to ask you about something if you don't mind, Mr. Bullock," he said as he sat back down and Callie served him cake and coffee. "I'm guessing you're familiar with the sixty acres on my farm that tuck into a sharp bend in Yellowleaf?"

Callie's father took a bite of his cake. "I am." He nodded toward his oldest son. "James has the land on the opposite side of the creek. He and Mary Alice live just over that big hill with the one sprawling oak tree on top."

"Can you tell me much about it?" Solomon reached for the dessert fork above his plate.

"The Cruzes called that piece of property their Little Delta because the black soil reminded them of the farmland around Leland, Mississippi, where they lived for many years," Callie's father said. "They were both originally from here, but he got a job with a county extension service over in Mississippi, and they didn't come back to Alabama till he retired."

Solomon sipped his coffee. "It looks like that field has never been cultivated. Is that because Yellowleaf floods?"

"It sure does. Gets out of its banks about twice a year, in the spring and early fall. But you know, I always thought that field could be trenched in such a way that the water would drain right off, and then there's no telling what all you could grow there."

"Daddy's right," James said. "That has to be some of the richest soil around here if you could figure out how to drain it."

"Why do you think Mr. Cruz never tried?" Solomon asked.

"By the time they moved back to Alabama," Callie's father said, "farming was just a hobby for him, and he left a lot of his land fallow. I guess he just never wanted to make the effort on that field. But you're lucky as you can be that he specialized in fruit trees for the extension service. The orchards and arbors on your land are very well thought-out, Solomon."

"That's what Callie told me." He stood to pull out her chair as she returned to her place at the table. "Would you consider coming to have a look at the creek bend sometime—tell me how you'd go about draining it?"

"Would he consider it?" Callie's mother asked. "You've made his day, Solomon. My husband loves moving dirt better than anybody I know."

"She knows me too well." Callie's father smiled at his wife. "I'll come first thing Monday morning. And don't you worry about buying any dredging equipment. I've got plenty around here from working fields on the river. You can borrow mine till you get your farm going."

"That's mighty generous of you, Mr. Bullock."

"Not at all. I'll enjoy seeing the farm again. I know it's a challenge right now, but there's some pretty land underneath all those bushes and scrub trees. You'll bring it back."

"Well, I'll take all the advice you're willing to give me."

Callie's mother turned to Knox and Emmy. "I don't suppose you two would care to reveal any of your wedding plans this evening?"

They looked at each other and nodded. "Actually, we would, Mama," Emmy said. "We'd like to get married at Christmastime, when the house is decorated so pretty and smells like evergreens and ambrosia. Just a small family wedding right here if that's alright with you and Daddy."

"You sure, Emmy?" her father asked. "No big whoop-de-do?"

"No whoop-de-do," Emmy said.

"What about just a whoop-de?" Callie asked her sister, bringing a laugh from the table.

"I'll hire some help for Hepsy, and we'll give the whole house a good going-over before we decorate," her mother said. "I'm assuming you'll want the ceremony in the living room, in front of the fireplace?"

"That would be lovely, Mama," Emmy said.

"Daddy can give you away dressed as Santa Claus, and the rest of us can be your wedding elves!" Sam said. Everyone laughed, even Callie's mother.

"Samuel," she said, "I doubt we'll require your input on the wedding plans, but it's good to know you're a wellspring of ideas, should the need arise. And *please* don't speak with your mouth full again."

"I have a little more news," Knox said. He looked at Emmy. "This is a surprise even for you. The first of October, I'm moving out of my parents' home and renting Miss Eva Clark's house from her son."

"What?" Emmy exclaimed. "Why, Knox, that house is right up the road!"

"Nobody's lived in it since she passed a couple of years ago, so they're working on repairs right now. It'll need some sprucing up—if y'all can think of anybody who might help me."

Emmy clapped her hands together. "It's such a pretty house— just needs a little spit and polish. And maybe a fresh coat of white paint. And a couple of wicker rockers for the porch, and maybe some ferns next summer—"

"And—and—and," George cut in.

"Oh, hush, George," Emmy said, laughing with everybody else. "I am officially getting carried away, and you'll have to live with it till I'm Knox's problem."

"Can't wait to have that problem," Knox said before his smile faded and he grew serious. "Listen, I know there's a troublesome question hanging in the air, so let me just answer it now. My brother has no place at this wedding. If my parents can accept that and they'd like to come, I'd appreciate it, Miss Aurelia, Mr. Ira, if you'd invite them. But if they insist on having Ryder and Lucinda, they'll just have to miss our wedding. That's their choice, but Emmy and I have made ours."

FOURTEEN

*S*olomon quickly became a regular guest of the Bullocks. On the last evening in July, the family gathered to celebrate James's birthday, and once again Solomon was seated next to Callie. They had just finished their cake when Callie heard the kitchen door slam and rapid, heavy footsteps in the hallway outside the dining room.

"Fisher?" her mother exclaimed as the carpenter appeared in the doorway. "What on earth?"

Fisher was nervously shuffling back and forth. He had taken off his hat and was clutching it in his hands. "I 'pologize, Miss 'Relia, Mr. Ira, but I couldn't make y'all hear me knockin' at the back door, and this is a 'mergency." He was breathing hard.

"What's the matter, Fisher?" Callie's father stood up at the table.

"It's Lily," he said. "I b'lieve her time's come early."

"Oh, dear heaven!" Callie's mother jumped from her seat. "George, you and Sam go fetch Hepsy from her church. She said they were having a social tonight. Ira, you and James please go and get Tirzah. Emmy, you entertain Knox. Mary Alice, I don't want you doing anything strenuous with a baby on the way, but maybe you could sit with Lily until Hepsy gets here?"

"Of course." Mary Alice stood, with James keeping his arm around her.

"Fisher, get a fire going and some water boiling in the laundry kettle. Callie, you and Solomon look after Theo and wrap up the rest of the cake so James can take it home with him when he leaves. Everybody, it's been a wonderful time together, but a baby's coming. Let's go."

In a matter of seconds, the room was empty except for Callie and Solomon.

She turned to him, his eyes wide, his mouth half open. "I don't think I've ever seen anything like that," he said.

"You mean you've never seen anything quite like *her*."

He leaned back in his chair. "I didn't know they even made women like your mother till I moved down here."

"Well, we have our marching orders, so we'd best get to it or we'll have to answer to her."

Solomon followed Callie upstairs to Theo's room, where they found him lying on the floor, sound asleep in his clothes.

"I was wondering why he never came down to get me," Callie whispered.

Solomon lifted Theo onto his bed, where Callie had pulled back the covers. She undressed her little brother and covered him with a sheet, then pushed the curtains open to make sure the night air could cool him.

"Think our work here is done?" Solomon softly asked her.

"Almost." Callie put Theo's favorite teddy bear next to him. "Now we're finished."

The two of them stepped outside the room, and Solomon quietly closed Theo's door behind them. Callie led him back downstairs. "Mama had planned to serve cordials in the parlor after supper. Would you like one?"

"Tell me something," he said. "What would you be doing right now if I weren't here?"

Callie looked down the hallway toward the empty dining

room. "Honestly, I'd probably clear the table and wash the dishes so Mama wouldn't fret over the silver when she gets back and Hepsy wouldn't have to face all of it before she starts breakfast in the morning."

Solomon began rolling up his sleeves. "Want me to wash or dry?"

❧

Callie and Solomon were finishing up in the kitchen when the back door swung open and George and Sam came inside.

"Solomon, Solomon, Solomon, what has our sister done to you?" George glanced at the clean, dry glasses and stacked plates on the table, ready to be put away, and a few pans peeking out of the sink, where Solomon stood with a dishrag in his hand.

"She told me it was an Alabama tradition—last guest to leave washes the dishes," Solomon said. "She wouldn't lie, would she?"

George nodded toward Callie. "This one? Without hesitation or remorse."

Callie threw a dish towel at her older brother. "Tell us some news, for heaven's sake!"

"Fisher's keeping watch on the porch, but Daddy's the only man allowed to peek in the door and even he can't go inside," George said. "Every now and then, Mama comes out to tell him what's happening. Lily's alright, but they think it'll be a while before the baby comes. Mary Alice wanted to stay a little longer, but I expect James will insist she come to the house and lie down pretty soon."

Callie heard a loud noise on the roof. "Is that rain?"

"More like a toad strangler," Sam said, "and probably set in for the night. Started building up right as we left."

Their father and James came running into the kitchen, dripping wet.

"Daddy, why don't you and James leave your shoes on the porch and I'll go fetch you some towels," Callie said.

"Thank you, my girl." Her father took off his shoes. "Solomon, you remember this—women are always worried about their floors. They're forever working to keep us from trackin' 'em up, scratchin' 'em up, and all such as that. I have no idea why."

"I'll remember that, Mr. Bullock," Solomon said with a grin as Callie left to get the towels.

When she hurried back, her father was urging Solomon to stay overnight. "If you try to make it home in this mess, you'll have pneumonia before you get there. The girls can get you fixed up in one of the guest rooms upstairs, and I'll ask Fate to bed down your horse. We'll feed you some biscuits in the morning and send you on your way in dry weather."

"Are you sure that won't be any trouble, sir?" Solomon asked.

"Not one bit." Callie's father hastily dried himself off. "James and Mary Alice will be staying in his old room, so we'll just make it a party in the morning."

"What kind of party are we having, Daddy?" Emmy asked as she and Knox came into the kitchen.

"A spend-the-night party."

Emmy put her arms around her fiancé. "Can Knox come too? I've been tormenting him with wedding plans and was just about to set him free when the rains came pouring down."

"Knox can come too." Her father kissed her on the cheek. "You and Callie can perk up a couple of guest rooms for our company."

"I appreciate that, sir," Solomon said.

Callie's father looked out the kitchen window. "Poor ole Fisher's been tending the kettle fire and pacing like a soldier on guard duty. I think I'll tell him he can rest up here on the big porch instead of trying to stay dry on that little bitty one at Lily's—I know he won't go home till the baby's here and

Lily's alright. Y'all go on in the living room and we'll have us a way-after-dinner cordial."

He went back outside, and the rest of the men except Solomon headed for the living room. He looked at Callie and nodded toward the few remaining dishes in the sink. "I believe in finishing what I started."

She smiled at him and started unrolling his shirtsleeves. "You've done more than you should have. If my brothers see you washing any more dishes, they'll tease you about it till the day you die."

Her father came back inside. "Come along, you two."

"Right behind you, Daddy." Callie took off the apron she had tied on to protect her dress. "I need to run upstairs and lower Theo's windows."

With her father gone, Callie turned to Solomon. "Before I take care of Theo, would you help me with one more thing?"

"Lead the way."

She took him to a closet in the central hallway of the house. "I can't reach the top shelf. Could you pull down one of those old quilts and that little pillow there—the blue one?"

He did as she asked and handed her the quilt and pillow.

"Thank you. Mama saves these to give away to poor families when we don't use them anymore. I don't think she would mind if we gave one to Fisher."

Solomon followed her back to the kitchen and out to the porch, where Fisher was sitting at the foot of a wicker chaise, dry but shivering in the rainy air.

"Everything's going to be fine, Fisher," Callie said. "Lily's in very good hands." She handed him the quilt and pillow. "I thought you might need these."

"'Preciate it, miss." Fisher got into the chaise, put the pillow behind his head, and covered himself with the quilt, pulling it up to his chin. "I sho' will feel better when this is all over and the baby's here and Lily's alright."

Callie dimmed the gaslight by the kitchen door. "I'll say a prayer for Lily tonight, Fisher—for Lily and for you."

❧

Long before dawn, Callie awoke to rolling thunder. The heavy rains of early evening turned out to be the prelude to a coming storm that had finally arrived. As lightning flashed out her window, she looked over to see Emmy sound asleep as always. But she wouldn't be there always.

Sitting up in bed, Callie hugged her knees to her chest and looked out at the flashes of light coming closer and closer together. So much had happened last night that her mind had been mercifully occupied. Just before midnight, Lily gave birth to a healthy baby girl. She named her Josephine. Tirzah wanted to sleep in her own bed, but since the weather was so bad, she finally agreed to a daybed in the Bullocks' sewing room. The guest rooms, she said, had "too much white folks mojo" in them. It would keep her up all night. Hepsy stayed at the cottage with Lily.

And then there was Solomon. Callie tried to push him out of her mind, but it wasn't working.

When the lightning flashed again, she began counting until thunder rumbled behind it. She didn't get far. The storm was swiftly moving closer. Again she looked over at Emmy and felt an ache in the pit of her stomach. In no time at all, that bed would be empty. There would be no more late-night laughter. No more secrets told by lamplight. No more Emmy assuring Callie that she was special and didn't need to change to suit other people's expectations.

Callie fought back the tears stinging her eyes. Not here. What if Emmy should awaken and see her crying? It would break her heart and spoil her joy.

The walls of their shared bedroom were closing in on Callie, stirring up her emotions but offering no privacy to release them. She slipped on her robe and crept out of the bedroom, then tiptoed down the main corridor to the kitchen and its back stairway. Upstairs, she took care not to step on the squeaky spots in the pine floor until she made it to one of three French doors leading onto the upper porch. This one opened onto the corner that would give her a view to the west, where strong storms always came from. The tall pines were swaying and sighing in the wind as the branches of oaks seemed to billow around their trunks, their leaves rustling so fast and loud that they hissed.

She turned her face to the wind and let it blow away the tears she could no longer hold back. Emmy was leaving her. The wedding plans, now a constant in family conversations, made it real. And Callie had never felt so desolate. Tears escalated to sobs, which were mercifully muffled by the wind and the thunder.

"Callie."

She gasped at the sound of Solomon's voice and turned to find him standing right behind her. There was nowhere to hide.

"Why are you crying?"

Callie was too distraught to give him anything but the unvarnished, painful truth. "She's leaving me, Solomon. I'm losing my Emmy. And I'm not sure who I am without her."

He said nothing but stepped closer and put his arms around her. Even with the damp air blowing in, she felt the warmth of his shoulder against her face, the calming rhythm of his breathing, the soothing touch of his hands against her back and in her hair. Without any words of comfort—or any words at all—Solomon gave her shelter.

FIFTEEN

Callie was sitting on the Bullocks' back porch with Lily, rocking the baby and trying not to daydream. Solomon had held her in the storm—she could still feel the strength of his arms, the warmth of his hands—and patiently offered comfort until she had no more tears to cry for Emmy. Then he had held her face in his hands and said, "I know you think Emmy's the special one. But you're wrong, Callie." He walked her back inside and gave her a lingering kiss on the cheek before they parted at the top of the stairs.

Solomon was gone before breakfast. Hepsy said he had stopped by the kitchen before anyone else got up and told her he appreciated their hospitality but had to get back to his farm. That was almost a month ago, and Callie hadn't seen him since.

She looked down at the baby in her arms and wondered what it would be like to have one of her own. "I can't believe how much she looks like you, Lily," Callie said. She and Lily were taking turns rocking the baby and peeling apples for the cider and applesauce Hepsy was making in the kitchen.

Lily reached over and laid her hand against her baby's face before picking up another apple. "Josie's my little angel. Sleeps good, eats good, and hardly ever fusses. Mama Tirzah says that's unusual for a newborn—'specially one that came early. Sure hope her daddy can see her from heaven."

"Were the two of you happy in Chicago?" Callie asked.

Lily shook the burlap bag where she was tossing apple peels so they would settle to the bottom and make more room. "We sure were. Wasn't perfect. Nothing is. But Levi was a good man— a kind and loving man—and we always enjoyed one another's comp'ny."

"Are you sorry you came down here?" Callie felt Josie relaxing into limp slumber and gently bounced her to sleep as they rocked.

"I really didn't have a choice," Lily said. "City's a hard place for a woman with a baby and no man to earn a living. My job didn't pay enough to keep food on the table and a roof over our heads. I knew I'd need my family to get by. Daddy's always been so restless. Him and Mama move around a lot, so I thought it'd be best for me to come to Grandmama."

"Must seem awfully quiet here compared to a big city like Chicago. Do you miss it?"

"Sometimes, 'specially on Saturday nights, when me and Levi used to go out to a restaurant or go dancing—or both!" Lily laughed, something she didn't do very often.

Hepsy came onto the porch. "Got another panful for me?"

"I do, Grandmama," Lily said.

Hepsy took the dishpan mounded with sliced apples into the kitchen and returned it empty. "Why didn't you go dress shoppin' with y' mama and Miss Emmy?" she asked Callie, who looked up at her with a grimace. Hepsy clapped her hands together and laughed.

"What's the joke, Grandmama?" Lily asked.

"Miss Callie despises shoppin' with women." Hepsy was still laughing. "Been that way since she's a little girl. Mr. Ira used to carry me with him to take her to town for her Easter dress 'cause I know what she like, and I could tell just by lookin' if something would fit her on accounta I made most of her clothes back then. I could get her through it real fast."

"Hepsy, can you even *imagine* what Mama and Emmy would be like, shopping for a wedding dress?" Callie asked.

"I bet you they don't get home till dark," Hepsy said.

"Dark and then some! They'll try on everything in the store and then end up going back to the first one they looked at—you wait and see."

Hepsy bent over the baby and lightly touched her nose. "She's gon' be a beauty just like her mama." She looked over at Lily peeling another apple. "I hope she has a easier time than you, my baby."

Lily smiled up at her. "I do alright, Grandmama. Don't you worry." Hepsy went back inside.

"Has Knox been able to help you, Lily?" Callie asked.

Apple slices pinged into the empty dishpan as Lily resumed her work. "He's a fine man, Mr. Knox. He must've come by the cottage three or four times, bringing news and telling me how things are going. Always comes straight from the court-house in his lawyer clothes, when you know he'd prob'ly like to go home and prop his feet up. One time he didn't get here till nearly eight o'clock on accounta him working late, but he still came. He says the railroad is talking about a settlement already. Guess they don't want to cross Mr. Knox in court like that factory owner did. Even colored folks know about that case and what he did for all those sick people. Hard to believe he's the brother of that other one."

A look of such sadness crossed Lily's face that Callie stood up from her rocker and said, "Let's trade."

Lily smiled and took Callie's seat. Callie gently placed Josie in her mother's arms before taking up the dishpan.

"If you could live anywhere you wanted, Lily—anywhere in the world—where would you go?"

Lily ran her finger lightly across Josie's forehead. "I don't know enough about the whole world to make that choice. But out of the world I *do* know, I reckon I'd like to go to Houston, Texas."

"Why there?" Callie picked up an apple to peel and slice.

"Well, they got several freedmen's towns around Houston— all over Texas from what I hear. You know what they are?"

Callie knew exactly what they were and was ashamed of how she did—by eavesdropping on Fisher and Lily. "Yes, I've heard of them. I can see why you'd like to live in a town like that, but why Houston?"

Josie stirred slightly, and Lily rocked her back and forth in her arms. "Because it's big enough to get lost in and it's close to the ocean. I've always wanted to live by the sea. You wouldn't ever feel trapped. There would always be boats and water to carry you away when you were ready to go."

"Sounds nice, Lily."

"Listen at me talkin' about livin' on the water and I can't even swim." Lily gazed out at the backyard, fenced in iron, as if it were a wide-open sea. She began singing to her daughter.

> *"Michael, row your boat ashore, hallelujah.*
> *Michael, row your boat ashore, hallelujah.*
> *The river is deep and the river is wide, hallelujah.*
> *Milk and honey on the other side—"*

Lily's song was interrupted when Sam came tearing through the open gate of the iron fence and bailed out of the saddle.

Callie jumped up from her rocker. "Sam! What's the matter? Is somebody hurt?"

He ran onto the porch as Hepsy came out of the kitchen. "Sheriff came to see Daddy. No time to explain, but Daddy told me to race home the back way and warn you to hide Lily and Josie right now. He says Hepsy should say Lily left for a few days to visit family. I've got to go hide myself so the sheriff won't know I beat him here and warned you."

"But Sam—" Callie felt frantic. Lily looked terrified, pacing with Josie like someone who wanted to run but had nowhere to go. Hepsy was clasping her hands together so tightly that Callie feared she might snap her very bones in two.

Sam grabbed the reins of his horse. "You only have a few minutes, Callie! Do what Daddy says. Now!" Sam ran with the horse, leading it through the gate toward the stables behind the house.

"What that sheriff want w' Lily and the baby?" Hepsy asked.

"I don't know," Callie said.

Hepsy paced back and forth for a few seconds before she stopped, stomped her foot, and nodded. She began quickly gathering up the apples and peels. "Y'all help me get this in the kitchen. We need it to look like I'm here workin' by myself. I'll tell the sheriff all the women in the family's out planning the wedding. Miss Callie, I'm gon' need you to do a little climbin'—and take Lily and Josie with you. Will you do that for me?"

Callie nodded as she and Lily helped Hepsy move everything inside. Then the two girls ran upstairs, Callie taking off her apron as they went. She quickly fashioned a sling out of it and tied it around Lily's neck so they could secure Josie inside. They both removed their shoes, and Callie hid them under the seat cushion. Then they climbed out the window and up the tree, making their way to the fork just before the county sheriff rode up on his horse, followed by Callie's father.

Hepsy came out to meet them where they had stopped, right under the tree. Callie looked down at Josie still sound asleep. She and Lily were both breathing hard from the hasty climb.

"Hepsy," Callie's father said, "Sheriff Cagle here's got a warrant that says he can traipse through our house looking for Lily and Josie."

"But they ain't here, Mr. Ira. They off visitin' family in north Alabama."

Josie stirred in Lily's arms. Callie held her breath as she and Lily watched her, but the baby relaxed again and kept sleeping.

"Mr. Bullock, I hope you won't hold this against me," the sheriff said. "I've got no choice, far as the law's concerned."

"I won't hold it against you, Sheriff," Callie's father said, "but I can't speak for my wife. You can expect to hear from her. And if I were you, I'd wipe my feet before I stepped on her floors."

"Yes, sir. This won't take long."

"What's this about, Mr. Ira?" Hepsy asked after the sheriff went inside.

"Let's wait'll he leaves, Hepsy. Everything's gonna be alright— long as he doesn't find 'em in the house."

"He won't, Mr. Ira. Me and the girls can promise you that."

Josie yawned and opened her eyes for a few seconds but then went right back to sleep in Lily's arms. Could she even sense, Callie wondered, that she was also cradled by a tree?

True to his word, the sheriff didn't stay long in the house, certainly not long enough for any kind of exhaustive search. Callie had to believe that fear of her mother's wrath had something to do with it. Aurelia Bullock had the persuasive power to convince every woman of means in the whole county to host fundraisers for the sheriff's next opponent, whoever that might be. She had unsaddled more than one local politician in her time.

"I didn't see anything I need to report," Sheriff Cagle said. "And again, I apologize for the inconvenience, Mr. Bullock."

"No harm done," Callie's father said. "Can we fix you a glass o' tea or anything before you go?"

"Tea?" Callie mouthed to Lily, her eyes wide. Her father might be pushing their luck.

"No, thank you," the sheriff said. "Best be on my way."

He mounted his horse and rode off down the road. From this high, Callie could even see him go left, heading back to town.

"You can come down now, Zacchaeus!" her father called up.

"How did you know, Daddy?"

"When you weren't in the house, I knew where Hepsy put you."

Lily and Callie carefully made their way down the tree and through the window, where Hepsy and Callie's father were waiting to help them in.

"Let's all have a seat," Callie's father said, leading them to the sitting area. Callie loosened the harness around Lily's neck and helped her with a yawning Josie before they all sat down.

"Lily," Callie's father said as he took a deep breath, "Ryder Montgomery is claiming that Josie is his child. Says they met when she was down here visiting family this past Christmas and kept it a secret."

"But that's not true!" Lily clutched the baby closer to her chest.

"I know, and it should be easy enough to prove. You can give me the name and address of your doctor in Chicago and I'll send him a telegram tomorrow morning. He ought to be able to clear this up right away."

"So there's nothing to worry about?" Hepsy asked him.

"I don't know if I'd say that just yet," he said. "Ryder's hired a lawyer outta Birmingham to fight for custody, and they're demanding that Josie become a ward of the county till the case is settled. I do not intend to let that happen."

Lily began slowly rocking Josie back and forth, clenching her jaw and shaking her head. "What's *wrong* with that man?"

Hepsy put her arm around Lily's shoulders and squeezed her tight. "I ain't never said this 'bout 'nother livin' soul, but I wish he'd drop dead."

"I doubt you're alone in that, Hepsy," Callie's father said.

"What are you going to do, Daddy?" Callie asked.

"For starters, hire Knox to represent Lily. Right off the bat, a court's gotta wonder why Ryder's own brother stands against him. And then we'll start locking the back gate so nobody can get to Lily's cabin without at least a tussle."

Lily kept bending down to kiss Josie on her forehead. Was she showing love to her child or frantically imprinting the memory of a mother's touch?

"Callie, why don't you help Lily and Josie settle down while me and Hepsy talk this over," her father said. "I'll stay close around here this afternoon. The boys can handle the fields. I think we've all had a bellyful of Ryder's nonsense."

SIXTEEN

Callie was happy to have an errand, something to take her away from the house and give her time alone to think. Hepsy wanted a croker sack of apples from "the good trees" by the creek on James's farm and had asked Callie to gather them. Why she needed so many—and why they suddenly had to come from the trees by Yellow-leaf Creek instead of the ones just a stone's throw from the house—Callie couldn't say. Nor did she question. She was too glad to get away.

She delivered a pound cake Hepsy had baked for James and Mary Alice, whose baby was due in November, before riding Daisy Bell down the hill behind their house, giving the mare time to step carefully on the slope. At the foot of the hill was the apple orchard, which stood in a small clearing just outside the woods surrounding the creek.

In the clearing, Callie dismounted and stroked the horse's neck. "Let's free you up too, girl," she said, removing the saddle, bridle, and saddlebags. She was surprised to find a picnic blanket under the saddle. "Hepsy went all out with our lunch today, Daisy Bell." She put the picnic blanket with the tack underneath a tree and fed the horse an apple from her pocket. "I don't think there's much to spook you here. Just don't wander far, okay?"

Daisy Bell nibbled the grass before taking a lazy ramble through the trees to the water.

There was no such thing as a bad day on a creekbank, Callie thought, especially this one. She wasn't sure where Yellowleaf began, but it widened and narrowed for miles and miles, some lengths of it deep enough to float in, others—like this one— shallow enough to wade. Surely no sound on earth was more soothing than that of water flowing over rocks, sighing and gurgling as it meandered through woodlands and pastures to the nearest river, in this case the Coosa just a few miles south. Oaks and cottonwoods shaded the banks, making shadows dance on the water where dappled sunlight broke through leafy branches overhead. Callie wondered if Solomon had spent much time here since his farm was just on the other side.

Ever since the night that Emmy's impending departure got the better of her, Callie hadn't managed any time alone with Solomon, no opportunity for her to apologize for crying like a baby in the middle of a thunderstorm. Maybe he didn't want any more time alone with her. Maybe he'd had quite enough.

She shook her head in a futile attempt to physically rearrange her thoughts like those shards of glass in the kaleidoscope that she and Emmy had loved as children. Miss Katherine would take it down from her mantel and let them play with it whenever their mother visited. Spellbound, they would take turns holding the brass tube and turning the ring to show each other endless patterns.

Callie needed to sort out her thoughts so she could put them in some order and stop them from tumbling around in her mind. Once the apples were gathered, she could think it all through, wading the creek and listening to the flowing water. But first, to the work—that had been her way since she was a little girl.

Ripe apples covered these trees, which held so much low-hanging fruit that Callie had no need for the ladder James kept propped against one of the trunks. She quickly and easily filled her croker sack, then set it under a cottonwood tree and laid her apron and wide-brimmed hat on top. She took off her shoes and stockings and pulled the back of her hem through her legs and up to her belt, where she tucked it in, making her skirt into breeches for wading, as Hepsy had taught her when she was little. Emmy hadn't been there to braid her hair before she left—something Callie would have to get used to—so she had pulled it all over one shoulder and tied it with a ribbon, making a single thick cascade that hung down to her waist. It looked "a bit vagabond," as her mother would say, but there was no one here to see it except Mary Alice, and she was family.

Rolling up her sleeves, Callie walked barefoot down the bank and onto a flat rock in the creek. She let the water swirl around her feet and ankles as she listened to the peaceful sound of Yellowleaf making its journey to the river.

Stepping off the rock and feeling the soft creek bed beneath her feet, Callie could see Daisy Bell up ahead. She looked down to watch a school of minnows swim by and heard the horse whinny. Daisy Bell took a couple of steps back, her eyes on the bank that lay on Solomon's property. Then she raised her head and whinnied again before climbing out of the water and disappearing behind some bushes covered with wild honeysuckle.

"Daisy Bell!" Callie called. "Daisy Bell, come back!" She waded up the creek as fast as she could with the current pushing against her legs. Just about winded, she spotted Solomon on the bank up ahead. He waved to her before taking off his boots and socks, rolling up his trousers, and climbing down into the creek. The apple in his hand lured Daisy Bell to follow. They met Callie just below the bend of the creek.

Still catching her breath, Callie held her hand over her eyes, shielding them from sunlight breaking through the trees. "Were you trying to steal my horse?"

Daisy Bell nuzzled Solomon's pocket in search of another

apple. "I was. But then I realized she'd eat every apple on my farm, so I'm giving her back."

Callie laughed and stroked the mare's face. "Daddy says I've spoiled her."

"Nothing wrong with a little spoiling."

Callie's eyes followed Solomon's hand as he ran it gently along Daisy Bell's back. What a difference between the hands of all the boys who had pursued her—smooth, pinkish, and fleshy—and those of a man like Solomon—strong, sinewy, and tanned from the sun, hands that could take hold and take charge with confidence. So focused was she on the movement of his hand that his question startled her.

"What brings you over this way?"

"I'm still trying to figure that out." Callie said, willing herself to stop "floppin' around in foolishness," as Hepsy would say. "Hepsy suddenly needed enough apples to feed the whole county, and for some reason they had to come from the trees back there." She pointed down the creek. "We've got all the same pippins near the house, but she said only these would do."

"That's curious."

"*And* she packed me a lunch and said she wouldn't expect me back till this afternoon, but the trees here are so loaded that I'm already done. Something's up."

Solomon shooed a fly away from Daisy Bell's ear. "You're right about that. Hepsy sent me over here too."

"What?" Daisy Bell sniffed at Callie's neck and tried to nibble the long, curly drape of hair hanging over her shoulder.

"Hepsy sent word by Lemuel that your father would be dropping off some idle workers who could help me start digging my trenches today."

Callie frowned and nudged Daisy Bell away from her hair. "Daddy said you weren't starting on that till after the harvest when you could get more help."

"That was my plan. But then Hepsy sent word that I should

wait for Mr. Bullock at the creek bend this morning around ten, and he'd drop off some of his workers who weren't needed right now."

Daisy Bell tried to nibble the sleeve of Callie's blouse. "Daddy doesn't have any idle help. Last night, he said he'd be leaving before daybreak to pick up extra workers in Wilsonville."

The horse decided to move along and soon occupied herself with a persimmon tree downstream.

Solomon tilted his head to one side. "Does Hepsy have a history of matchmaking, by any chance?"

"Of *what*?"

"Well, think about it. She put you here. She put me here. She fibbed a little to do it and packed a lunch . . ."

Callie felt a hot flush on her cheeks, and her hands flew up to cover them.

Solomon smiled. "Are you blushing, Miss Bullock?"

"No. Maybe. Probably." She lowered her hands. "Am I scarlet?"

He scrutinized her face and lightly touched her cheek. "A little pinkish maybe."

Callie dropped her arms to her sides. "I always seem to make a fool of myself in front of you."

"Since when?"

"All the crying."

"There's nothing foolish about crying for somebody you love."

Callie stared down at the water, making circles with her foot below the surface. "I suppose not." She looked up at Solomon. "I've just always done my crying alone."

"Should I have left you alone in the storm?"

The waters of the creek babbled over rocks in the silence until Callie finally said, "No. I'm glad you were there."

"So am I." He took her by the hand. "Come on. Let's go see if our theory is correct and Hepsy packed lunch for two."

They waded back to the spot where Callie had left the saddle-bags, and Solomon helped her climb up the bank.

"Now we know why there was a picnic blanket under my saddle," Callie said, holding it up so he could see. They spread it under an oak right by the creek and sat down with the saddle-bags. Callie had to laugh when she opened them. "Hepsy's pulling out the big guns." Their matchmaker had packed fried chicken, homemade rolls, and tea cakes in one bag; napkins, a jar of tea, and two tin cups in the other.

Solomon took a bite of the drumstick Callie handed him. Hepsy's fried chicken was unmatched. "Do us both a favor," he said after he had a few bites. "Tell Hepsy you think a long courtship is in order."

Callie poured him a cup of tea. "You'd court all five Bartell sisters if they could fry chicken like this."

"Shamelessly."

"Mama Bartell's a widow woman, so you could make it an even six."

They were quietly enjoying their lunch, watching Yellowleaf drift by, when they heard a loud noise.

Solomon jumped and looked around. "What in the daylights was that? Sounded like a cross between a crow and a cat."

Callie giggled and pointed to the hill behind them. "Mary Alice loves peacocks. Sometimes her flock wanders."

"That's a relief," he said. "I thought we were about to be carried off."

Callie handed him a tea cake. "I was beginning to think something carried *you* off. Or that I scared you off. You haven't been around lately."

"No, I haven't. But it isn't because I didn't want to." He took a bite of the thin, buttery cookie. "That's hands down the best cookie I ever ate. You know how to make these?"

"Everybody knows how to make tea cakes." She smiled as he took another bite. "Well, everybody but Emmy. Somehow she always rolls the dough too thick. George teases her about her 'famous tea muffins.'"

He finished the cookie before he said, "My father died. I had to go to Hannibal. That's why I haven't been around."

Callie laid her hand on his arm. "Oh, Solomon, I'm sorry. I know he was difficult, but still—he was your father."

He smiled at her as she quickly withdrew her hand, afraid she had gone too far. "It's alright—but I really do appreciate your sympathy." Solomon looked out at the creek and sighed. "True to form, he left no will. His lawyer called everybody up there to settle the estate."

"Did you get it all taken care of?" She refilled his tin cup.

"Right away, my brothers and sisters started fighting over the land, the money, the house—anything of value. I stayed with them for a week, but that was all I could take. Spent the rest of my time up there going to auctions and looking at livestock. I've decided once and for all that I don't want anything *from* my so-called family and I don't want any part *of* them." His voice, so hard when he talked about his kin, softened when he looked at Callie and said, "This is my home now. At least, it's where I hope to make one."

"Tell me about it," she said. "Tell me everything you want to do with your farm."

Solomon shared all his plans for crops and livestock.

"If you didn't already have the perfect house," Callie said, "I'd say you should build one right on this creek. It's so peaceful."

"I've seriously thought about it. Anything close to the water would have to be on pilings, but that's manageable for a small house."

"What about a little fishing cabin?" With her index fingers, Callie drew a rectangle in the air. "Maybe just one long room, with a screened porch on the water so you could sit out there at night and listen to the creek? You could even sleep out there."

He gave her a puzzled frown. "That doesn't sound like something I'd expect you to get excited about."

"Why not?"

"Because you live in a mansion."

"But I didn't choose it. Daddy did."

"You don't like the big house with the white columns?"

"Of course I do. And I'm grateful for it. But it's not what I would choose for myself." An unexpected image of Lily and her cabin flashed in Callie's mind. *Nobody asked me.*

"What's the matter?" Solomon asked.

"I was just thinking about Lily, something I heard her say one time—that she was grateful to have the cottage in our backyard, but nobody asked her if she wanted to live there. We just assumed she'd be happy with whatever Mama thought was best for her."

"Nobody ought to decide what's best for somebody else," Solomon countered.

Callie stretched out her legs and leaned back on her hands. It was the first time she realized that she still had her skirt tucked into her belt, making trousers that hit far above her ankles. Miss Nicey would be scandalized. But Miss Nicey didn't matter much right now.

Solomon lay on his side and propped himself on his elbow to look at her. "So what house would you choose for yourself?"

Callie smiled at the thought of it. "I'd choose your house—or a one-room cabin on stilts with a screened porch overlooking this creek."

"Would you really, Callie? No joking?"

"No joking."

His eyes never stayed quite the same color, subtly changing as the light shifted, but they were always honest. They were the kind of eyes you could never lie to.

"You've always had fine things," he said. "Don't you think you'd miss them if you suddenly had to do without?"

"No, because I've never cared about things—except maybe hats. I do love a good hat. A good hat and a good horse."

"Not the silver and the crystal?"

"Emmy's the one who loves those. I don't mean she would ever put things ahead of people. She'd give you anything she owns if you needed it or if she thought it would make you happy. I just mean it gives her joy to make things special for other people, so she loves all the china and silver and pretty linens." Callie smiled at him. "I prefer fried chicken from a saddlebag."

Solomon lay back on the quilt, staring up at the sky before turning to look at her. "I've never met anybody like you."

Callie suddenly had the same feeling she got on the roller coaster that came to the county fair every fall. It was a small one with only one substantial hill, but Callie would ride it again and again with her brothers just for the excitement of feeling her stomach dip and flip when the speeding coaster cars went over the top.

She crossed her arms over her knees and rested her chin there. "Do you have any regrets about coming here, Solomon? Moving to a strange place and starting from scratch, I mean?"

"No," he said. "I haven't left behind anything that matters. And there was something about the old place—tangled mess though it was—that just roped me in. I took one look at that house and knew I wanted to live in it one day."

"How did you even find it?"

"An ad in the newspaper. There was a hazy picture of the house and an attorney's address—Knox's address. I didn't even write. Just caught a train and came down here to see it."

"You're very lucky to choose your own path and follow it like that." Callie was surprised by the sad sound of her own voice.

He raised up, sitting cross-legged. "Can I ask you something without making you mad?"

"Yes."

"Are you as happy as the rest of your family?"

"What do you mean?"

"Are you really happy?"

She raised her head and took her time before answering honestly. "No."

"That's what I thought. But I'm not sure why."

"Because my brothers and sisters all know who they are and where they belong, but I don't."

"You belong as much as they do."

"To Mama and Daddy, sure. But I'm talking about here." She held her arms out wide. "Where do I belong here, in the world? Do you understand?"

"Yes."

"James will always be happy farming, and he's very good at it," Callie went on. "So Daddy's crop lands will be in good hands. Theo is the same. He's just a child, but already he lives and breathes plows and harrows and red-dirt fields. George isn't much for hands-on farming, but he has a head for business, so Daddy's helping him move in that direction. And then there's Sam." Callie smiled at the thought of her most rambunctious and adventurous brother. "The cotton fields will never hold him. He's always wanted to join the Navy. As long as he can travel and see new things, he'll be happy. And Emmy, of course, just wants to be with Knox, wherever that takes her. They all seem so sure of where they belong—so well suited to something."

"But not you?" Solomon reached over and brushed an ant off her ankle.

"Not me."

"Does the farm make you restless—like you want to run away and work on a riverboat?"

Callie shook her head. "I love the farm. What makes me restless is not getting to be part of it—all of it. I can carry lunch to the men and deliver soup to the field hands when they're sick, but I can't help run the farm and work it like my brothers. And

I can't be happy just getting married and having children and hosting suppers and tea parties the way Emmy can. I want to be a mother, but I'd much rather tend livestock or help raise a crop than make punch and plan party menus."

"Plowing all day is wearisome business," Solomon said.

"Not half as wearisome as the conversation at tea parties," Callie argued.

"You have a point. I'd rather plow."

"So would I," she said with a sigh.

"Callie, I think it would be a terrible waste to try and confine you to tea parties."

She looked at him straight on. "Do you really believe that, Solomon—truly?"

"I do."

They both grew quiet, watching the creek flow and listening as doves began calling across the water. Solomon looked at her and smiled. "There's no better sound than that, is there?"

Callie smiled back at him. "Even when I was little, I'd stop in my tracks to hear the doves. Hepsy says they're my spirit bird. Maybe they're yours too."

"Maybe so."

They listened to the birds again before he asked her, "Would it be alright if I asked your father's permission to see more of you?"

"Yes." No roller coaster had ever made Callie's heart beat so fast. She had to pause for a minute before she could speak. "Would we have to court?"

"Court?"

"Would we have to go to house dances and church socials, or could we do things we might actually enjoy?"

He raised an eyebrow and grinned at her. "What did you have in mind?"

"Stop!" Callie felt her cheeks flame and covered them with her hands, which made Solomon laugh.

"I apologize. But not too much. Do you like to fish?"

"I love to fish. But I hardly ever get to. Would you really take me?"

"I would."

"I could pack us a picnic."

"You could."

"What if Mama thinks we need a chaperone?"

"I nominate Theo. He has trouble staying awake."

Callie laughed at the thought of a sleeping Theo tagging along. "Yes, if we must have a chaperone, an unconscious one would be the best choice." Another silence fell before she said, "There's something I want to show you—something in the creek, I'll add, before you make me turn bloodred again."

Solomon held up his hands in protest. "I don't cause the blushes. I just observe them."

She wrapped up the leftover chicken and rolls in a napkin and tied it. "There. I just made you supper. Let's go look at the castle."

"What castle?" He stood and helped Callie up.

"Come on. I'll show you."

He held her hand as they waded the clear water south of the bend. It came to Callie's knees in a few spots but was mostly shin or ankle deep. As they followed a serpentine stretch of the creek, trees and other flora along the banks became especially dense and lush as the water wandered downhill and the banks rose four or five feet above the creek bed.

Callie looked up at Solomon. "Almost there." When the creek straightened, she pointed straight ahead. "The castle gates."

Two stone pillars, each about eight feet high, protruded from the banks of the creek. Beyond them was a remarkable sight. On either bank, oak trees had been uprooted and tilted toward the water, meeting in an arch high above Yellowleaf. They appeared to have broken each other's fall in midair. The result was a giant green teepee above the water. Solomon gaped at the sight, his eyes wide as could be.

"Come inside." Callie gave his hand a tug and nodded toward the pillars.

They waded between the tall columns of rock and stopped underneath the arch of green now cemented together by years of honeysuckle and morning glory vines. In the center of the structure, water was bubbling up, sending out ripples from a spring-fed fountain beneath the surface of the creek.

Solomon was staring up at the arch overhead, which cast the creek in a strange and beautiful light as the sun streaked through the green from high above. The tunnel effect of the trees played tricks with the normal sounds of the water, which echoed like a cistern inside a cave.

"What in heaven's name happened here?" His voice was hushed, just as Callie's always was when she came here.

"A tornado," she explained. "It skipped instead of staying on the ground and touched down right in the creek for a few seconds. The trees had such deep roots that they held on to the ground. That's why they aren't dead. They tipped over on both banks and fell into each other. Now so many vines have grown over them that they couldn't fall if they wanted to. This has been here forever."

"What about the stone pillars we came through?"

"They're the ruins of an old bridge that was here years ago—before I was born."

They walked toward the ripples. Here the creek bed took a dip and the water deepened, rising just above Callie's knees. She and Solomon stood facing each other in front of the fountain.

He cupped his hands, scooped up the spring water, and held it to Callie's mouth. She lowered her face into his hands and tasted the cool sweetness of it. He lightly ran his fingertips over her mouth, where the water was dripping.

Callie silently cupped her own hands, dipped water, and held it up to his mouth. She felt his face in her hands as he tasted it. Without words, he put his arm around her waist and pulled her against him. He laid his hand against her face as he kissed her forehead, her cheek, and then her mouth.

Callie stopped thinking or listening to anything except the sound of Solomon's breath. As they stood together in the creek, his arms around her, Callie wanted only to feel. She wanted to feel Solomon forever.

SEVENTEEN

allie? Are you alright?" Emmy came into the bedroom, where Callie stood by the window, staring out at the Lookout Tree and replaying every moment of her time on Yellowleaf with Solomon.

"I'm fine, why?"

Emmy joined her at the window. "You seem a little—I don't know—distracted?"

Callie nudged her and laughed. "Look who's talking, Miss Bride-to-Be."

"Am I truly obnoxious?" Emmy looked worried.

"No! I'm just giving you trouble. You're excited, that's all. And I'm happy for you, Em. I'll miss you like all get-out, but I'm very happy for you."

They sat down on Callie's bed. "Did you find Josie some pretty things while you were wedding shopping yesterday?"

"Yes," Emmy said. "I just gave them to Lily. I'm hoping they take her mind off that woman from the court."

"What woman?"

"The one Ryder's lawyer sent over here today to try and take Josie. Mama gave her what for and sent her packing. We'll never have any peace—Hepsy's family or ours—as long as Lily and the baby are here. She already received her settlement from the railroad, so she has some financial security. I'd love to see her take Josie out of here and go someplace safe where Ryder will never be able to find them. Then we could all be happy again."

"Your eyes look tired, Em."

Emmy rubbed them. "I'm sorry I didn't understand how hard it was for you, never sleeping through the night the way I used to do. Now I know what it's like to lie awake with your thoughts and your troubles."

Callie took her sister's hand. "Try not to worry so much. We've got Knox and Daddy and Mama and Hepsy and Tirzah, so Ryder's outnumbered." Callie grinned at Emmy. "If it comes down to it, I'll shove him in the river again, only this time, Lily can hold his head underwater."

That brought a smile to Emmy's face, which had been drawn with worry. "Everybody thinks I look after you," she said, "but they've got it backwards. They've always had it backwards."

❦

Callie didn't remember going to bed. She woke in a strange haze, her vision dark and cloudy. Something wasn't right. One minute she was sitting with Emmy, talking about baby clothes, and the next she was here in bed, lying in darkness, with no idea of what had happened in between. She didn't remember going to supper or telling everyone good night or putting on the gown she now wore. She didn't remember anything between the day and the night. Or was it night? She wasn't even sure of that.

Voices swirled all around her. *Can she hear us? . . . Mama, what do you think? . . .* A familiar figure stood over her—tall and stately. In a flash of fleeting clarity, Callie saw a strand of red beads around her neck. Tirzah. What was she doing here?

❦

Callie had no idea how much time had passed when she finally came to herself and saw Tirzah leaning over her and looking into her eyes. "Go fetch Young Miss," Tirzah said to someone in the room. "Say Baby Girl depart the angels. She comin' back."

A few minutes later, Callie's mother hurried into the room, followed by Emmy. Callie reached out from her bed. "Mama?"

"Thank the Lord," her mother said, sitting next to her and clutching her hand.

Emmy knelt on the floor beside them. She was crying but smiling. "You gave us such a scare, Callie. I thought I'd lost you. If Solomon hadn't found you when he did, we might have."

"Solomon? Is he here?" Callie struggled to piece together what was happening to her. She felt like she had made some strange leap through time and space, leaving her completely disoriented.

"He's not here now, but he'll be back," Emmy said, laying her hand against Callie's cheek.

"What—what happened?" Callie asked. She touched her forehead and felt a large bandage running all the way across it. She tried to sit up but couldn't.

Her mother put her hands on Callie's shoulders. "It's a little too soon for that. We were hoping you could tell *us* what happened, Callie. Solomon was coming to see your father early yesterday morning and spotted you lying under the Lookout Tree. You were in your nightgown with one shoe on, and your head was bleeding. He carried you into the house and fetched Dr. Embry for us."

Every new piece of information just made Callie more confused. "Why was I outside in my nightgown? And in one shoe?"

"We don't know," Emmy said. "It looks like you climbed the tree sometime during the night and fell out, but we can't imagine why you'd be up there. You don't remember?"

Callie reached up to touch her head again.

"What's the last thing you do remember, Callie?" Her mother blotted her cheeks with a cool cloth.

Callie stared at the ceiling as if her memories were floating up there, waiting to be pieced together. "I remember . . ." The strongest memory she held—the one she was clinging to—was of Solomon. But even in her current state, she didn't want to share it. "Hepsy sent me to pick apples . . . and take a cake to Mary Alice."

"Anything else?" Emmy asked.

Callie blinked her dry, scratchy eyes. "I remember the two of us . . . talking . . . about Lily and Josie. You had just taken them . . . new baby clothes."

"Good, Callie!" Emmy said. "That's exactly right. We sat on your bed and talked after I took Lily the baby clothes. That was the day before yesterday. Do you remember anything else?"

Callie thought hard but saw only flashes and fragments. "Voices . . . the baby . . . I think . . . maybe I dreamed something about Josie. Is she alright?"

"Josie and Lily have gone, Callie," Emmy said.

"Gone where?" Callie tried to rub her head, but her mother gently pulled her hand back down.

"We don't know," she said. "They must've left the same night you fell. Apparently with Fisher."

Callie couldn't take it in. "But . . . are they alright?"

"We hope and pray," her mother answered.

"Their things are gone," Emmy said.

"And Lily left a note," her mother added. "Show it to her, Emeline."

"Oh, Mama, do you think we should? It might upset her."

"It's alright," Callie said. "I'd like to see."

Emmy handed Callie the note, which must have been hastily written—some words printed, some in cursive. Had Lily been scared when she wrote it? Callie was far too groggy to focus. The words kept blurring together. Her head was starting to hurt.

"I'm too . . . too fuzzy to read it, Em."

Emmy took the note back. "That's alright, dearie. It just says that Lily was tired of being tormented by Ryder and was leaving with Fisher—and taking Josie, of course. She didn't say where they were going. Just thanked us for everything and said she hoped we'd understand."

"You . . . you really think . . . they're alright, Emmy?"

Her sister softly squeezed her hand. "I think they are likely right where they should be. I just feel it in my bones."

"What about Hepsy?" Callie asked.

"Hepsy seems oddly at peace with it," her mother said. "I guess she knew there could be no life for Lily and Josie here, not with Ryder and his foolishness. Fisher is capable of taking care of them wherever they may be. Even so, I was surprised at how well Hepsy took it."

Callie stared at Emmy, struggling to remember whether she might've seen them leave, but nothing came, and her eyes began to sting. "I can't . . . I can't remember anything, Emmy. Nothing after . . . the apples and the baby clothes. What's wrong with me?"

Her mother stroked Callie's cheek. "Time and rest will make it right. Tirzah says you'll be fine. Tirzah is never wrong."

"She was really here?" Callie asked her mother. "I thought I might've dreamed her."

"She just left. Your father took her home."

Callie lay still and quiet for a moment. "Something smells good."

Her mother nodded. "Tirzah made a steam to soothe you last night. You were so restless and agitated."

"The creek," Callie said, her voice weak and drowsy. "It smells like the creek."

EIGHTEEN

Callie had fallen back to sleep after talking with her mother and Emmy. She didn't stir again till the next day. But now she was wide awake and felt like herself for the first time since the accident—whatever it was.

Sitting up slowly, she gingerly touched her head, feeling a smaller bandage than before. She swung her legs over the side of the bed, cautiously stood up, and made sure she could balance before walking to the window and looking out on a beautiful fall day. To her surprise, the sun lay low in the sky. She had expected morning.

At the washstand, Callie poured a basin full of water and bathed as best she could. A tub bath would have to wait. She put on a powder-yellow cotton dress and gathered her hair over one shoulder, tying it with a ribbon just as she had done the day she met Solomon on the creekbank. Or did she? Callie didn't trust her own memory right now.

Reaching down for her shoes made the room spin. Her head felt light, and a dark tunnel began to close in around her. She grabbed hold of the bedpost to steady herself while her head cleared and the darkness dissipated. Shoes and stockings would have to wait for a better day. Opening the bedroom door, she stepped barefoot into the central hallway of the house and followed voices to the front porch.

"There's my girl," her father said as he came to her and gently put his arms around her. "How are we feeling, Miss Callie?"

She smiled up at him. "Much better now, Daddy. I think I've had enough of the Rip Van Winkle life."

He kissed the top of her head. "Come on over and join us."

Her parents were sitting on the front porch with Solomon, who stood up from the porch swing when he saw her. His brow was furrowed as his eyes darted from the bandage on her head to her hands, to her bare feet peeking from beneath her skirt, and finally back up to her eyes—perhaps assuring himself that all the pieces were there.

Callie's mother came and kissed her on both cheeks. "Are you sure you're ready for this, Callie?"

"I'm ready, Mama."

"Come over to the swing. I'm sure Solomon won't mind sharing."

"Not at all." He steadied the swing for Callie and held her hand as she sat down.

"Do you feel surefooted?" her mother asked, standing next to Callie's father.

"Barefooted but surefooted," Callie said, slightly lifting one foot.

Her mother raised an eyebrow. "You would never get away with that if I weren't so relieved that you're up and around. Since you're in good hands here, I'll go and see how Hepsy's coming with supper. You need some solid, nourishing food to get your strength back. Solomon, I'm so glad you could join us."

"Thank you, Miss Aurelia," he said. Callie noticed the shift from "Mrs. Bullock" to the more familiar "Miss Aurelia" and wondered how that came about.

Callie's mother touched her father's shoulder. "Ira, would you be good enough to help me?"

"Right behind you." Callie's parents disappeared into the house, leaving her alone with Solomon on the porch.

Slowly rocking the swing, he took her hand, raised it to his mouth, and kissed it. "You gave me such a scare, Callie. I don't think I've ever been that scared in my life."

She reached up to touch his face. "I'm sorry. I didn't mean to. The truth is, I don't remember what I meant to do. No matter how hard I try, it just won't come."

"You'll remember soon enough." He put his arms around her, and she lay her head on his shoulder. He lifted her bare foot with his boot as he had done in the Lookout Tree. "I think you're at your best when you're shoeless."

"Good, because I hate wearing shoes."

They rocked together in the swing before she had a question. "Solomon, what were you doing here that morning—when you found me under the tree, I mean?"

"I was coming to talk with your father before he went to the fields. I wanted to ask him if it would be alright for us to see more of each other."

"And did you? Talk to him, I mean?"

"Not right then, but later. You kept me a little occupied for a while."

"What did he say?"

Solomon smiled at her. "He said he'd let me court his youngest daughter in exchange for my sixty acres in the creek bend."

"I'll bet he did it with a straight face too." Callie smiled at the thought of her father testing Solomon. "What did you tell him?"

"I told him if he'd throw in a good mule team and a plate of Hepsy's fried chicken, he had a deal."

Callie laughed. "Well, what was the outcome?"

"We have his blessing—and I get to keep my land. Also, your mother seems to be trying very hard not to terrify me anymore."

Callie was suddenly worried that the Bullock clan might be too much for him. "It's a lot, isn't it, Solomon?"

"What?"

"My family, with all our suppers and crises and bumps on the head. As long as you've been on your own, we must make you feel like you've run slap into a big, loud train wreck."

"I wouldn't say that." He gently squeezed his arms a little tighter around her for a moment. "More like two train wrecks."

"Nobody would blame you if you ran for the hills."

"Always been more of a creek man."

"Speaking of the creek," she said, lifting her head so she could look at him, "I can clearly remember *some* things that happened before I fell."

"Like what?"

"You promised to take me fishing."

"I did."

"And you kissed me."

"I did that too."

"For a long time."

"Not long enough."

NINETEEN

$\mathcal{A}$s the family gathered in the dining room for supper, Callie and Solomon had to give up their private spot on the porch. They took their usual seats as Callie's mother directed, between George and Sam. But right after Callie and Emmy served supper, Knox started coughing and couldn't stop.

"Are you alright?" Emmy had her arm around him and handed him a napkin, which he used to cover his mouth. "Would you like some water?" He shook his head, unable to speak.

Callie and Solomon looked at each other, their faces showing the same concern as everyone else's. Knox's raspy, labored cough sounded unnatural and unnerving.

Finally, he caught his breath enough to say, "Please forgive me, Miss Aurelia, Mr. Ira. I thought—" He started to cough again but regained his composure. "I thought I was over whatever bug has been keeping me home from work. But I think I should go." He tried to stand but fell back into his chair.

"You aren't well enough to go anywhere," Emmy said. "You're coming upstairs. George, would you help us?" George hurried to the other side of the table, put Knox's arm around his shoulders, and lifted him out of the chair. Together, he and Emmy guided her struggling fiancé upstairs.

"Ira, should we ask Tirzah to come?" Callie's mother asked. "I believe Knox might be more comfortable with Dr. Embry, don't you, Aurelia?"

"Yes, of course. We should send for him right away. Sam—"

"On my way, Mama," he said. "Y'all excuse me."

Sam left the table but returned before he had time to get outside. Sheriff Cagle came into the dining room with him.

"Mama, Daddy," Sam said, "you've got company."

"Come in, Sheriff," Callie's father said. "Sam, we'll fill you in when you get back. We need you to go on and get the doctor."

Sam grabbed a couple of rolls from the buffet and left again as Callie's father offered the sheriff a chair.

"I'm afraid I have some very bad news, especially for Miss Bullock—Miss Emeline, that is." The sheriff sat down and removed his hat.

Callie's heart began to pound. She suddenly envisioned a flawless Lady Baltimore cake tumbling off the fellowship table and landing in ruins on the floor.

"There's no easy way to say this," Sheriff Cagle went on. "We found Miss Emeline's fiancé dead in the river this afternoon—shot twice in the back."

Callie's father frowned. "There's been some mistake, Sheriff. Knox just left the table a few minutes ago. He's upstairs and feeling unwell. That's why we've sent Sam for Dr. Embry."

The sheriff leaned forward in his chair, slowly twirling his hat in his hands. "I don't understand. We found the victim—somebody we all recognized—in a suit that everybody at the courthouse had seen Mr. Montgomery—Mr. Knox Montgomery—wear many times. It had his monogram on the inside coat pocket."

"Was it light blue?" Callie asked.

"Yes, that's the one," the sheriff said.

"Daddy," Callie said, "Emmy told me that Ryder once tried to pass himself off as Knox in that suit—as a prank. The suit was a gift from the judge when Knox graduated law school, so he wears it in court a lot. The man in the river—do you think he could be Ryder?"

"Are you all sure the man upstairs isn't Ryder?" the sheriff asked. "You said he's been known to pass himself off as Knox."

"He could never fool Emmy," Callie said.

"Who could never fool me?" Emmy asked as she and George returned to the dining room.

"You'd better sit down, dear," her mother said. "We've sent for Dr. Embry."

"Thank you, Mama. I just gave Knox some of Tirzah's elixir to help him sleep. He's resting quietly now." Emmy and George sat down together.

"The sheriff has brought disturbing news," their mother said. "A man was found dead in the river."

Emmy's hand flew to her mouth.

"Do they know who he was?" George asked.

"He looked like Knox and was wearing Knox's suit," their mother said. "Callie tells us Ryder has tried passing himself off to you before, Emeline?"

Emmy gave Callie a fleeting, fearful look across the table. Callie kept her eyes on her sister. "I told them about his silly joke, Emmy—the prank he tried to play on you that time, remember? He thought he was so clever and funny?"

Relief flooded Emmy's face. "Yes, his silly prank. It was ridiculous. I'd never mistake Ryder for Knox. They look so different."

"Not to most people," the sheriff said. "Are you sure that's not Ryder you're tending to upstairs, Miss Bullock?"

"It most definitely is *not*." Emmy looked disgusted by the thought.

The sheriff fidgeted even more with his hat. Callie felt a little sorry for him. He thought he had come to deliver sad news, which was hard enough, but now here he was in her mother's grand dining room, struggling with the unpleasant task of interrogating the family.

"Is there any proof of Knox's identity you can give me, Miss Bullock—anything besides your own assurance, sound though it may be?"

"Actually, yes," Emmy said. "After Ryder tried to—tried to fool me, Knox showed me a birthmark. He has it but Ryder doesn't. It's here, on his right arm." Emmy pointed to her wrist. "And it's shaped sort of like a small crescent moon. I can show it to you right now if you like. His parents can confirm—oh my goodness. Have you told his parents yet?"

"No, ma'am," the sheriff said. "I came here first, just in case there was any doubt about the victim's identity—for the sake of his family, you understand."

Callie's mother tersely corrected him. "Emeline is Knox's family."

"Yes, Mrs. Bullock," the sheriff said. "I didn't mean any disrespect."

Emmy stood up. "Come with me, Sheriff, and I'll take you to Knox. He'll be sleeping, but you can see his wrist without disturbing him."

The two of them were upstairs only briefly. "It appears we were mistaken," the sheriff said when they rejoined the others. "I'll need Knox's parents to confirm the birthmark, but absent any discrepancies there, it's likely his brother we found in the river. Of course, that opens up a whole 'nother kettle o' fish. We were pretty sure there was only one man who might want to harm Knox—that factory owner—but with Ryder . . . well . . . Any idea who he was trying to fool this time, dressed in his brother's clothes?"

"I'm sure we have no idea what was going through Ryder Montgomery's mind." Callie's mother had begun tapping a finger against the base of her wineglass.

"Have your people found anything else in the area where he was?" Callie's father asked.

"We found a loaded shotgun about a quarter mile from him, but it had only been fired once. All the other shells were still in it. Ryder's wounds looked more like rifle shots to me, just based on the skin tearing—"

"Ira," Callie's mother said, her tapping growing more rapid by the second.

He nodded and stood up. "I'll walk you out, Sheriff."

The sheriff started for the doorway but turned and looked at Callie. "Hit your head, Miss Bullock?"

She touched the bandage on her forehead.

"Good night, Sheriff," her mother said in a tone that would brook no argument.

"Yes, ma'am. I'm very sorry I interrupted your meal."

The sheriff took his leave, and the family tried to resume their supper, with Callie's mother quickly silencing any morbid talk of dead bodies in the river. But when Sam returned with the doctor, he couldn't let his questions rest until someone told him what had happened. Callie fixed him a plate and set it in front of him as her father briefly explained the nature of the sheriff's visit. Sam listened, watching as Solomon helped Callie with her chair.

"Well," he said, "the sheriff would have an easier time finding somebody who *didn't* have a reason to shoot at Ryder. Then again, do they even know if the killer got the brother he was after?"

"Samuel!" His mother shot him a warning look.

"Sorry, Mama." Sam was quietly eating his supper when he suddenly stopped, looked around the table, and asked, "Have the rest of y'all figured out that Solomon's sweet on Callie?"

TWENTY

*H*e's been up there for an eternity." Emmy looked as distraught as Callie had ever seen her, nervously twisting and untwisting the handkerchief she clutched and taking deep breaths to try calming herself. The family had gathered in the living room, waiting for Dr. Embry to finish examining Knox.

Her mother laid her hands over Emmy's. "Now, Emeline, we will not think the worst until we have good reason."

Emmy looked like she was trying to smile, but her lips trembled so that the corners of her mouth could barely form a wobbly curve. "Yes, Mama."

She sat between her parents on a long formal sofa. Callie was with Solomon on a settee near the fireplace, where George and Sam stood flanking the mantel. James hovered near his expectant wife and brought Mary Alice a small velvet stool, insisting that she prop her feet up while they all waited. Quiet, occasional conversation replaced the Bullocks' usual rowdy banter, and the room fell completely silent when they heard footsteps on the stairway. Dr. Embry removed his mask as he came into the living room, his head bowed, his mouth a tight line, holding back words that threatened to spill sorrow all over them.

"Please sit down, Doctor," Callie's mother said, motioning to an armchair next to the sofa. "May we get you anything?"

"No, thank you." Dr. Embry took his seat. "I wish to goodness I had better news for you all. But the truth is, Knox is very sick."

Callie looked across the room at Emmy, whose eyes were already welling.

"There was blood on the handkerchief he'd been using. I didn't like what I heard when I listened to his lungs through the stethoscope. I'm afraid he looks and sounds like every tuberculosis patient I've ever treated."

Emmy's face turned snow white. Her mouth was open, trying to speak, but it emitted no sound. She collapsed onto her mother's shoulder. Callie felt frozen, barely able to breathe. She longed to comfort Emmy, to tell her everything would be alright, but she couldn't move. Solomon silently slipped his arm around her.

"How long has he been like this?" Dr. Embry asked.

Emmy did her best to collect herself. "He—he was worn out by that big court case—the one for tuberculosis patients. I just th-thought he was having trouble getting his—his strength back."

"So it's been mostly fatigue that he's experienced?"

"Until a c-couple of—of days ago," Emmy answered. "He hasn't wanted anything—to eat. Yesterday he ran a little fever. Tonight he started—coughing so badly—"

The doctor nodded. "That's the pattern for many patients, I'm sorry to say. Knox could've had what we call latent tuberculosis. The bacterium that causes the disease was in his body but sleeping, in effect. Now it's active and very dangerous—to him and to all of you."

"I thought only people in those tenement houses in big cities got TB," Sam said.

"No, Sam," Dr. Embry explained. "If you can breathe, you

can get tuberculosis because it's airborne. Once you breathe in the bacterium after a sick person coughs or sneezes, everything depends on your body's immune system—how strong it is and how resilient you are."

"Has Knox been contagious all this time, Doctor?" Callie's father asked.

"Hard to say. A patient isn't contagious until they have symptoms. But since there's no way to tell whether his previous fatigue was caused from working long hours or from the active disease, we don't really know how long he might've been spreading it—unknowingly, of course. It could be that he's had the infection for a while, and then the recent strain of the trial weakened his immune system and essentially woke up the disease. In any case, he's definitely contagious now, and you all should take precautions."

"What do you recommend, Dr. Embry?" Callie's mother asked.

"First and foremost, nobody enter that room without something covering your nose and mouth. I expect his parents will want to send him out west to a sanatorium, but for now, open the windows so that Knox gets lots of fresh air. But block the crack under the door, just as a precaution for the rest of the family. Give him plenty of fluids and anything you can get him to eat, though it likely won't be much. And wash your hands religiously after you've had any contact with him, which should be extremely limited."

"Can the rest of us spread it?" George asked. "Do we need to be careful about contact with other people?"

"Keep to your farm for the next couple of weeks," the doctor advised. "See if any of you becomes symptomatic. Some people can carry latent tuberculosis for months or even years. As long as you don't have any symptoms—fever, nausea, extreme fatigue, and most of all a persistent cough that doesn't go away—you shouldn't have anything to worry about and you can't give it to anyone else. But at the first sign of symptoms, you need to send for me and stay away from other people. Emmy, since you've spent the most time with Knox, I'm afraid you're at the highest risk. You probably shouldn't sleep in the same room as Callie until we can make sure you haven't been infected."

"We'll do as you say, Dr. Embry," Callie's father said.

The doctor said his goodbyes. George showed him out. And the living room grew silent again, except for Emmy's sobs. Her mother held her tight, gently rocking her as she wept.

"Ira," she said quietly, "please ask Tirzah if she'll come."

TWENTY-ONE

*I*n the days ahead, the Bullocks established an entirely new routine. Theo slept on Callie's trundle in the girls' room. George and Sam carried twin beds from the attic onto the upper porch. Emmy stayed in an upstairs guest room, where she could hear Knox if he called out for her.

Callie came to dread the sight and sound of her mother's grandfather clock in the main hall, for it seemed now to be ticking away Knox's life and Emmy's happiness. He grew weaker by the day—sometimes by the hour.

"His parents still haven't come?" Callie stood in the doorway to Knox's room, masked like Emmy.

Her sister shook her head, adjusted the bedcovers, and came out to join Callie. "You shouldn't be up here," Emmy said. "Let's go outside where it's safer."

On the upper porch, they took off their masks as Emmy sat down in the swing, Callie pulling up a rocker several feet away.

"I just can't believe it," Callie said. "Even for the Montgomerys, this is low. To ignore your own son when he's so sick . . ."

"They didn't support him when he was healthy and making a name for himself. Why would we expect them to come when he's sick and weak?" Emmy rubbed her forehead.

"Another headache?" Callie asked. Emmy nodded, and Callie joined her in the swing.

"Don't sit so close to me, Callie. We don't know if I'll get sick, and I couldn't stand it if anything happened to you because of me."

Callie slid down to the far end of the swing. "Hush up and rest your head in my lap."

Emmy smiled and lay down, using Callie's lap as her pillow. Callie rocked and stroked her sister's hair until Emmy fell asleep. She was exhausted from sleepless nights, listening for the faintest sound of discomfort from Knox's room. Callie knew without a doubt that if Knox were himself, he would never let Emmy near him right now, fearing for her safety. But the sickness had taken over, and he called for her day and night.

Hepsy stepped onto the porch and saw Callie holding her sister in the swing. She clasped her hands tightly together. "That's dangerous, Miss Callie."

"I know." Callie looked up at her. "But how can I not?"

❧

For Knox, the end came quickly, just as Tirzah had predicted. "Almighty done call this man," she had told Callie's mother. "It's his time."

Dr. Embry explained that the infection would not confine itself to Knox's lungs and had gotten into his bloodstream, where it spread without mercy. He died with Emmy sitting at his bedside, holding his hand. She was inconsolable.

The sight or smell of food made Emmy violently ill. Her skin grew pallid, her eyes darkened with circles drawn by sleepless nights. But on the day of Knox's funeral, an odd calm came over her. Callie could see it in her steady hands as she pinned a black hat onto her blond hair, which was beautifully styled for the first time since Knox had fallen ill at the Bullock table.

"Can I help you, Em? Can I do anything at all?" Callie stood behind her sister as she sat at their dressing table, the two of them reflected in the mirror.

Emmy smiled at her. "I don't need anything."

Until now, she had been a wreck, barely holding herself together enough to care for Knox, while Callie had remained strong, ready to lend support and comfort. But now, faced with the finality of Knox's funeral, Callie feared she herself might no longer be in control of her emotions, while Emmy seemed the picture of serenity.

Callie rested her hands on Emmy's shoulders. "What's happening, Em? You seem . . . different."

Emmy looked at her in the mirror, reached up, and laid a hand over Callie's. "I *am* different. He spoke to me."

Callie frowned and stared into the mirror. "You mean Knox?"

Emmy nodded. "Don't worry. I'm not hearing voices from the great beyond. It's more like . . . I felt him. I felt him being healed and at peace. He was . . . transformed. I can't explain it. I just sensed him changed and in a beautiful place, telling me that he wasn't here anymore and that I shouldn't grieve for the body being laid in the ground because he wasn't in it. Do you think I'm crazy?"

Callie kissed her sister on the cheek. "I don't think you're crazy. I think you're able to feel things the rest of us miss."

Emmy stood up and put her arms around Callie. "I love you, dearie. So very much."

❦

The day after Knox's funeral, Callie came down to the kitchen early in the morning just in time to see Hepsy spring back from the sink. "You look like you just saw a snake, Hepsy."

Callie stepped closer and peered into the sink, which held one of the garden baskets Tirzah had woven for them. Inside it was a small doll that George had given Callie for her sixth birthday. It was covered with a dishcloth.

"What's Polly doing in the sink?" Callie frowned as she pulled back the dishcloth to reveal the doll's familiar pink dress.

"You didn't put it there?" Hepsy asked her.

"Why would I do that?"

"They's some bad juju around this here." Hepsy backed farther away from the sink, pulling Callie with her.

Hepsy's unease only intensified once it became clear that no one in the Bullock household had any idea how the basket with the doll had gotten into the sink.

Though Hepsy had been raised in the Baptist church and lived her whole life in Alabama, her mother came from St. Helena Island in South Carolina. For most of her life now, Tirzah had devoutly followed Almighty but married her adopted Christian faith to the traditions of her Gullah community. She had taught Hepsy about the dangers of "bad juju," which they now met not with spells or incantations, as in the old days, but with prayers for the protection of Almighty.

The doll was just the beginning. Soon after she found it in the kitchen sink, Hepsy made another discovery.

"Miss Callie! What you doin' out here? You been under that tree all night?"

Callie opened her eyes to see Hepsy kneeling over her as she lay on the ground underneath the Lookout Tree, right where Solomon had found her before. She was wearing her nightgown.

"What happened, Hepsy?" Callie's voice trembled with fear, and her whole body shook.

"I don't rightly know, but we gon' see to it. Don't you worry. Come on and let's get you inside." Hepsy put Callie to bed with a cup of tea and some of Tirzah's special elixir to help her rest.

Then came the worst night of all. Callie came to herself in her brother's arms. George was hurrying down the stairs, carrying her and calling out to their parents. "Mama! Daddy! You need to get up!"

George told them he had been sitting up late to finish reading a book when Callie came up the stairs in her nightgown. Her eyes were wide open, but she was sound asleep. She silently opened the window by the Lookout Tree and started to climb out. George stopped her, carried her downstairs, and alerted their parents, who came running into the living room, where George laid her on the couch. They summoned Dr. Embry.

Hepsy sent word to Solomon that he might want to come and get Callie out of this "house o' sorrow" for a little while. Maybe that would calm her nerves and quiet her mind. Maybe it would free her from the juju.

Solomon and Callie stood fishing on the bank of Yellowleaf. "Want to tell me about it?" he asked her.

"About what?"

"Whatever made you ignore the last two fish."

They stood side by side on the creekbank, but Callie had to admit that she had been far, far away the whole time. She sighed and pulled her line out of the water. "I'm sorry."

"No need to be. Maybe we just weren't meant to fish today."

Solomon propped their cane poles against a tree, picked up their picnic basket, and took Callie by the hand, then led her through denser woods on the back of his farm to a spot where the creek was wide and shallow. It was sprinkled with cascades as the water made its way downstream.

Callie smiled at him. "It's beautiful here."

He took the quilt she had brought and spread it beneath a tall pine, where they sat down together.

"Now," he said, "forget about the fish and tell me what's bothering you."

Callie looked at him and realized for the first time how tired he must be. When he wasn't working on his farm, he was spending every minute with her. She laid her hand against his face and felt his soft beard against her skin. "I don't want to tell you any of my troubles right now. I want to hear yours." Leaning against the tree, she stretched out her legs. "Rest your head in my lap."

Solomon lay down and stretched out.

She slowly ran her fingers through his hair and looked down at his handsome face. "Now, talk about anything but me."

"Do I have to talk?"

"No."

"Good." He closed his eyes and took a long, deep breath.

Callie relaxed against the tree, listening to the doves call and the creek water splashing against rocks. Such tranquil sounds. She didn't want to think about her disturbing night rambles. She didn't want to think at all.

❦

Callie awoke to an afternoon breeze. Solomon was looking up at her. "Did I sleep very long?" she asked, rubbing her eyes.

"I don't know," he said. "I just woke up."

Callie smiled at him and rested her hand against his chest. "Aren't we exciting?"

He covered her hand with his. "Anyplace you'd rather be?"

She stroked his hair. "No. It's so peaceful here with you. Makes me forget everything else."

"Tell me what you'd like to forget. You'll feel better, and I will too."

Callie took a deep breath and blurted out, "There's a very good chance I'm losing my mind."

"That's a new development."

"I'm serious."

"I know. But I also know you aren't insane."

"I've started sleepwalking," she said.

"When?"

"Right after Knox's funeral. The first time, I went only as far as the kitchen, where I apparently took a garden basket from the pantry, put a doll inside, covered it with a dishcloth, and set it in the sink. I went back to bed and didn't remember doing it. Mama and Hepsy didn't figure out it was me until I walked in my sleep again."

"There was a second time?"

"And a third." She told him about the other two incidents when she had wandered from her bed unawares.

"What does your family say?"

"They think we should listen to Dr. Embry and let him send me to a healing springs resort in Talladega—for my nerves."

"Is that what you want?"

She looked down at him and sighed. "I think whatever is wrong with me started at home. Something made me get out of bed and go outside the night Lily and her baby left with Fisher, which could've been the same day Ryder was shot. I just can't remember what drove me out there. And I think the best way to bring it back is to stay where it happened."

"But you'll go anyway because your parents want you to?"

She lightly ran her fingertip over his brow. "I don't know. If Mama and Daddy feel strongly about it, I guess so. They'd never force me, of course. They're just worried. What do you think?"

"I think you should trust your own judgment. Never let anybody else tell you they know best."

"My family must be so tiresome for you."

"Your family's been very good to me. I just like to keep things simple. And I like to make my own decisions." They grew quiet for a moment before Callie raised a question that had been troubling her.

"Solomon . . . you seem different around them—different toward me, I mean."

He sat up and leaned against the tree with her. "I would say the same about you."

"Really? Do I treat you differently in front of my family? Because I don't mean to."

He rubbed the back of his neck as he considered it. "I always thought it was you—but maybe it's me."

"And I thought it was you," she said, "but maybe it's me."

They said it together: "Maybe it's them." Then they began to laugh—really laugh—something Callie hadn't done for weeks.

Solomon leaned over and gave her a soft kiss. "Come along, Miss Bullock. I have something to show you." He stood and pulled her up. "But it's in the creek, so you'll have to take off your shoes and stockings. I think all the other underpinnings can stay."

Callie laughed and stepped behind the tree to get ready for a wade. Solomon was already in the creek when she started down the bank. He held her hands as she made her way into the clear water and led her upstream until the channel narrowed to about eight or ten feet across, where Callie saw something that left her speechless. It was an open A-frame structure, one side anchored on each bank, with a porch swing hanging by long ropes from the top so that you could swing over the water and look down the creek.

"I knew you couldn't come and sit with me on my front porch without a chaperone, so I decided to build us our own porch in the creek," Solomon said. "What do you think?"

She stared at the swing, thinking about all the work he had put into it, just for her. Then she looked up at Solomon. "I love it. And I love the hands that made it."

TWENTY-TWO

Callie wouldn't let Solomon see her off at the train station. She told him she just couldn't bear it. Instead, he came for supper the night before, and her family allowed them privacy afterward. As they stood beneath the Lookout Tree, he had kissed her goodbye and said, "Promise you'll come back to me."

Now she sat next to her father on a train bound for Rosemont Springs and the healing waters that were supposed to cure her memory.

Through the train window, Callie could see a landscape that she would have found breathtaking if it weren't separating her from everyone she loved. They passed creeks and streams and rolling hills splashed with fall color as the oaks and maples turned to orange, yellow, and red. Now and then a cotton field would appear out the train window, its bolls open, releasing puffy clouds of white up and down the stalks.

Her father took her hand and smiled. "I'll bet ten bales of cotton I know who you're thinking about."

"What if he gives up on me, Daddy?" Callie had never kept secrets from her father.

He kissed her hand. "Solomon won't give up. He's got sense enough to know what he's found."

Callie looked up at him. "I don't know if I can do this. The truth is, I'm scared to death."

Her father put his arm around her. "Me too. But I'll promise you this. If we aren't happy with what we see, we'll be on the next train home. I don't care what the doctors say. Nobody's gonna force you to stay here if you don't want to."

Callie lay her head against his shoulder. "I'm glad you're here. You in particular."

❧

It was almost lunchtime when the train pulled into Rosemont Station. Callie's father tipped a porter to take care of their bags before they followed a stream of travelers to the two-story, white clapboard hotel, which had double porches and tall windows all the way around. It was surrounded by shade trees. Paths leading away from the hotel had wooden signs pointing the way to the indoor and outdoor pools, as well as the social pavilion, stables, and kennels.

Callie's father held the door for her as they stepped inside the hotel lobby—a large parlor with heart pine floors and Victorian furniture. A Victrola sat in one corner by the fireplace, which was opposite the front desk. Her father gave his name to the hotel clerk, who was standing next to a boy about Sam's age.

"Ah, yes, Mr. Bullock—I have your reservation right here," said the clerk. "We're so pleased to have you and your daughter with us. I believe you have an appointment with Dr. Martin at two o'clock this afternoon?"

"That's correct," Callie's father said.

"Alright then. I'm Rosa Hayes. My husband, Otto, and I own the hotel. He's also the minister at the Methodist church. My sister Olean oversees the kitchen and is our head cook—a fine one at that. We'll think of your daughter as part of our family while she's with us. Fall and winter are our off-seasons, so the hotel isn't at all crowded. If you don't like your rooms for some reason, we can easily make a change. Our son Robbie here will be happy to show you upstairs and get you settled in. And we'll start serving lunch in the dining hall shortly. Dr. Martin will meet you right here in the lobby at two. Robbie, here are their keys. Enjoy your stay, Mr. Bullock, and do let us know if there's anything you need."

"Thank you, Mrs. Hayes," Callie's father said. "We appreciate your hospitality."

Callie and her father found their luggage already in their rooms, which were on the second floor of the hotel, Callie's in the corner and her father's next door. They freshened up from their journey and had lunch in the dining hall, then took a walk around the resort grounds before returning to the hotel lobby just before two. Soon they were greeted by a kindly man who was tall and lean, with silver-white hair and sky-blue eyes. He wore a white coat over his dress shirt and tie.

"Mr. Bullock, I presume?" he said as he shook hands with Callie's father. The doctor's eyes twinkled when he smiled.

"I'm Ira Bullock and this is my daughter Callie. You must be Dr. Martin."

"I am indeed. If you'll come right this way, Mrs. Hayes has kindly offered us the use of a private parlor where we can talk."

They followed him to a small but cozy room with tall windows. It was furnished with a green velvet sofa facing two similarly upholstered wingback chairs, a cherry coffee table in the center. The three of them sat down together.

"Miss Bullock, as I understand from Dr. Embry, you suffered a fall and a head injury, followed by memory loss," the psychiatrist began. "Is that correct?"

"Yes, sir," Callie answered.

"And so far you've been unable to recall the accident itself, but you have no trouble remembering what came before it or what happened once you were fully conscious again. Is that correct?"

"Yes, sir. I remember talking with my sister, Emmy. She had bought baby clothes for a friend who was staying with us. We sat together on my bed. But after that, nothing. Nothing until I saw Tirzah—she's the midwife who delivered all of us—standing over me. She's also a healer. My mother calls on her when she's worried about one of us."

"I see," Dr. Martin said. Callie already liked this man, with his comforting voice and kind eyes. He listened to her as if she were the most important person in the whole state of Alabama. "Now," he said, "do you have any memory at all of where you fell and hit your head?"

Callie shook her head. "No, sir. I know that Solomon—he's my—that is—he's a family friend—he found me the next morning when he came to see Daddy. He told my parents that I was underneath a big tree in our yard—one I've climbed many times—and I was wearing my nightgown and one shoe."

"How curious," the doctor said. "And you have no idea what prompted you to get out of bed, put on your shoes, and perhaps climb a tree?"

"No, sir. I've tried and tried as hard as I can, but it just gives me a headache. If I had been fully dressed—or in my nightgown with no shoes—it would make a little more sense. Not much more, but a little."

"And I understand there's been some sleepwalking?"

"Yes, sir. Three times since Knox's funeral. Knox is—was—my sister's fiancé. He died of tuberculosis recently."

"Oh, I'm very sorry to hear that," Dr. Martin said.

Callie described all three sleepwalking incidents to the doctor, who listened intently as he wrote in a leatherbound notebook. "Of course, I don't remember the things I do while I'm asleep, but once somebody wakes me up, I remember everything from that point on."

"Mr. Bullock, what are your thoughts on your daughter's condition?" Dr. Martin asked.

Callie's father leaned forward in his chair, his hands clasped together. "I feel like she just took a bad bump on the head and her mind needs time to recover. I believe her memory will come back soon enough, but even if it doesn't, she'll be alright. Dr. Embry, though, felt pretty strongly that she should see you, and we—my wife and I—trust his judgment. We don't want to take any chances with Callie's health if there might be more to this."

Dr. Martin nodded as he wrote in his notebook. "Well, I'll tell you both what I recommend, and then we can discuss whether you and your wife are comfortable with it, Mr. Bullock—and whether *you* are comfortable with it, Miss Bullock. That's very important. First, I'd like to send you to the hospital in Talladega for some X-rays. Are you all familiar with this technology?"

"No," Callie's father said.

"It's completely painless, and it allows us to essentially take a picture of the bones and organs inside the body. We'd be able to see, for example, if your daughter had any fractures to the skull. What I'm trying to do is rule out any physical causes for her continued memory loss and sleepwalking episodes. Once we do that, we can proceed with other forms of treatment."

"And what would those be?" Callie's father asked.

"Mostly I'd have her get plenty of rest and take the waters from the hot springs in the indoor pool since it's a bit too chilly to swim outdoors. She'd also receive a daily glass or two of water from other mineral springs on the property, ones which we believe can help restore imbalances that affect the chemistry in the brain. I'd meet with her a couple of times each week to talk about any flashes of memory, however small they might be. She'd receive a journal so that she could record her thoughts any time of the day or night. And we'd make sure she has proper nutrition and lots of fresh air. The hardest part would be isolation from her family. You wouldn't be able to visit each other for a little while."

"Sir?" Callie's heart was suddenly racing, a wave of heat

flushing her whole body. She wished she could run to the nearest window and throw it open for some fresh air.

"Doctor, I don't think we can go along with that," her father said.

The doctor smiled and nodded. "I fully understand your trepidation. Every family feels that way at first. But solitude is an important part of your daughter's treatment, though certainly not for the duration of her stay here—only in the beginning."

"But why?" Callie asked.

"Picture yourself listening to the Victrola in the hotel lobby," Dr. Martin explained. "When the room is full of people laughing and talking, you can't hear the music very well. But once they've all gone and there's no extraneous noise covering up the sound, you can hear every note. It's the same with your memory. Right now, you have all kinds of distractions making noise around the message you're trying to hear in your brain. If we can pull you out of that, put you in a place that's peaceful and quiet so that the only thing you can hear is the voice of your own memory, I believe you'll begin to hear it loud and clear—provided there are no physical impairments, of course."

Callie turned to her father. "What do you think, Daddy?"

"It makes sense, I suppose . . . Even so, it's hard enough for us to be separated from her, Dr. Martin. If we can't even visit her, I'm not sure how any of us could stand that, especially her mother."

Dr. Martin took off his wire-rimmed spectacles and cleaned them with his handkerchief as he talked. "I'll tell you what. I'll give you a specific time frame. You'll refrain from visiting for one month, Mr. Bullock. We'll see if that makes a difference in your daughter's memory. Then I'll write you with my recommendations, and we'll reevaluate where we are. Would that help allay everyone's concerns?"

Callie and her father looked at each other and nodded in agreement. "I want at least a weekly note in her handwriting, letting me know she's alright and happy here," Callie's father said. "If I don't get that note, you can expect a visit from me. And I don't want any restrictions on her ability to contact me— by letter or telegram—if she should grow unhappy here. As long as she's content, why, we'll abide by your rules."

Dr. Martin nodded. "I would expect nothing less. And I want to assure you both that there's nothing strange or mysterious or in any way secretive about this process. Both the brain and the body have the power to heal themselves, but they sometimes need a little help."

"Does that include strong drugs?" her father asked, concern on his face.

"For a patient like your daughter, no. She appears to me in complete control of herself, and her mental faculties are very sharp. I'm sure you've heard horror stories about morphine addiction and the like, but nothing of the sort will be given to your daughter. The strongest medication I would prescribe might be a mild sedative to help her sleep if she's struggling to rest in a strange place, but whether she takes it would be entirely up to her."

"What about the sleepwalking?" Callie's father asked. "What if it continues here?"

"I don't believe it will," Dr. Martin said. "What your daughter described to me sounded very specific, almost a reenactment of something she had done before or perhaps something she had seen. That won't be possible here because her surroundings are so unfamiliar. Some doctors lock sleepwalking patients in their rooms at night, but I don't believe in that. Just knowing they're confined creates undue stress, in my opinion. What I would recommend is that you hire a sitter to keep watch outside her door at night for the first week or so. I'll be happy to arrange one for you—someone I know and trust, of course."

"I think that would be best," Callie's father said. "Thank you."

"What about you, Miss Bullock?" Dr. Martin asked. "How do you feel about all of this?"

"A little anxious, of course," Callie said. "And sad to be separated from my family. But if I can get well here, it will be worth it. I'm willing to try my best."

Dr. Martin smiled at her. "That's all we can ask. I believe, at the end of the day, you'll be very glad you came. I'll arrange for a sitter and give Mrs. Hayes a schedule for my visits with Miss Bullock. The two of you enjoy the rest of your day."

The men stood and shook hands, then Dr. Martin left the parlor.

"Let's take a walk, my girl," Callie's father said. "I think better outside."

They followed a wide path to a string of mineral springs—some like small ponds, others no bigger than the well behind the Bullock house—and sat down on a park bench.

"This has been a hard year, Callie," her father said.

"I know. I'm sorry I've made it harder."

He gently patted her hand. "You did no such thing. You can't help what's happening to you right now. And I meant what I said in there. If you get to feeling the least bit unhappy here, you send me a telegram. When we go back to the hotel, I'll open up an account for you and tell Mrs. Hayes there are no restrictions on it whatsoever. Anything you want or need—from a new hat to a train ticket—you put it on there."

Callie grinned and nudged her father. "How many bales of cotton can I spend?"

Normally, he would've joked with her about spending all his cotton money, but Callie could see that he was too worried for that right now. "You spend whatever you like," he said. "You've never been the least bit extravagant. Now might be the time to start. Just as soon as they give me the okay, Solomon can come up for a visit. But if he doesn't mind his manners, he'll have me to deal with."

TWENTY-THREE

Callie soon discovered one advantage to living alone. She didn't have to keep quiet as she tried to subdue the turmoil in her mind. Until Knox became ill, Emmy had always slept soundly from the moment her head hit the pillow. Sharing a room with her, Callie had to devise ways to get free on those many nights when her thoughts simply wouldn't lie still and let her rest. Sometimes she would slip out to the study and read. Or she might take a pillow and cover to the upper porch and lie down on the swing, letting its gentle rocking lull her to sleep.

Here at the resort, however, she was the only person in the room. She could be as noisy as she liked while she brewed herself a cup of tea in a kettle over the fireplace. She could let her mind roll and tumble with abandon while she wrote in the journal Dr. Martin had given her, purging the chaos until she was ready to sleep.

Callie quickly fell into a pattern—journaling at night and writing letters in the afternoon. On Saturday during her first full week at Rosemont, a chilly autumn rain was falling. Hepsy had mixed up a tin of Tirzah's special tea blend and packed it for Callie, who brewed herself a cup and pulled her rocker in front of the window to write.

October 9

Dear Emmy,

Is it raining at home? It's pouring here, but you know me—I love the rain.

It's so strange to be all alone. Every morning when I wake up, the first thing I do is look across the room where your bed should be.

Earlier this week, Dr. Martin took me to Talladega for something called an X-ray. Can you believe they have a machine that can see inside your head? I was afraid of what they might find in mine. But the news was good—no fractures or anything. No bats in my belfry!

Dr. Martin thinks I had a concussion but nothing more. I had my first appointment with him yesterday. He is kind as can be and makes me believe this will all get better soon. And he was right about the solitude being good for my memory. I've already started to see snippets here and there, but they're so hazy, like looking "through a glass darkly."

Yesterday I was taking a walk and had a sudden flash of someone's back—just the back of a person standing by the river. I couldn't say if it was male or female, let alone anyone I knew. Maybe I didn't remember anything at all. It's frustrating.

Tomorrow will be my first Sunday in a strange church with people I don't know. I wonder what it will be like. Mr. and Mrs. Hayes—I guess I should say Brother Hayes since he's a minister—they own the hotel, and they're taking us to the local Methodist church in a wagon that has long benches and a top of sorts in case it rains. Brother Hayes is the pastor there. The resort also has what they call the "chapel in the meadow" for private reflection. I can see you smiling. You know I'll do most of my praying there. But I'll give this church a try and see what it's like.

*How are you, Emmy—truly? I feel like I've abandoned
you when you need me most, and my heart is broken for
you. I know you said you're at peace and you know that
Knox is in a better place. But that doesn't make you miss
him any less.*

Take care, sweet sister—
Love,
Callie

❧

October 14

Dear Callie,

*I'm thinking of you this morning and wishing I were at
Rosemont Springs with you. I'd give anything to get away
from where I am, but the trouble is that "where I am" is in
a life without Knox, and it will follow me wherever I go.
Up until now, I've been able to answer all of life's great
questions with one look at him. Who am I? Why am I
here? I'm the one who loves Knox best, and I was put here
to share his life, have his children, and make him happy.
That's all I ever wanted from the moment I met him. And
now I'm lost.*

*That doesn't mean I am not happy and relieved to learn
that you suffered no serious physical injuries. But that's
just the beginning of your healing, isn't it? I wish I could
help you remember, Callie, but I can't fathom why you
would've been in the Lookout Tree that night—or when
and why you would've left our room and gone anywhere
else outside.*

Please remember that, even though we're apart, I am right

by your side in your struggle to remember. I am searching here, and you are searching there, but we remain together, always.

Much love,
Emmy

P.S. Give those Methodists a fair shake—they might surprise you.

TWENTY-FOUR

Callie was just into her third week under Dr. Martin's care, and as he'd predicted, she was no longer sleepwalking. The sitter outside her door had been dismissed. More and more, she saw "snippets," as she called them, not fully realized memories of the night she fell but stronger and stronger flashes. She now carried her journal with her everywhere, even to the indoor pool, where she would wrap it carefully in a towel and tuck it into the knapsack Mrs. Hayes had given each of her guests—a handy tote as they traveled between the hotel and the springs or stables.

Rosemont's indoor pool was large, rectangular, and spring-fed, covered with a barnlike structure and surrounded by wooden decking that provided a smooth surface for lounge chairs and benches. It had separate dressing rooms for men and women. Because the water came from a hot spring and the early morning air around it was cold this time of year, a cloud of steam rose from the surface. Callie found it both eerie and inviting, especially when the pool house was empty and quiet. Something about this unusual environment seemed to stimulate her memory. At her request, Dr. Martin had spoken with Mrs. Hayes and arranged for Callie to take the waters early in the morning, before the pool officially opened for the day.

It was about six thirty when she used the key Mrs. Hayes had given her to unlock the door to the pool house and then relock it from the inside. No one would disturb her.

Callie spread a towel over one of the lounge chairs and placed her knapsack on it. She sat down and took out Emmy's latest letter, which she had already read twice, missing her sister more than she could have imagined.

October 15

Dear Callie,

I know I should wait to hear from you before I write again, but there was a thunderstorm this morning, so of course I am thinking of you. I guess I just needed to talk with my sister.

I wish I could see a picture of Rosemont Springs. Then I would have an image in my mind of where you are and what you might be doing. Daddy says it's a beautiful place and that he is very impressed with your doctor. But I know a beautiful place can be a lonely one, and a doctor is no substitute for family.

Unless I'm not as smart as I think I am, you are missing Solomon terribly. It's alright to talk about him, you know, to be happy that you've found your soul mate at last, as I suspect you have. I've lost Knox, but that doesn't mean I'm not happy that you have found Solomon. He's the one, Callie. I just know it in my bones.

I have been thinking about the night you fell. And the more I consider it, the less sense it makes that you would've been in the tree. You always liked to take your shoes OFF to climb it, not put them on. And surely your lost shoe would've turned up by now if you had indeed fallen right there. I don't believe that's where you were. Unfortunately, the question remains—where were you?

I know it must be frustrating, but do not give up hope,
my dearie. I will not give up on you. Not ever.

All my love,
Emmy

Callie tucked the letter inside her knapsack, which she covered with the heavy robe she had worn from the hotel. After stepping into the warm water, she slowly waded toward the deep end, thinking of Emmy and trying not to feel so alone. She swam the length of the pool at an easy pace before relaxing and floating on her back.

She looked up at the high-pitched ceiling of the pool house with its rounded gambrel roof and heavy timbers. The shape of it reminded her of Tirzah's handwoven garden baskets. They were as solid as the roof above and so tightly woven that they could float on water. When she and Emmy were children and Miss Katherine taught them the story of Moses in Sunday school, they had carried a baby doll and one of Tirzah's baskets to the creek. They took turns pretending to be Miriam, watching over her baby brother hidden in the reeds beside the Nile, and Pharaoh's compassionate daughter, who rescued God's chosen deliverer. Sometimes Callie and Emmy couldn't resist setting their "Moses" afloat, sailing the baby doll back and forth to each other in the basket.

There in the stillness of early morning, the warm water enveloping her and steam drifting up from the water, Callie saw those images clearly—the basket, the baby doll, the creek, her sister . . . and something else. Callie stood up so abruptly that she almost went underwater. Scrambling out of the pool, she hurried to her journal, quickly drying her hands and arms so she could scribble down everything she remembered. That night, after supper, she would share her recovered memory in a letter to her sister.

October 20

Dear Emmy,

Today I saw something—something important, I think. But I don't know what it means.

Dr. Martin arranged for me to have private early morning swims in the indoor pool filled by a hot spring. I was lying on my back in the warm water, looking up at the curved roof of the barn that covers it, and I thought of Tirzah's baskets. Remember how we used to carry one to the creek and take turns playing Miriam and Pharaoh's daughter? I just saw a snippet, Emmy—you as a child with a doll in Tirzah's basket, floating it on the creek the way we used to. But as I kept thinking about it, I saw something else—my missing shoe, sort of hovering in midair, dangling in front of me. I couldn't see where it was. And now I just feel more confused.

I miss you, Emmy. And something else. I miss Solomon. I can't begin to imagine how you must miss Knox. My precious sister, you never leave my thoughts.

> *Take care, sweet Emmy—*
> *Love,*
> *Callie*

❀

The next morning, Callie was delighted to find that Dr. Martin had slipped a note under her door, suggesting that they meet in the lobby and take a "nice, brisk walk" during their visit today, rather than meet in the hotel's private parlor as they usually did. She buttoned her wool coat and put on her hat and gloves. With Thanksgiving just a month or so away, the air had grown crisp and cool, dipping into the low forties in the evening and early morning, but it was still warm enough for a walk on a sunny day like today.

She was always happy to see Dr. Martin, who waited for her by the fireplace in the hotel lobby. There was something about his warm smile and the what-might-we-discover-today twinkle in his blue eyes that made her hopeful.

"Hello, Miss Bullock!" He took her hand and clasped it between his.

"Hello, Dr. Martin," she said with a smile. "I trust you come ready to unravel the entanglement that is my brain."

"No, my dear, I come to celebrate it with wonder."

Callie laughed. "Well, let the celebration begin."

"Shall we?" Dr. Martin held the door open for her. "I thought we might take a walk down by the stables and then circle back up to the little coffee shop in the train station, if that's agreeable to you."

"Perfect." As they set off on their walk, Callie admired the grounds of the resort in all their fall splendor. "It's a shame more people don't come here this time of year," she told Dr. Martin. "The trees are just gorgeous. And it's not too cold to be outside."

"I couldn't agree more," he said. They followed a path through maple, oak, sassafras, and persimmon trees alight with red, orange, yellow, and purple. "Tell me about your morning swims, Miss Bullock. Any revelations?"

She sighed as she stopped to pick up an especially brilliant maple leaf from the ground. "Yes and no. I saw something, but it doesn't make any sense." She told him about the childhood game she and Emmy had played and about her intruding vision of the lost shoe. Then she dropped the leaf and watched it land at her feet.

"Well, let's see now," Dr. Martin said. "You told me during one of our previous visits that your family had a guest at the time of your fall—a young woman with a baby, if I remember correctly? Lily, wasn't it?"

"Yes, sir. That's right."

"And she was in some kind of difficulty?"

"Very much so," Callie said.

"I'll admit I am at a loss about the displaced shoe, but I doubt you need me to point out the connection between your Moses game and the real-life mother and baby your family has been caring for."

"No, sir, but I just can't fully connect them the way I need to."

They had reached the stables, where a groom was helping a boy about Theo's age climb into his saddle. Callie hoped her little brother understood why she had to go away for a while.

Inside the barn, the horses were having their morning sweet feed and hay. Callie stopped now and then to pet the ones who stood at their stable doors and leaned down to sniff her hat. "Next time, I'll bring apples," she promised a mare named Birdie.

"Unless I miss my guess," Dr. Martin said, "you could hop on that horse bareback and persuade her to take you anywhere you wanted."

Callie smiled as she combed Birdie's mane with her fingers. "I love horses. Mules and cows can be ornery, but horses are generally agreeable companions as long as you treat them fairly. They have a strong sense of justice."

"And what about you, Miss Bullock? Do you have a strong sense of justice?"

"I like to think so." She patted Birdie's neck before they moved along.

"Tell me all about Lily and her baby," Dr. Martin said. "Try not to leave anything out."

As they walked together through the hall of the horse barn and back outside to the main path, Callie told him everything she knew about Lily—her husband and baby, her move to Alabama, the way she sang and inadvertently caused a stir at the May Day celebration, and Ryder's relentless pursuit of her, including his nighttime appearance by the river and his attempts to take Josie. Finally, she told him about Lily's disappearance and Ryder's murder.

"If Lily were wealthy and white, Ryder would've thought twice before trying something so vile," Callie said. But then she considered what he had done to Emmy. "Then again, maybe he wouldn't. In any case, with Lily being colored and poor, Ryder was *sure* he'd get away with it. But he hadn't counted on Mama."

They arrived at one of the mineral springs, where Dr. Martin directed her to a park bench in a warm, sunny spot. "And what does your mother have to do with all of this?"

"She's very devoted to Tirzah—the midwife and healer I mentioned when I first told you about my fall—and her daughter, Hepsy, who runs our house," Callie explained. "Hepsy is Lily's grandmother and Tirzah is her great-grandmother. Tirzah came to cook and keep house for my parents when they were expecting my oldest brother. She did a lot more than run the house, though. Mama says that Emmy and I both would've died at birth without her."

"She must be quite the midwife," Dr. Martin said.

"Oh, she is. And then Hepsy came to work for us when Tirzah decided it was time for her to rest. Tirzah personally trained her own daughter to run our house. Naturally, we're all very grateful to them. When Mama saw what Ryder was trying to do to a member of their family, it made her furious. At first, she kept him away from Lily herself, but eventually, she had to involve Daddy."

"What did your father do?"

"He paid Ryder a visit and told him that if he set foot on our farm with intent to bother Lily again, he could expect buckshot," Callie said.

"And do you think this Ryder fellow believed him?"

"Ryder was useless, but he wasn't stupid. He knew Daddy didn't make idle threats."

Dr. Martin's demeanor changed, his lips a hard line, his eyes focused straight ahead. "Miss Bullock, I'm afraid I have to ask you something difficult." He turned to face her. "Is there any chance that the memory you've blocked was a crime? That perhaps you witnessed your father putting an end to this man who was causing so much trouble for Lily and, by extension, your family?"

"No, sir," Callie said. "No chance at all."

"How can you be so sure?"

"Because I know him. When Lily disappeared, she was living in our backyard. Ryder would've had to come to our very door to get near her. Daddy or my brothers would've stopped him right there and sent for the sheriff themselves. And they wouldn't have killed him. They would only have stopped him. Ryder was shot in the back by someone who wanted him dead. And they dumped him in the river—a stretch of it that doesn't cross our farm. Daddy wouldn't hesitate to defend his family on our property, but he'd never hunt a man down and shoot him in the back. Neither would my brothers."

"Well, I must say I'm relieved to hear it. And I hope you won't fault me for asking."

"Not at all. Your questions are helping me get well."

"I believe we just made it over a hump of sorts," the doctor said. "Shall we go and have some coffee at the train station?" He checked his pocket watch as he and Callie stood. "Excellent. We should have plenty of time for coffee before the lunchtime train arrives with all those hungry diners following the scent of Miss Olean's fried chicken."

At the station, they found a table next to a window and ordered their coffee. Dr. Martin smiled as Callie filled hers with so much cream that it became the color of burlap. "My daughter does the exact same thing," he said.

"It's how Hepsy served it to Emmy and me when we were little—only she used milk—and I never outgrew it," Callie said.

"We had this tea set Daddy bought for us in Mobile. Hepsy would fill our cups almost full of fresh milk and then add a little splash from Mama's coffeepot. We thought we were so grown up—and that Hepsy was letting us get away with something. But we were drinking a lot more milk than coffee."

They sat quietly, the clink of their cups and saucers the only sound before Callie raised a question. "Dr. Martin, I wonder if we need to keep thinking along the lines of what you suggested about Daddy."

"You mean you believe you *did* witness a crime?"

"No, sir, not necessarily a crime. But what if I saw something I wasn't supposed to see? Or something I didn't want to see? Would my mind try to block it out?"

Dr. Martin nodded as he stirred his coffee. "That's not uncommon. Is that what you think is happening to you?"

"I'm not sure. But it makes sense. I keep thinking about my shoes. The one I was wearing when Solomon found me was relatively clean. The shoe I remembered while I was swimming was its mate, but it was caked with mud—black mud, which you would see near a river or a creek. Only it wasn't on a river-bank or a creekbank. It wasn't anywhere. It was just sort of floating in midair."

"And what do you make of that, Miss Bullock?"

Callie frowned at the doctor, whom she now considered a trusted friend. "I don't know. Maybe I was near a creek or the river before I fell?"

"In other words, you've come to believe that you didn't just fall out of the tree you were found under. Is that correct?"

"Yes, sir, that's correct. I wouldn't have gone outside at night in my gown unless there was some sort of emergency. And I wouldn't have put on shoes to climb the tree. Emmy reminded me in her letter—I usually take my shoes *off* to climb it. Also, why can't anyone find the lost shoe, which is nowhere in or around the tree?"

"There's nothing wrong with your logic," the doctor said with a smile. "I want you to continue refusing to accept the easy answers when they do not make sense to you. Trust your own judgment. Believe in yourself and the reliability of your own mind."

"You sound like Solomon," Callie said.

"Am I to deduce, from your wistful expression, that Solomon is more than a family friend, Miss Bullock?"

"Are you asking as my doctor or are you just meddling?" she asked with a grin.

"Just meddling," he said, making Callie laugh. "I'm sure you must be eager to get back to him, but as your doctor, I would discourage you from pushing yourself too hard or trying to force progress. Best to let it come to you. It won't be much longer before Solomon can visit. In the meantime, I want you to continue your early morning swims, and I also think I'll prescribe a trail ride with that mare we met this morning."

Callie raised her coffee cup. "To my favorite medicine."

TWENTY-FIVE

*C*allie was standing before her bureau mirror, pinning on a burgundy velvet hat, when she accidentally knocked off the tin of Tirzah's tea that Hepsy had blended for her. Thank goodness the lid was on tight. Bending to pick it up, she saw something she hadn't noticed before—a small piece of paper taped to the bottom. On it was written a name, Ura Prospect. Nothing else. Callie didn't know anyone, colored or white, by that name. Maybe the tin had once belonged to a friend of Hepsy's or Tirzah's. She set it back on her bureau but couldn't stop staring at it. Was that really all the strip of paper held—the name of a previous owner—or had Hepsy sent her a message?

More questions without answers. More days without Solomon. More reasons to remember, but the memories wouldn't come. Not until they were ready. Not, according to Dr. Martin, until Callie was ready for them.

She put her change purse, room key, and gloves in the pockets of her dress coat, which she would leave in the lobby as she joined the other guests for Sunday breakfast in the dining hall.

Mrs. Hayes believed in a hearty Sunday breakfast—scrambled eggs, creamy grits, bacon, smoked sausage, and country ham; biscuits with red-eye gravy, freshly churned butter, blackberry jam, and fig preserves; hot coffee for the adults, cold milk for the children, and spring water for all. Her guests could not receive a blessing, Mrs. Hayes said, if their stomachs were growling during the call to worship. A bountiful Sabbath day breakfast, served family style, was sure to silence any potential rumblings during the service, thus opening hearts and minds to "things that are higher, things that are nobler."

As Callie and the other guests enjoyed their breakfast, Mrs. Hayes made the morning announcements. "You all are in for a treat this Sunday," she said. "Mount Nebo Primitive Baptist Church is hosting its fall Sacred Harp singing today, and there will be a fellowship dinner at noon. They always extend an invitation to our guests, so we'll be taking you there right after breakfast."

"I don't understand," said a guest from Pennsylvania. "What is Sacred Harp?"

"It's a very old method of teaching harmony to singers who can't read music," Mrs. Hayes explained. "The notes have different shapes, and the shapes represent sounds on the musical scale—one shape for 'fa,' another for 'sol,' another for 'la.' That's why some people call it 'fa-sol-la singing.' It's fascinating and quite moving to hear. Some of the church members get so excited about these gatherings that they start early. But there will be plenty of music for you to enjoy once we arrive."

Callie joined the other guests as they made their way to the wagons, climbed aboard, and settled into the long benches bolted down the middle and along each side. It was probably a sin, but Callie was looking forward to the open-air ride more than the service itself. She had never heard Sacred Harp singing and wondered if it would make her homesick for the church choir back home, where Emmy sang soprano and her mother was the star alto. Callie had seriously considered skipping the group church outing today and saying her prayers at the chapel in the meadow, but now it was too late for that.

She chose a seat in one of the rear corners so she would have a clear view out the back of the wagon. This time of year, fall leaves draped Whitestone Mountain in a coat of many colors. It was breathtaking. Surely the Lord would forgive her, just this one Sunday, for preferring His creation to His house, given that she was all alone, worshiping with strangers for the second time.

If Emmy were on this wagon right now, she'd be greeting all the other guests, asking where they were from and how they'd heard about Rosemont Springs, which activities they most enjoyed at the resort, and whether they preferred the fried chicken or the pot roast from the dining hall since both were absolutely delicious. Callie had always marveled at her sister's ability to feel right at home—and put others completely at ease—wherever she went. That wasn't Callie's gift. She often wondered what was.

Tuning out the chatter, she listened to the *clomp-click* of horses' hooves as the wagons left the resort drive and turned onto the main road, running parallel to the railroad tracks. They had gone about two miles when Mr. Hayes drove the horses onto a much narrower road—more of a wagon trail really—that went straight into the woods. Callie could hear the soft thud of hooves striking loose dirt and an occasional snort from the horses as they pulled the wagon through sunlit oaks, maples, elms, and pines towering overhead. The main road quickly disappeared behind them as the wagon traveled deeper into dense woodlands. It crested a small hill before the trail turned sharply and hugged a crystalline creek that reminded Callie of Yellowleaf—and Solomon. She could see the clear water cascade over boulders and hear it splash into shallow pools before babbling over smaller rocks in its path.

Then she heard something else, faint at first but growing stronger with every turn of the wagon wheels—a cappella voices creating a sound both ancient and spiritual. It kept growing louder, but still its source was veiled by the woods.

Only when the wagon rounded one final bend did Mount Nebo come into view. A log structure with only a small clearing surrounding it, the church looked like it had sprung from the ground of its own volition, as native to the woods as the pinecones and acorns. A tall door in front was open to the fresh air. Up on a small hill behind the church stood a large canvas tent, so weathered that it looked to Callie like a relic from the war.

As she silently took in the church and its surroundings, all the other hotel guests were excitedly chattering about the music and speculating about the food to follow the service. Why would anyone want to laugh and talk or even breathe in the presence of such an otherworldly sound surely touched by divinity? You could feel its transformative power. All you had to do was "be still and know." And yet the irreverent hotel guests chattered away. They might just as well have been swapping recipes at the foot of Mount Sinai. This log cabin of a church, hidden in the woods, was a sacred place. The singers and the God they worshiped made it so.

When at last the others were inside the church, Callie stood alone by the front steps and communed with the songs, which were sung in four-part harmony but different somehow. As she listened, she realized that both men and women were singing all the parts, just an octave or two apart. And they sang loudly, with great emotion—sometimes words, sometimes just "fa-sol-la." Callie heard some songs that were completely unfamiliar. Others had words she knew, but their melodies were foreign.

The jubilant "On Jordan's Stormy Banks" that she had sung since childhood was here transformed into an eerie, mysterious reflection on the hereafter, sung in a minor key. Its exultant invitation—"Oh, who will come and go with me? I am bound for the promised land!"—was replaced with an exquisite pastoral vision:

"O, the transporting rapt'rous scene
That rises to my sight;
Sweet fields arrayed in living green
And rivers of delight."

"Miss? Oh, miss?"

Without realizing it, Callie had closed her eyes to block out any distractions from the music. She opened them to see an elderly man in worn black pants and a pressed white dress shirt, likely his best, standing on the top step of the church.

"Would you like to come in, miss?"

Callie smiled at him and nodded. "Yes, sir, thank you."

She followed him inside the church and was surprised to see that the pews were not arranged in the usual way, flanking a center aisle. Instead, they formed a hollow square, all facing the empty center.

"Where should I sit?" Callie whispered to the man.

"Anywhere you like, miss," he answered. "If you plan to join the singing, tenors are there." He pointed to the section with the most pews. "Altos are there, trebles there, basses there. If you'd rather just listen, why, take a seat behind the singers in any section you like. Most newcomers like to sit with the tenors because they sing the melody."

Callie smiled and thanked him. She looked at the pews behind the tenors and saw all the hotel guests seated there, no doubt talking. She chose an empty pew at the back of the alto section and took a seat.

A woman stood in the center of the square, holding a hymnal. "My lesson is 'North Port.'" She called out the hymn number, and Callie was suddenly enveloped in sound that resonated off the log walls and the heavy timbers of the high-pitched roof. The windows of the church had no glass panes but were open to the woods when their shutters were thrown wide, as they were now.

Closing her eyes, Callie listened to one of the most beautiful songs she had ever heard—also sung in a minor key—filled with longing for union with God. It seemed to reach way down into her soul and touch the homesickness she had tried to deny ever since her train pulled out of the station, carrying her away from all things familiar and beloved.

> *"Jesus, my all, to heav'n has gone,*
> *Glory, hallelujah;*
> *He, whom I fix my hopes upon!*
> *Glory, hallelujah!*
>
> *"I want a seat in Paradise,*
> *Glory, hallelujah!*
> *I love that union never dies,*
> *Glory! Hallelujah!"*

A man about the age of Callie's father was coordinating the singing. He would draw a small piece of paper from a basket, then call out the name written on it, prefaced by "Sister" or "Brother." The designated leader would come to the center of the square, announce the name and number of their chosen hymn—their "lesson"—then sing the pitch and lead the singers, who all kept time by raising one arm up and down like a rhythmic knee slap that stopped in midair.

A young man who reminded Callie of Sam had just finished his lesson when the director called out another name. "Sister Ura Prospect."

Callie thought her heart would stop as a woman stepped from her pew in the tenor section and came to the center of the square. She looked to be in her fifties, with a slight build and an attractive though serious face. Her clothes were simple—a long skirt and a jacket of olive-green wool, a black felt bucket hat covering most of her salt-and-pepper hair, and a small gold cross pinned to her wide lapel. She looked like the picture of humility.

"My lesson," she said, "is 'Amsterdam.'" She called out the number, hummed the pitch for the singers, and then began to lead them, facing the tenors as all the other leaders had.

The first "fa-sol-la" verse complete, the church members sang emotional words of homecoming.

> "Rise, my soul, and stretch thy wings,
> Thy better portion trace,
> Rise from all terrestrial things
> T'wards heav'n, thy native place."

As Ura continued leading her song, she did something very odd. Slowly and deliberately, she turned away from the tenors and faced the altos. Callie saw some of the singers begin whispering to each other as they cast puzzled glances in their leader's direction. Ura's brow furrowed, though she continued with her lesson, one hand holding her hymnal, the other moving up and down to keep time. She took a few steps toward the altos and scanned the pews until her eyes landed on Callie and remained there during the last verse of the song.

> "Rivers to the ocean run,
> Nor stay in all their course;
> Fire, ascending, seeks the sun;
> Both speed them to their source;
> So a soul that's born of God
> Pants to view His glor'ous face;
> Upwards tends to his abode
> To rest in His embrace."

The song ended, and the leader called the next singer's name, yet still Ura faced the altos, staring at Callie, who had never felt so completely shaken. She considered fleeing the church, but where would she go—into the woods?

"Sister Ura?" said one of the altos on the front pew, standing to put an arm around her as the others began the next song.

Finally, Ura turned her gaze away from Callie and looked at the alto. She hurriedly returned to her seat. The singing continued, uninterrupted. Then the director announced lunch in the fellowship tent.

Callie wasn't very hungry. The episode with Ura Prospect had her so rattled that she feared a big lunch, followed by the jostling wagon ride home, might inflict an unpleasant gastric spectacle on the other resort guests. She took a dinner roll and placed a small slice of country ham inside, then stepped outside the crowded tent. Nibbling on her roll, she drifted down the wagon path just a bit, still within sight of the church. Doves called overhead, and she stopped to listen.

"There ain't no more peaceful sound on God's green earth," said a quiet voice behind her.

Callie turned around and was startled to see Ura standing just a couple of yards away. "No, there isn't."

"I scared you, didn't I?" Ura bowed her head as if she wished this sort of thing would stop happening. "That was not my intent. I ask your forgiveness."

Callie couldn't find her voice. She only nodded until she could manage to say, "Of course."

"May I have a word with you?" Ura asked.

"Yes, ma'am."

Ura came closer until Callie could see that her brown eyes were filled with kindness. Nothing about her demeanor appeared remotely threatening.

"I . . . I have a gift," Ura said hesitantly, no doubt wondering if the revelation would chase Callie away. "I have the gift of sight. And I can see you're looking for something—a shoe."

Callie froze and had to will herself to speak. "How did you know that?"

"It's not that I knew—it's that I saw," Ura said. "It's real hard to explain. Just the sight, that's all. I've had it since I was a little girl. Not the easiest spiritual gift to manage, but I'm grateful for it just the same."

"And you—you believe you saw my shoe?" Callie heard the tremor in her own voice.

"I know I did," Ura said. "It's by a river. Less than a quarter mile south of the blue water. I don't know why that patch o' water is so blue, but it is. You'll find your shoe on the eastern bank of the river beneath the tallest pine tree—the one with a heart carved in it and the initials 'M.A.'" Ura handed Callie a piece of paper. "By your fine dress, I reckon you're a guest at the hotel. That there's a map from Rosemont Springs to my house. You come to see me if you want to. We can talk some more. Blessings on you, young miss."

Ura turned and walked quickly back to the fellowship tent, leaving Callie trembling, clutching the scrap of paper, and staring after her, unable to take a step forward or back. She hadn't even asked this woman how she knew Hepsy—or *if* she knew her. And Ura had called her "young miss"—the same thing Tirzah called Callie's mother.

Callie was suddenly overwhelmed by it all—her lost memories, the separation from Emmy and her family, and a deep longing for the comfort of Solomon's arms around her. Her eyes began to sting, and she knew the tears were coming. For once in her life, she welcomed them. Any kind of release, even a tearful one, would be better than the pent-up frustration and profound loneliness she felt right now.

She fled off the wagon trail and through the trees to the creekbank. In her mind, she could hear Emmy singing Callie's favorite hymn, leaving out words here and there, as she always did. Callie sat down on a stump, sobbing loudly and uncontrollably. She hoped the church crowd would keep to their tent and their food and their chatter and grant her the only solace she could find—"the beauty of the earth" and "the glory of the skies."

When Callie didn't show up in the dining hall for Sunday night supper, Mrs. Hayes brought a plate to her room. But she wasn't hungry. She wanted to go home. Desperately. Until now, she had been relatively content at the resort because she trusted Dr. Martin and knew she was making progress. Something about the encounter with Ura Prospect, however, convinced her that she could no longer travel this road alone, even with the doctor's help.

Callie put on her nightclothes and climbed into bed with her notepaper, using a large book as a desk. Leaning against the headboard, she poured out her day to Emmy, telling her all about the church in the woods where she had found, on one hand, a new kind of spiritual communion, and on the other, a frightening sense of her own—what would she call it?—*otherness*, for lack of a better word. Her lost memory set her apart from everyone else. Her eerie encounter with Ura Prospect was proof of it.

As she ended her letter to Emmy, she knew her sister would understand.

> *If only I could turn back the clock, Emmy. If only Knox could still be here, and Ryder had never laid eyes on Lily, and I had never seen whatever it is that I saw. Do you think I'm the reason I can't remember, Em? Am I such a coward that I'm hiding away in this resort rather than letting myself remember something that might be hard to face? Look at what you're facing. And you're doing it without me because I'm not as strong as I thought I was. I'm not as strong as you need me to be. Well, enough. I refuse to be that weak and scared. I'm going to remember, Emmy. And I'm going to come home to you.*
>
> Take care until then, sweet sister—
Love, Callie

TWENTY-SIX

*I*t does no good to wallow and stew. That's what Callie's mother always said whenever she thought one of her children had let some problem or disappointment take hold of them for too long. Callie felt she had begun to do just that—wallow and stew. What she needed was a change of pace. So for the second day this week, she would skip the pool and go instead to the stables, where she would saddle Birdie and take the mare for a long ride on the resort property. Callie had found that she was rarely lonely in the company of a horse.

Besides the healing mineral waters that drew so many visitors to Rosemont Springs, the resort also encompassed scenic woodlands, lakes, and streams, and its riding trails all were well marked. Whitestone Mountain was about as reliable a landmark as you could ask for. As long as Callie kept it in view, she couldn't really get lost.

As usual, she stopped by the kitchen for a couple of apples on her way out. Birdie always seemed to appreciate the gesture of friendship. Callie had also packed a lunch in her knapsack so she wouldn't need to hurry back to the dining hall at mealtime. Mrs. Hayes had suggested something called the meadows trail because it was very sunny and likely warmer than the others this time of year. Also, it led to spectacular views of the mountain and had a clear, cold stream where Birdie could drink—Callie too if she felt so inclined. Best of all, it would take her to the resort chapel she had yet to see.

Though Mrs. Hayes offered to have Robbie saddle the horse for her, Callie declined. She thought preparing a horse was an important part of the ride. Not only did it build trust between horse and rider, but it reintroduced them if they had not traveled together for a time.

At the stables, Callie took her time brushing Birdie, whose temperament was very similar to Daisy Bell's—a little pampering brought a world of cooperation. Horses, Callie believed, liked to feel appreciated.

Once in the saddle, she completely relaxed. Birdie would ask no questions about her strange encounter at the church singing, as some of the resort guests continued to do. How on earth could she possibly answer them—"A seer thinks she found my shoe"? It sounded ludicrous even to her.

It does no good to wallow and stew. Callie would not allow herself to dwell on Ura Prospect. Even so, she could picture in her mind the exact spot where Ura saw her shoe. It was underneath the pine tree that James had carved for Mary Alice, whose initials, "M.A.," Ura had seen.

Once James knew something, he knew it. And from the first time he danced with her, he knew he was going to marry the soft-spoken eldest daughter of Mr. Harold Chesser, who ran the town mercantile. James carved the tree after their first date and likely never expected any of his siblings to notice it. Callie and Emmy were gathering wild muscadines for Hepsy one day and stumbled onto it. It struck them both because it was so uncharacteristically romantic and whimsical for their quiet and serious brother. It was the kind of thing George would do, but not James. Still, there it was, a proclamation of his devotion carved in a towering pine by the Coosa River.

The sun shone warm and golden, the November air crisp, as Callie and Birdie followed the trail that took them through open meadows lying at the base of the mountain like the colorful skirt of a Christmas tree. Across the meadow grasses, Callie could see sweeps of purple asters, black-eyed Susans, and blue globe thistle. She closed her eyes and took a deep breath, inhaling the autumn air with its woody fragrance of fall leaves, then traveled along a stream so close to the base of the mountain that she had to lean back to see the top of the peak.

At last, Callie spotted it—the chapel in the meadow. The white clapboard structure, its paint worn and weathered, was shaped like a typical church, with a steeply pitched roof and even a simple wooden steeple on top. But while the front and rear walls were solid, the chapel had no sides—just well-defined corners with support columns in between. Beyond that, the sanctuary was open air. Double front doors were propped open so that Callie could look straight through the church and see the altar. Five or six rows of rough-hewn pews, which looked as old as the landscape, lined either side of a center aisle. The entire church was built of heart pine.

Callie climbed out of the saddle and grabbed the light halter and lead rope she had looped around the horn. Birdie deserved to enjoy such a place too. After replacing the bridle and bit with the halter, Callie fed the horse an apple she had brought along. "There you go, girl," she said as she stroked Birdie's neck. "Have some grass and a drink while I go inside for a bit." The mare nuzzled her shoulder as she tied the long rope to a tree.

Ordinarily, Callie would never set foot in a church wearing her riding skirt and hunting jacket. It would feel so irreverent. But this place made it alright somehow. She walked quietly down the center aisle and took a seat on the front pew, breathing in the scents of the meadow and coaxing her turbulent thoughts into a tenuous quietude. She grew still and began to pray, asking God to comfort Emmy in her grief, give Solomon the strength to restore his farm, and grant her enough courage to face whatever memories she was hiding from and return to the people she loved—people she gave thanks for every day.

Callie felt a peace fall on her, light as snow the few times she had seen it. She knew she would soon remember. She knew she would go home. Most of all, she knew she was done with inertia, with standing still, frozen by fear and frustration, waiting and hoping for something to happen. For better or worse, she must move forward.

No longer stumbling in the dark, Callie felt led. Most immediately, she felt led to Ura Prospect.

TWENTY-SEVEN

*T*he next morning brought brisk weather to Rosemont Springs, but Callie was warming up as she brushed Birdie, who was beginning to get her winter coat. She fed the mare two apples at the stables. Then she saddled her and set off for the mountain.

Hepsy always said that nature was God's medicine chest. It could heal when nothing else would. Callie felt the need for healing today. Her spirit had been broken, but traveling across the meadows with Birdie was restoring it. She could smell smoke in the air and see it drifting up from the mountain as local cabins chased away the morning chill with warm fires and woodstoves.

Callie followed Ura's map to a well-traveled path up the mountain, listening to the fall leaves crunch under Birdie's hooves as the two of them climbed about halfway up and found the cabin with a small purple flag by the mailbox, just as Ura had drawn on her map.

The seer's cabin looked cozy and inviting. Two washtubs flanking the front steps overflowed with mums, asters, and pansies in rich fall colors. Smoke drifted out of the chimney, offering the promise of warmth. Two rockers on the porch were draped with heavy blankets—a sure sign that the inhabitants couldn't resist being outside, even in cold weather, and Callie couldn't blame them. The view from up here was awe inspiring, a colorful fall tapestry underneath a sky too blue to be real. Callie draped Birdie's reins over the small hitching post in front of the cabin, took a deep breath, and climbed the front steps.

On the porch, beside the entrance, was a small table that held a yellow basket and a sign that read, "10 Cents If You Can." Callie took her change purse out of her pocket and dropped her money in the basket. She was about to knock when Ura opened the door and smiled.

"You knew I was coming?" Callie asked.

"No, young miss," Ura said. "I just heard footsteps on my porch."

"I put my money in the basket."

"Oh, you needn't have. I invited you. I had to put the basket out on accounta all the people comin' here, wantin' me to see somethin' for 'em. It took me away from my chores so much that my husband had to hire somebody to help out. That money pays for the help so I can use my gift."

"I'm happy to contribute," Callie assured her.

"Come on in and warm yourself."

"Thank you." Callie stepped inside the cabin, which was simple but spotless. She unbuttoned her wool jacket as Ura ushered her to one of two rockers in front of the fireplace, where logs crackled and the embers glowed. Callie thought of all the times she had rocked her little brother in front of the fireplace back home. Anytime she had trouble getting Theo to sleep, the fireplace would do the trick.

Ura poured them both a cup of hot tea from a kettle on the woodstove at the opposite end of the cabin and brought one to Callie before taking a seat next to her.

"I wasn't sure you'd come at first," Ura said. "But then this morning, I just got the feelin' you might."

Callie held the steaming cup, letting it warm her hands. "I wasn't sure myself."

Ura's eyes narrowed, and she tilted her head to one side. "You prayed over it, didn't you?"

"Yes, ma'am." Callie took a sip of her tea. "This is very good. I don't think I've ever had anything like it before."

Ura smiled and nodded. "Thank you. I make it myself—gather everything in it from the mountain. But you didn't come here to talk about tea, did you?"

"No, ma'am. I guess not."

"Reckon you could quit callin' me 'ma'am' and tell me your name so we could just be friends?"

"That would be nice," Callie said with a smile. "My name is Callie—Callie Bullock."

Ura nodded. "Alright then, Callie. You call me Ura and tell me what questions you have for me."

"Well, I was wondering why your name was taped to the bottom of a tea tin that our housekeeper, Hepsy—Hepsy Jordan—packed for me when I came to the resort. Do you know each other?"

Ura frowned and tapped her chin. "I don't believe I know anybody by that name. 'Course, I could be wrong."

"What about her mother, Tirzah?"

"Tirzah Randolph?"

"Yes!" Callie leaned forward eagerly. "You know her?"

"Tirzah took me under wing when I didn't know what on earth was happenin' to me. I wasn't but ten years old when I found out I wasn't like ever'body else. Scared me to death. And Mama didn't have no idea what to do about it."

Callie relaxed in her chair. "So what happened?"

Ura slowly rocked back and forth as she remembered. "Well, Mama finally went down the mountain to see Miz Caldwell—her and her husband owned the hotel before the Hayeses—and asked her to please let us know if she run across any guests there who might know somebody that seen visions—somebody grown. Mama figured it would *take* somebody like me to *help* somebody like me."

Callie took another sip of her tea. "And she found somebody at the hotel?"

"Musta been a year or so passed, but by and by, in come a lady from over in Shelby County said she knew of a colored seer named Tirzah Randolph. Mama carried me to her house—took us two days to get there—and Tirzah, she taught me not to be fearful of my gift. She said it come from Almighty and He meant for me to use it for the good. That's what I been a-doin' all these years, best I can. I use it for the good."

"How do you do it—see things, I mean?" Callie asked.

"It's not anything I do. It's something I receive. Just like your shoe. I was leadin' my lesson in the hollow square when I seen that shoe, plain as day, underneath that tall pine tree with them initials carved in it. The tree wasn't no place I'd ever been before, so I knew that vision belonged to somebody else—belonged *in* somebody else. Took me a minute to figure it out—to feel where the vision was comin' from—but then I spotted you, settin' on the back row of the altos. Right away, I knew you belonged to that shoe and it belonged to you. Can you tell me about it—what it means?"

Callie told Ura about her fall and memory loss, about the shoe and two strange events that likely happened around it—the disappearance of Lily, Fisher, and Josie, and the murder of a man who may or may not have been mistaken for his twin brother.

"Merciful heaven, sister," Ura said. "What you ain't been through ain't been thought of." She stared at the fire, rocking a little faster. Then she abruptly stopped, holding her cup in her lap and keeping her eyes on the flames dancing in the fireplace.

Callie didn't know what to do, so she waited and watched.

Finally, Ura set her cup on the floor. She looked at Callie with eyes full of sadness and laid a hand on her arm. "Your sweet sister. So many tears to shed."

Callie nodded. "Yes, I know. That's one of the main reasons I want to get home—for Emmy."

Ura turned away from Callie and again stared into the fire. After a short silence, she said, "Emmy had a baby in her basket when she went down in that river."

Callie stopped rocking and became so still that she swore she could hear her own heartbeat. Ura's words were a bright light illuminating the cloudy dreams and hazy visions where Callie had wandered in her personal wilderness. The river, Emmy, the basket that cried—they all came into focus, and not in her imagination but in her memory. Callie still had no idea what had compelled her to follow Emmy that night—to spy on her—and she didn't remember the trip to the river. But she could clearly see what happened there, and it made her feel sick. *Emmy went down into the river with a basket that cried and came back empty-handed.*

Callie stood so abruptly that she spilled her tea all over the floor. "Oh!" she cried. "I'm sorry, Ura! Let me—"

Ura stood up and took her by the shoulders. "Don't fret over the tea. It's time for you to go, my sister. I expect you hurried up the mountain, but you must take care going back down. It's the same with the visions. They can present theirselfs quickly, but you got to take your time findin' out what they mean. You got to pray over it. And then go home, Callie. It's time for you to go home."

Callie couldn't speak. She could only nod. But before she left the cabin, she put her arms around Ura and hugged her. "You unlocked a door I couldn't. Thank you."

"Wasn't me that done it," Ura said, holding Callie at arm's length and looking at her. "That was the good Lord. And He revealed something else to me. You can trust that man with them pretty eyes. You can trust him with all of it. And you got to. You hear me? You really got to. Else you won't get to live the life Almighty's stored up for you. Hear me?"

"I hear you, Ura," Callie said. "And I believe you."

On her way out the door, Callie emptied her change purse into the yellow basket. Then she mounted Birdie and set off. She could see her path clearly now, and she was on her way, not just to Rosemont Springs but home—all the way home.

TWENTY-EIGHT

Callie and Dr. Martin were taking one of their walks around the resort when she told him about her visit with Ura Prospect. "I remembered what I saw, Dr. Martin. But it can't mean what I think it does. That's just not possible."

"Are you comfortable sharing the details of your memory?" he asked.

Callie hesitated. What if her memory caused trouble for Emmy? "No, sir. But it's not because I don't trust you. It's just that what I remembered involves someone else, someone I love very much. I saw them do something they would never do. I think that's why my mind has been so confused. I know I didn't imagine it. I know I saw what I saw. But there has to be something about it that I don't understand. I think that's what I have to find out now. That's why I feel ready to go home. The 'what' I found here, but the 'why' is back there."

They had circled back to the front porch of the hotel. Dr. Martin smiled at her. "You've come a long way in a very short time, Miss Bullock. I believe you will find your 'why' because you aren't afraid of it anymore."

"I didn't do it by myself," Callie said. "Do you allow patients to hug you, or is that against the rules?"

"Some rules are meant to be broken," he said with a twinkle in his blue eyes. Callie hugged him and kissed him on the cheek. He tipped his hat to her and said, "I'll speak with your father, and we'll see about continuing our talks through correspondence as long as you need to."

She stepped inside the lobby, where Mrs. Hayes was handing a room key to a new guest. "There you are, Miss Bullock. Did you have a nice walk?"

"Yes, ma'am, thank you," Callie said.

"You have a guest in the parlor," Mrs. Hayes said. "I've already had a tea service sent in for you."

"Thank you." This was a puzzle. No one but Dr. Martin and Ura knew Callie was ready to come home, and her family still thought visitors weren't allowed.

She stepped around the corner to the parlor door and opened it. There, by the window, stood Solomon. Callie gasped, too shocked to speak.

He smiled at her and asked, "Aren't you even a little glad to see me?"

All the emotions that had built up over the past few weeks came at her in a swirl. She just stood there trembling, unable to move, until Solomon came to her and wrapped his arms around her. "It's alright, Callie. Everything's going to be alright."

She remembered the story he had told Sam—of clinging to a tree to keep from drowning in the Mississippi. That was how she felt right now, like she might drown in her own deluge if she didn't cling to Solomon.

He kissed her and guided her to the sofa, where they sat down together.

Staring into his eyes, she said, "Never in my whole life have I been so happy to see anybody."

He kissed her again before Callie began peppering him with questions: Why was he here? How was Emmy? How was Theo? How long could he stay?

"Mrs. Hayes got worried about you because you weren't eating," he explained. "She spoke with the doctor, and he telegrammed your father that he thought you needed a visitor from home."

"And Daddy sent you?" she asked.

He looked down. Maybe this was all just too much for him. Maybe he had come to say goodbye. "Actually, your mother asked me to come here today."

"*Mama* sent you?"

"Yes." He looked up at her with such sadness in his eyes.

All the joy of seeing Solomon drained away as Callie realized he had likely been coerced into coming. "You didn't want to come?"

"No. I mean yes. It's just that—"

Callie felt physically ill. She forced a quivering smile and laid her hand over his. "It's alright. Nobody could expect you to take all of this on. You need to think about your farm and your future. You don't need all my—"

Solomon silenced her with a kiss. "What I'm trying and failing miserably to say, Callie, is that I very much wanted to see you. But I have to tell you something that I wish I didn't. It's Emmy. She's sick."

Callie felt the blood drain from her face, her head so light that she thought she might faint. "The same as Knox?"

Solomon nodded. "But not nearly as bad right now. She has hope, Callie. But I won't lie to you. She's very sick."

"We have to go to her, Solomon." Her voice was shaking.

"We can't."

"But—"

"She's not at home anymore, Callie."

"Where is she?"

"Your father has taken her to New Mexico by train. Dr. Embry found a sanatorium in a place called Silver City. Emmy will have the best doctors, the best food, the best everything.

Your father plans to stay with her until she's well enough to come home. That's why your mother asked me to come. I didn't want to be the one to tell you. But then again, I couldn't stand the thought of anybody else doing it, so when your doctor telegrammed that you could have visitors . . ."

"I couldn't have stood it coming from anybody else," she said. She was quiet for a moment. "We should go home."

"Are you sure you're ready?"

"I'm ready."

"Alright then," he said. "I came on the only train running today, and tomorrow the only run is in the afternoon. But I promise we'll be on it. In the meantime, is there someplace we can talk? Someplace outside where there's sun and air?"

Callie nodded. "I know a place."

TWENTY-NINE

*S*olomon and Callie had saddled two horses, Birdie for her and a stallion named Sonny Boy for him. Callie wanted to show him the church in the meadow.

"That's incredible." Solomon was looking up at Whitestone Mountain. "I never saw such color."

"I know," Callie said. "It really is a beautiful place—but it looks different when you're by yourself."

"So does Yellowleaf."

Solomon stopped his horse. Callie reined Birdie in and brought her closer to Sonny Boy.

"I've missed sharing the creek with you, Callie," Solomon said. "I've missed sharing everything with you. It's scary for somebody like me who's never missed anybody to suddenly feel like there's not much point to getting up in the morning if I'm not going to see you. I don't know what to do about that."

Callie stroked Birdie's mane. "What do you want to do about it?"

Solomon looked at her for a moment before reaching around her waist and pulling her off Birdie and onto Sonny Boy's saddle so that she rested on his lap. He kissed her gently at first, but then her hands were in his hair, and she felt the softness of his mouth and the heat of his breath.

At last, he stopped and held her face in his hands. "I want to marry you. I know it's not the time or the place to ask. I know your family's all torn up over Emmy and Knox—and worried to death about you. There couldn't be a more selfish thing for me to do right now than ask you to leave them and come make a life with me. But I love you too much to pretend I don't. I might never be as rich as your daddy, but I'll spend every day of my life doing anything I can to make you happy. So. There it is."

She silently stared into his eyes, smiling. Then she said, "There's a courthouse in Talladega."

❦

Halfway to their destination, Solomon and Callie stopped by a creek to let the horses rest and drink. They were sitting together on the bank, leaning against a tree, when she said, "I remember what I saw the night I fell."

"It all came back to you?"

"I don't remember everything, but I remember the part that frightened me into forgetting." She hesitated until he reached over and took her hand.

"It's alright," he said. "You don't have to tell me if you don't want to."

"No, I do. It's just hard—" She closed her eyes, feeling the need to shut out the present and revisit her memory, just to make sure it was still there, unchanged. Then she turned to Solomon. "I saw Emmy. I saw her go down into the river with a basket, and I could hear Josie crying inside it. Emmy waded out into the river until I couldn't see her anymore. And when she came back, she didn't have the basket. She didn't have the baby."

Solomon stared at her, his eyes wide. "You think you saw Emmy *drown* Josie?"

"It's not possible, I know. Emmy would never hurt a living

soul, especially an innocent baby. But I know what I saw. And I know I didn't dream it. I just can't fathom what it means."

"I wonder if Lemuel had anything to do with all this."

"Lemuel? Why?" Lemuel Abrams was her father's most trusted field hand. He had worked for the Bullocks since he was a teenager.

"About two weeks before you fell, he asked me if I knew any riverboat pilots who might be able to help a colored family get down to the gulf to visit a sick relative. I told him where to find a pilot I knew and trusted—the only colored pilot I ever met. He used to work the Mississippi but moved to the Alabama rivers a few years ago—uses a dock near Wilsonville. You think the 'family' was really Lily and Fisher?"

Callie rubbed her forehead, which ached with the familiar pain that always came when she tried hard to remember. "I don't know. I can't imagine the two of them leaving without Josie. It doesn't make sense."

"No, it doesn't." He kissed her on the cheek. "Should we stay here and try to figure it out or get to the courthouse before it closes?"

Callie didn't hesitate. "Courthouse."

THIRTY

*T*alladega had a pretty town square lined with shops and cafés, but Callie was so eager to get inside the courthouse that she barely noticed. Solomon held her hand as they hurried up the steps and walked through heavy double doors flanked by white columns. On the main floor of the courthouse, they followed signs to the justice of the peace and approached a long wooden counter with one of its windows labeled "Marriage Licenses."

"Afternoon," said a grim clerk behind the window. She was one of the tiniest women Callie had ever seen, no more than five feet tall and probably less than a hundred pounds. Her salt-and-pepper hair was pinned into what looked like an ill-fated attempt at a pompadour, and she wore wire-rimmed spectacles.

"We'd like to get married—today if that's possible," Solomon said.

"Alright." The woman sighed like someone who had greeted so many happy couples that she found them exhausting. "Come around the counter and have a seat at my desk."

Solomon thanked her as he and Callie stepped around the counter and sat down. The nameplate on the woman's desk read "Doris Simpson."

Doris opened her desk drawer, pulled out a white form with

pink carbon paper attached, and rolled it into her typewriter. "We'll start with you," she said to Solomon. "Full name?"

"Solomon Lucas Beckett."

Callie smiled at him and whispered, "I didn't know Lucas was your middle name."

"Date of birth?"

"March 12, 1883."

"Age?"

"Twenty-six."

Doris lowered her spectacles on her nose and peered over them at Solomon. She studied his face like someone examining a piece of furniture to make sure it didn't have any nicks, then typed. Solomon and Callie stole a glance at each other.

"Place of birth?"

"Hannibal, Missouri," Solomon answered.

"Current place of residence?"

"Shelby County, Alabama."

Again, Doris peered at him over her glasses. "Town?"

"The closest one to my farm is Shay's Bend. That's where the mail comes."

"Then that's where you live," Doris said. She turned to Callie. "Full name?"

"Calinda Jane Bullock."

"Callie Jane," Solomon whispered. "I like it."

"Date of birth?"

"January 20, 1891."

"Age?"

"Eighteen."

Doris leaned forward in her chair. "You sure?"

"Of course."

Doris tilted her head sideways and looked at Callie. "Who's the first president of the United States you remember?"

Callie frowned and looked at Solomon, but he nodded toward the clock on the wall. The courthouse would close in an hour, and they needed this woman's help. Callie did her best to remain cordial. "A little bit of President Cleveland, but I think I'm just remembering things my parents told me about him. The first one I remember well for myself is President McKinley. Daddy used to read me stories from the newspaper about the war in Cuba and then of course his assassination. He thinks it's important for children to know what's happening in the world around them."

"My daddy never read a word to me," Doris said. "So you're seventeen?"

"No, ma'am," Callie said. "I'm eighteen and will be nineteen on January 20, 1910."

"Just making sure. Don't want some lecher robbing the cradle." Doris glanced at Solomon. "No offense." She began typing again. "Place of birth?"

"Our family farm in Shelby County, near Shay's Bend."

"Current place of residence?"

"The same."

"And the two of you are not close cousins?" Doris asked.

"We aren't related in any way," Solomon answered.

Doris kept typing. "You want the date of your marriage to be today?"

"That's correct," Solomon said.

Doris stopped typing and suspiciously eyed Solomon. "How come you're not getting married in a church?"

Solomon seemed too surprised to answer, but Callie wasn't. "Mr. Beckett is acting out of consideration for me," she said.

"This a have-to wedding?" Doris asked.

Callie sprang from her chair. "It most certainly is not!"

Solomon stood up and put his arm around her. "Ma'am," he said calmly, "what she means is, there is sickness in her family, and a church wedding would put a strain on her parents."

"Had to ask," Doris said flatly.

"No harm done," Solomon said with a smile as he and Callie sat back down.

Doris finished typing, pulled the form out of her typewriter, and laid it on her desk. Pushing it toward Solomon, she said, "You sign here, she signs there, judge'll sign the bottom, and we'll need two witnesses. I take it you didn't bring any?"

"No, ma'am, I'm sorry we didn't." Solomon signed the form and handed Callie the pen.

With the paperwork complete, Doris got up and lightly knocked on the judge's door. There was no answer. She knocked louder. Then louder. Finally, she opened the door and called out, "Judge Cooley!"

"What in the Sam Hill, Doris?" the judge grumbled.

"We got a marriage," she said, motioning for Callie and Solomon to step inside the office.

The judge, who was clean-shaven and a little on the pudgy side, took the robe hanging from a hat stand and put it over his shirt and pants. He yawned as he motioned for Callie and Solomon to stand in front of his desk. "We need two witnesses, Doris," he said.

"I know." She left the office and came back shortly with a woman holding a wet mop.

"We don't need anything mopped up, Coweta," the judge said. "We just need you to witness a marriage. Doris, hand me the license." He yawned again as he studied the form. "Looks like everything's in order." He looked at Solomon. "Do you, Solomon Lucas Beckett, take this woman, Calinda Jane Bullock, to be your lawfully wedded wife?"

"I do," Solomon said.

The judge looked at Callie. "And do you, Calinda Jane Bullock, take this man, Solomon Lucas Beckett, to be your lawfully wedded husband?"

"I do," Callie said.

"Then by the powers vested in me by the state of Alabama, I pronounce you man and wife." The judge signed the license, then handed it to Doris so she and Coweta could sign their names. Doris gave Solomon the original and kept the carbon copy.

"Congratulations," the judge said, "you're married." He took off his robe, picked up his suit jacket, and headed for the door, with Doris following behind.

Callie heard a desk drawer open and slam, then watched Doris leave through the main door, her purse in hand. Coweta picked up her mop and went on her way, leaving Callie and Solomon standing alone and dumbstruck in the judge's office. They looked at each other in silence for a few seconds before they both burst out laughing.

Callie mimicked the judge's gruff voice. "You do, she does, now kiss her and *git*!"

Solomon put his arms around her and kissed her. "'Callie Jane Beckett.' That sounds like a woman who could handle a shotgun."

"Don't cross me," she said.

Solomon sat down on the edge of the judge's desk, held Callie's hands, and sighed. "Even *I* don't feel married, and I'm sure you don't. You probably weren't looking forward to spending your wedding night in a hotel with strangers either."

"It's alright," Callie said with a shrug.

"No, it's not. And we're going to fix it." He pulled her closer to him, and she put her arms around his neck.

"How?"

"Well, when we get back to the hotel, you'll go to your room and I'll go to mine. In the morning, we'll find a preacher and get married in that little church in the meadow. And then we'll get on a train, come home, and spend our wedding night in *our* house."

"Solomon, do you really mean it?" Callie was so excited she could hardly breathe.

"I take it you agree?" he said with a grin.

"I agree so very much."

"Let's practice." He picked her up and carried her out of the courthouse.

Callie laughed. "What are we practicing?"

"Carrying you over the threshold."

"What else do we need to practice?"

"Believe me, Callie Jane, I cannot wait to show you."

THIRTY-ONE

allie finished writing in her journal, then closed it and packed it away in her steamer trunk. She shut the lid and locked it, put the key in her purse, and laid her purse and coat on top of the trunk. She turned and stared at her reflection in the mirror. Unlike Emmy, she had never given much thought to her wedding day, mostly because she couldn't imagine finding anyone she wanted to spend her life with. But now she had. And Mrs. Hayes had just come by to let her know Solomon was waiting for her downstairs in the hotel lobby.

After their courthouse wedding, she and Solomon had gone to a small jewelry store on the square and bought gold wedding bands. All other arrangements Mrs. Hayes volunteered to handle.

Today Callie wore a pin-tucked day dress of pale blue silk with a square neck and a flounce that dropped from her knees to the floor. It had a matching knee-length jacket trimmed in ivory lace and blue velvet, cinched at the waist with a wide silk belt tied into a bow. She wore her long, curly hair partially up, with the sides pulled back and secured with a pearl comb on the back of her head. The comb was a gift from Emmy.

Callie felt a huge lump in her throat as she thought about

her sister and the promise Emmy had made to her in happier times, when she was anticipating a future with Knox, far removed from his embittered family. *A few miles can't separate you and me. Even Knox can't do that.* But in the end, he had—through no fault of his own. He had unknowingly given Emmy the sickness that took her far away, but it wasn't just the miles that separated her from Callie now. It was the chasm between one sister's joy and the other's heartbreak.

Callie picked up her coat and purse. Robbie would take her trunk to the train station. She was about to walk downstairs to the lobby, where Solomon waited. How strange that only a flight of steps separated one from the other—the past from the future, the daughter from the wife.

Callie left her room and closed the door behind her. She did not look back.

❧

The sun was high and golden, the air cool but not too cold, as Solomon helped Callie out of the carriage, which was driven by Brother Hayes and decorated with a large white bow on the back—his wife's handiwork.

Callie and Solomon stood together, looking at the open-air chapel, where fall wildflowers seemed to have multiplied overnight. "Oh, Solomon, there's someone you have to meet!" Callie cried as she saw Dr. Martin step out of the chapel. She hurried to him with her groom in tow. "Dr. Martin, I want you to meet Solomon!"

"Ah, the so-called family friend I've heard so much about." The doctor smiled and shook Solomon's hand. "I never believed that for a minute. And I'm happy my intuition proved correct."

"Pleased to meet you, sir," Solomon said, "and I want to thank you for helping Callie."

"No thanks necessary," the doctor said. "This beautiful wedding day is reward aplenty. Let's be about it, shall we?"

Inside the church, Mrs. Hayes had tied wildflower tussie-mussies to the pew ends flanking the short center aisle and placed a basket of flowers at the altar. Seated in the pews were the Hayes family and those of the hotel guests who thought it might be nice to see a country wedding.

Brother Hayes was officiating. "And who will be standing up with you?" he asked Solomon and Callie.

They looked at each other. They hadn't had time to consider it. Callie asked Mrs. Hayes and Solomon asked Dr. Martin, who had already agreed to walk Callie down the aisle.

They were all about to take their places when Callie looked up the church aisle and saw Ura standing in the doorway. Callie motioned for her to come in. Ura tentatively stepped inside the church, and Callie brought Solomon to meet her. "Solomon, this is Ura. She helped me get pieces of my memory back. Ura, this is Solomon—the man with the pretty eyes."

He looked puzzled. Callie hadn't had a chance to tell him about Ura's visions just yet. "I'm pleased to meet you, ma'am," he said.

As Ura stared at him, her eyes narrowed. She slowly raised her hand above her head. "Tomatoes. I see tomatoes by a creek that floods." Then she turned and walked away.

Solomon looked at Callie with wide eyes, his mouth slightly open. She laughed at his stunned expression. "I'll explain later," she said. Turning to the back of the church, she saw that Ura had not taken a seat but had joined a small group standing just inside the front door of the church, some of whom looked vaguely familiar to her. She realized they had been among the singers at Mount Nebo.

Brother Hayes motioned for Solomon to join him at the altar. Mrs. Hayes led Callie and Dr. Martin to a spot right in front of Ura and her group before taking her place for the ceremony. Brother Hayes quieted the wedding guests. As Dr. Martin escorted Callie down the aisle, the Mount Nebo group began to sing.

"Now shall my inward joys arise,
And burst into a song;
Almighty love inspires my heart,
And pleasure tunes my tongue."

In a house of worship open to God's creation, Brother Hayes married Callie and Solomon.

∽

The sky was dark when Solomon drove their wagon onto the small patch of land he had cleared around what was now Callie's home. He helped her down and carried her trunk inside before leading their mule team to the barn behind the house. While he tended the livestock, Callie sat down in a rocker he had placed on one of the curved porches she loved so much.

Solomon returned to the house to find her rocking, her eyes closed, a faint smile on her face. "I thought you'd be inside," he said.

She opened her eyes and shook her head. "No, you have to carry me over the threshold like we practiced."

Solomon picked her up and carried her inside, past the stairs, to the only bedroom on the ground floor. "I love you, Callie Jane Beckett," he said as he lay down with her on the bed.

"I love you too, Solomon Lucas Beckett." She held his face in her hands as he looked down at her. Callie smiled at him and said, "Let's practice all those other things."

THIRTY-TWO

*Y*ou're married." Callie's mother announced it before she and Solomon could. It was their first morning as husband and wife, and they had come to tell her mother. The three of them sat down together in the parlor.

"Mama, how did you—"

Her mother put a hand up. "Tirzah saw it and told me. But even if she hadn't, I would've known the minute I looked at you together."

"Miss Aurelia," Solomon said, "I hope you know that we didn't intend any disrespect to you and Mr. Ira. We just didn't think it was right to have a big celebration right now."

"Are you angry, Mama?" Callie asked, her voice a little shaky.

"Of course not," her mother said. "I'll admit, I was hurt at first, but Tirzah helped me see. I'm just saddened by the circumstances that made you feel you didn't have the right to celebrate what should be such a happy occasion. Both of you come here." She stood and held her hands out to them. Callie and Solomon each took one of her hands and kissed her on the cheek. She laid her hand against Solomon's face. "You'll take good care of my child?"

"Always," he said.

She turned to Callie and put her arms around her. "Be happy, my daughter. Be as happy as you can. And be a good wife to Solomon."

Callie had never seen this side of her mother, whose confidence and iron will had always made her seem so indomitable. Losing Knox and being forced to send Emmy far from home had taken something out of her. Now that Callie was married, she could understand how awful it would be to endure the kind of distance that separated her parents, whom she had never thought of as a married couple before—just her mother and father.

"Let's sit down," her mother said. "Tell me about Rosemont Springs."

Callie told her mother all about the resort and Dr. Martin, how he had helped her overcome her fear of remembering and stopped her sleepwalking. The one thing she didn't share was what she had remembered about Emmy and the river.

"Mama, have you ever heard of Ura Prospect?"

"Of course," her mother said. "Everybody knows about Ura. Tirzah herself helped her understand her gift. Why?"

"Because I met her," Callie said. "Someone taped her name to the bottom of a tea tin Hepsy packed for me."

"I wonder who could've done such a thing," her mother said with a smile.

"Mama!" Callie exclaimed. "You?"

"'There are more things in heaven and earth,' Callie. What did Ura find?"

"My shoe. She says it's by the river, under the tree where James carved Mary Alice's initials."

Just outside the parlor door, they heard the crash of a dish being dropped.

"Is that Hepsy?" Callie asked. "She's never dropped a dish in her life."

She rushed out to find Hepsy mumbling to herself and picking up the pieces of a cup and saucer. She looked up at Callie, then her eyes drifted to the gold band on Callie's finger. As upset as she seemed about the teacup, Hepsy broke into a smile. Callie pulled her up from the floor and hugged her.

"Well?" Hepsy asked with a grin.

"I felt the heat," Callie whispered. Hepsy threw her head back and laughed as Callie ran to the kitchen to get the mop and broom.

"You can't be helpin' me clean house no more, Miss Callie," Hepsy said as she swept up the last of the broken cup and Callie mopped up the tea. "You a married woman now."

Solomon stepped out into the corridor. "I reckon I ought to thank you, Hepsy."

Hepsy grinned as she took the mop from Callie. "I reckon you should, Mr. Solomon. Lemme go try again with the tea."

Solomon and Callie returned to the parlor. "Mama, how is Emmy?" Callie asked.

Her mother took a deep breath. "I don't know what to tell you. Her doctor says she is responding to the fresh air and high altitude, but . . ." Sorrow shrouded her mother's whole demeanor.

Callie went to sit next to her. "But what, Mama?"

"Tirzah says that I should prepare myself," her mother said, looking into Callie's eyes. "She says some people were meant to be together for all eternity."

Callie feared her whole body might dissolve right into the settee, seeping through it to the floor and the ground below. She took her mother's hand, which was trembling. "May I write to her in New Mexico?" Callie asked.

Her mother nodded and laid her free hand over Callie's. "Yes, but nothing upsetting. Her doctor doesn't want any additional strain on her reserves, which are terribly low right now."

"Should I tell her about Solomon and me? It seems cruel somehow to talk about our happiness when she has lost Knox."

"Callie, I know how much you love your sister, and maybe it would be better to wait till she comes home to tell her so that we can gauge her strength. But at the same time, your life can't stop because of Emmy's sorrow and sickness—and your happiness has not come at the expense of hers. The two have nothing to do with each other. Be considerate of Emmy, as you always have been, but do not stifle your own light because her journey has taken a dark turn for now."

Solomon knelt beside his mother-in-law. "Miss Aurelia, do you want us to come here and stay with you until Emmy and Mr. Ira can come home?"

Both women looked at him with surprise. Callie had never felt such gratitude in her life.

"You would do that for my daughter, wouldn't you?" her mother said.

"And for you," he said.

"No, son. I will never forget that you offered, but your place is not here. It's on your farm. And Callie's place is by your side. You must walk your path and I must walk mine. It's enough for me to know you're both close by. You have a life to live together. And life is very short—no matter how many years we're given."

THIRTY-THREE

Solomon and Callie had ridden together on Diamond when they came to see her mother, who told them to take Daisy Bell and consider the mare part of her wedding present. When her father came home, he would decide the rest. Now they were riding past the Bluing on the Coosa River, heading for the pine tree where Ura had seen Callie's shoe.

At last, they neared the riverbank, and Callie pointed to the tree. "There it is." Under the towering pine, they dismounted their horses and walked to the edge of the bank. "Solomon, look." There, at the edge of the water, was Callie's shoe, mired in the mud.

As she bent down to pick it up, Solomon put his hands around her waist so she wouldn't fall. She pulled it out of the reeds and stared at it as he helped her up. Holding the shoe, Callie vividly remembered the sensation of one foot slipping, almost making her fall into the river, and having her shoe pulled off by the thick mud. What made her leave it behind? Right now, the river sparkled with sunlight, but Callie could picture it cloaked in darkness as it had been that night. And then a flash of light—from where, she couldn't see.

Callie looked down at the roots of the tree and remembered

a coat falling onto them—Emmy's heavy winter coat. Then the sound of water splashing. Emmy coming out of the water. A baby's cry. Emmy picking up Hepsy's basket. And then the images faded like smoke drifting from a chimney on a cold winter morning.

Callie took a deep breath and looked up at Solomon. "I saw it all again, only a little more. A flash of light from somewhere. Emmy taking off her coat and coming out of the water before I saw her go back in with the baby. Still nothing before the riverbank."

"That's alright, Callie. In the beginning you couldn't remember anything at all. It might come slower than you'd like, but it'll come. Just give it time."

She put her arms around him and held on. "Let's go home, Solomon. I want to be in our house with you. I want that pretty desperately right now."

November 14

Dear Emmy,

How's my favorite sister this morning?

I've been given the privilege of sharing the best news—Mary Alice had her baby! It's a boy—very healthy—and they've named him Harold Ira after both grandfathers. They're going to call him Hal. Mary Alice is doing well, and of course James is a proud papa. He'll have to add on to his house if Mama and Daddy don't stop carrying presents over there.

You missed a historic first at the Bullock house yesterday: Hepsy dropped a teacup! She has never dropped a single dish as long as I can remember. I was telling Mama about the seer I met at a little country church near Rosemont.

Her name is Ura Prospect, and it turns out Mama and Tirzah knew her already. Anyway, I was telling Mama how Ura had a vision about my missing shoe—she saw it by the river, underneath the pine tree with Mary Alice's initials—when we heard the cup shatter outside the parlor. Hepsy was mighty rattled, as you can imagine, but we cleaned it all up and set her to rights again.

I think she's as out of sorts as Mama. I'm so relieved to be back home, and I can't imagine how hard it must be for you and Daddy, so far away. But you'll be coming home soon, Emmy, I just know it. We'll talk like we used to and laugh about silly things that aren't funny to anybody else.

> *I love you dearly, my*
> *precious sister—*
> *Callie*

She had agonized over this letter especially. As her mother had advised, she said nothing that might disturb her frail sister. On the other hand, she hoped to hint that her memory was returning and that whatever had happened that night on the river, Emmy could tell her. The pieces of memory Callie had recovered made her less concerned about herself and more worried about Emmy. It pained her to think that her sister was carrying around a terrible secret all by herself. If there was one thing Callie understood now, it was the loneliness of bearing a burden all by yourself.

❧

The day before Thanksgiving, Callie was working her way down the stairway of her house—she still couldn't believe she and Solomon had one of their own—cleaning every step and polishing every inch of the handrail. At last, she made it to the elegant leaf carvings on the newel posts. She took her time, cleaning the intricate patterns the way she had seen Hepsy bring out the luster on the mantel carvings at her parents' home.

When she finished, she stepped back to look at the stairs, remembering all the times she had climbed them as a child or run a little finger over the leaves carved into the wood. "Solomon!" she called out. "Can you take a minute and come in here?" He was repairing the woodstove while she worked on the stairs. She smiled when he came in. "Chimney sweeping got you down?" She brushed some soot from his cheek.

"Almost, but I think I've finally fixed it," he said before the stairway caught his attention. He was speechless for a moment. "I had no idea what was under all the dust. It's incredible, Callie, just like you said."

She put her arms around his waist.

"You'll get sooty," he said.

"I don't care."

He held her tight. When he spoke, she could hear in his voice a mix of disbelief and profound gratitude. "We have a home, Callie. A real home."

❧

Callie and Solomon were about to leave for Thanksgiving dinner at the Bullock house when Fate Barbour came up their narrow driveway in a handsome black two-seat buggy pulled by two mares Callie had never seen before. One of her father's horses, a palomino named Butterscotch, was saddled and tied to the back.

"Happy Thanksgiving, Fate," Solomon said as he and Callie went outside. "What's this?"

The stable manager climbed down from the buggy. "They's a note on the front seat, Mr. Solomon. It's for you and Miss Callie. Miss 'Relia said if I wouldn't mind deliverin' the buggy this mornin', she'd provide me a saddle horse to get on home to my family. Buggy's a beaut, ain't it?"

"Sure is," Solomon said. "Appreciate you bringing it to us."
He shook Fate's hand.

"You welcome."

The buggy was black and sleek with very little ornamentation. The harnesses were all brand new as well.

"Please tell Ida and the kids we said happy Thanksgiving,"
Callie said.

"I sure will. Y'all have a good one." Fate untied the saddle
horse and rode away.

Callie picked up an envelope on the front seat and read the
note out loud.

To Solomon and Callie—

> *This small gift carries our wish for many years of happiness. All our love, on the occasion of your marriage.*

> *Daddy and Mama*

"You think she was afraid I'd drive you to Thanksgiving
dinner in a farm wagon?" Solomon asked with a grin.

Callie laughed, petting the mares. "That's exactly what she
thought. We can accept it, can't we? It would hurt her feelings
if we didn't."

Solomon smiled and kissed her on the forehead. "I surrendered to Miss Aurelia a long time ago."

Around the Bullocks' Thanksgiving table, Callie's brothers
initiated her husband into the family.

"I hate to tell you, Solomon, but Callie'll never truly be
yours," Sam said. "Her heart belongs to old man Chester."

Solomon winked at Callie. "I wondered why she made me
fix up a room for him at the house."

Everyone laughed, even Callie's mother, who didn't smile
much these days.

"If your bride should turn up missing, just climb the highest tree on your farm," George said. "Trust me, she'll be up there."

"I won't need to climb trees at our house because I won't have annoying brothers to escape from," Callie retorted.

"Am I annoying, Callie?" asked Theo, who had insisted on sitting at the "big table." George had given up his regular seat next to Callie so Theo could have it.

Callie put her arms around her baby brother. "*You* are my precious angel, Theo, and you could never be annoying."

It was James who formally welcomed Solomon, raising his wine glass. "To our sister and her new husband—much happiness to you both."

The family toasted Callie and Solomon with Hepsy's muscadine wine.

As usual, conversation eventually turned to the farm. In public, Callie and Emmy weren't allowed to join the men in discussing crops and farm economics. But in private, with just the family, they could hear or say whatever they chose. For the Bullock daughters, it was a strange dichotomy. They couldn't participate in the farm or make decisions about it, yet they were encouraged to understand the family business as fully as possible.

As Callie brought her little brother a second slice of Hepsy's pecan pie and cut it into small bites, her mother announced, "Your father telegrammed me that he thinks we need to reopen the sawmill."

"How soon, Mama?" George asked.

"Right away. Emmy's care is very expensive, but it's absolutely essential. Your father feels that the sawmill could fund her stay at the sanatorium, while the cotton crop takes care of everything else. What are your thoughts?"

"Whoever runs the mill will have to camp down there," George said. "It's too far to travel back and forth. So I think I should do it. We all know James is the better farmer—doesn't matter right now in the dead o' winter, but it will in a few months. And he's got Mary Alice and a new baby to think about."

"We appreciate that," James said. "We really do. I'll see if I can find you a good carriage setter for the mill. You need somebody who knows what he's doing. None of the field hands have any experience in a mill. They can cut timber, but they don't know anything about milling it."

"I'll come and help you, George," Sam offered.

"No, Sam," their mother said. "You don't know anything about the mill, and you've been looking forward to visiting your cousins in Mobile. There's no point in ruining your trip when you wouldn't be able to give George the help he needs."

"I can do it," Solomon spoke up.

Everyone at the table turned to look at him.

"I worked in a lot of mills along the river—last few times as the carriage setter," he explained. "I can help you run it."

"What about your farm?" James asked.

"I think this has to come first."

"Solomon," Callie's mother broke in, "I want you to consider something, and I know your first impulse will be to say no. But you are a part of this family now. You have brothers around this table. And we have resources that are as much yours as ours."

"Daddy pays the field hands year-round," James said, "whether they're working or not. It's how he keeps the best help. If you're willing to go with George and run the mill, I can send plenty of workers and mule teams to clear your land, now that our crop's in."

Solomon waved his hand in protest. "I could never ask you to do that."

"You're not asking," James said. "I'm offering. You can do something for this family that nobody else can do. Let us return the favor."

It was quiet around the table while Solomon thought about it. He took Callie's hand and looked at her.

"It's up to you, Solomon," she said. "Whatever you decide."

Finally, he nodded. "Alright. I'm grateful for your help."

"And we're grateful for yours," Callie's mother said. "I believe we have reached the point in our dinner where your father would say it's time for cordials. Happy Thanksgiving, children. Keep those absent from our table in your prayers and in your hearts."

⇝

Thanksgiving night was blustery. Callie and Solomon got home late and were now lying together, listening to the wind rustle the tree outside their window.

"Are you sure about the sawmill, Solomon?" she asked. "Or did you just feel overrun by my family?"

He kissed her forehead. "Nobody pushed me into anything. It just pains me to admit how badly I miscalculated. I could never get all this land cleared in time for spring planting, not with just a couple of field hands working with me. And I've never depended on anybody but myself—not till you came along."

"We have to depend on each other," Callie said. "Otherwise we'd be out there all alone. Out there in the wind and the rain."

THIRTY-FOUR

The week after Thanksgiving, George secured a contract with the railroad to mill its ties and specialty lumber for a new stretch of tracks. The railroad would supply the timbers. Overnight, the sawmill went from closed to booming.

Callie volunteered to cook for the crew. She couldn't stand the thought of being away from Solomon, and she wanted to do something—anything—to help Emmy.

"Hepsy, do you think I need more cast-iron skillets?" she asked as the two of them transformed her father's rolling store into a chuck wagon.

"Not unless you got forty mules to pull you."

"I guess I'm packing a little on the heavy side," Callie said. "I just don't want to get there and find I'm missing something I need."

"You got the essentials, I promise you." Hepsy surveyed all the skillets, boilers, Dutch ovens, and utensils. The wagon was stocked to the gills with flour, sugar, cornmeal, lard, beans, rice, and coffee. "Here's your medicine chest in case you got to doctor any cuts and scrapes." She handed Callie a rectangular metal tin about the size of a bread box. "I put you a bottle o'

Mama's elixir in there, and they's a big sack of her tea in the corner over yonder."

"Thank you, Hepsy." Callie found a safe spot for the medicine chest and slid it onto a bottom shelf in the wagon.

"M' George says he got you set up to buy eggs and meat and such from a farmer in Talladega Springs."

"That's right."

"Well then, you ought to be all set," Hepsy said. "You scared?"

"A little," Callie admitted. "I hope they like my cooking. But I'm excited too, even though I hate the reason we have to go."

Hepsy smiled. "I remember a few adventures w' my husband before he passed. You make the most of 'em, you hear? Won't hurt Miss Emmy none for you to put the sadness out o' y' mind while you do something good to help her. You know well as I do, she'd want it that way."

❧

Before daylight the next morning, the sawmill caravan was ready to head out, with Solomon and George driving the equipment wagons and Callie following in the chuck wagon. Lemuel was traveling behind her with a wagonload of tents, cots, lanterns, and heavy wool blankets, as well as plenty of shotguns should any local moonshiners decide to cause trouble. Bringing up the rear was Slim, driving a covered wagon carrying the workers.

Even on this cold December morning, Callie was warmed by adrenaline and the hope that they could make a difference for Emmy. It was thrilling to have a sense of purpose, to do something about her sister's sickness instead of helplessly grieving it.

Just before he climbed into his own wagon, Solomon came to hers and kissed her. "Feel okay driving this thing?"

"I think so," Callie said. "But if I throw a skillet at you, that means I need help and you'd better come running."

Solomon rubbed his head. "I can feel it now. Listen, from

what George tells me, it's pretty smooth going until the river crossing in Childersburg, but if you have any trouble, just give me a shout."

Callie saluted. Solomon laughed as he climbed down from her wagon and boarded his own. Then they were off.

George had hitched Callie's wagon to the mules Rogue and Buster because he said they were a flawless team and wouldn't give her any trouble. Just to be on the safe side, she had fed them treats and brushed their necks and manes before beginning the journey.

She could hear hooves striking the earth and the mules snorting in the brisk December air as their caravan pulled onto the main road that ran south. They followed it for about three miles before they took a southeasterly jog toward Childersburg, where they would cross the Coosa River and continue to her father's timberland.

The moon still lit an inky sky, and Callie could see the fog from her own breath in its silvery glow. Not a sound came from the covered wagon carrying the workers, who were likely napping and trying to stay warm. Callie might be napping herself if she weren't driving a mule team.

The landscape here was mostly flat, covered with cotton fields laid by for the winter, their cleanly picked stalks cut to the ground. In the moonlight, the fields looked silver dusted. Callie could tell the caravan was drawing close to the Coosa. A river's surroundings tended to the extremes—high bluffs or tabletop bottomlands. She could picture the river flowing through these flatlands.

They had traveled a few more miles when Solomon shouted something to George, who whistled loudly then jumped down from his wagon and held up his arm. The caravan stopped while the two men talked. Then George went to the covered wagon and returned with Deacon Randolph, Tirzah's grandson, whom Callie's brothers considered the best mule driver on the farm. Deacon took over the equipment wagon for Solomon, who climbed up beside Callie.

"Give me a ride, ma'am?" he asked.

"It'll cost you," Callie answered. "Why did we stop?"

"The ferry landing is coming up, and river crossings can be a little tricky with mules."

She started to hand him the reins, but he pushed them back. "No need. You can do it. I'm just here in an advisory capacity."

Callie kissed him on the cheek. "Do more than advise if it looks like I'm about to drive us into the river."

"Yes, ma'am."

The moon had slowly disappeared as the dark sky began showing signs of light, first with subtle hints of a still-hidden sun backlighting the darkness, then in vivid streaks of pink and orange as blades of sunlight ripped the dark cloak covering the sky. The streaks grew bigger and wider until Callie could see her surroundings, near and far. And she could smell the earthy waters of the river.

Soon the ferry landing appeared, and Callie gripped the reins tightly as she watched first George and then Deacon make the crossing. Their wagons were so heavy—each pulled by three teams of mules—that the ferry could take only one at a time.

Next it was Callie's turn. Her hands trembled and her heart raced as they approached the water, but she gained confidence as Solomon patiently coached her so she understood how to guide the team.

"Look at you, an expert mule driver," he said when she had the wagon in place. "We should probably climb down till we get across, just in case the mules get spooked or we hit any snags in the river."

He got off the wagon and helped Callie down. Though she knew the Coosa was likely muddy from fall rains, right now it was reflecting the early morning light, the surface of the water painted with soft, rosy blues and grays.

Standing beside Solomon at the guardrail, she was mesmerized by the rhythmic splashing of the river against the ferry slicing through the Coosa in the chill morning air. The waters parted around the front of the vessel as it continued a steady forward push toward the opposite bank.

Suddenly the scene changed in Callie's mind. It wasn't the ferry she saw parting the river, but Emmy, her back to Callie as she hurried toward the bank. Callie clutched the rail with clenched fingers, her whole body shaking as they drew closer and closer to land, Emmy walking through the water just ahead of the ferry. Once on dry land, Emmy stood under the pine tree, fell to her knees, and wept.

"Callie? Callie! What do you see?"

She jumped at the banging of the ferry ramp against the riverbank. The loud noise brought her back to Solomon. Her voice trembled as she looked up at him and recounted her vision. "I saw Emmy crying. I saw her wade out of the river, kneel down under the tree, and cry."

Solomon put his arms around her. "You still don't know what it means, Callie. You don't have the whole picture yet. Give Emmy time."

She nodded and allowed herself the comfort of lingering in his arms, feeling his face against her hair and his hands on her back. Then they climbed onto their wagon and completed the crossing.

For the rest of their journey, Solomon didn't leave her. Neither did the memory of sweet Emmy wading a troubled river and weeping on its bank.

THIRTY-FIVE

Setting up the mill was an undertaking. Though Callie had never been particularly interested in machinery, the mill fascinated her. A long carriage moved the timber forward and back against huge circular saw blades. George worked the sawyer's position, watching each log to determine where the cuts should be made, while Solomon rode the carriage, following George's direction and adjusting the machinery to keep the log positioned correctly for the saw. The field hands loaded the timbers onto the carriage and then stacked the finished lumber.

Callie's job was to feed everybody and doctor their cuts and scrapes. Slim and Lemuel built her a long serving table outside a tiny cabin that functioned as the mill's kitchen. The cabin was just large enough for a woodstove, a worktable, and a few essentials like the biscuit pan and a huge cast-iron skillet. Everything else Callie kept in the chuck wagon parked out back. Each morning, Solomon would go ahead of her and start the woodstove so the kitchen would be warm when she came to cook breakfast.

A few days after they set up camp, George was coming back for seconds at breakfast. He handed his empty plate to his sister. "Callie, if I didn't know better, I'd swear you could cook."

She put two biscuits on his plate and covered them with sausage gravy. "Hush your mouth or I'll quit feeding you." She served him more bacon and eggs and refilled his coffee.

"I believe you've taken to camp life," he said. "Beats those tea parties, huh?"

Callie took a sip of hot coffee. "A toothache beats those tea parties."

"True. Here I always thought marriage was a ball and chain, but it seems to have set you free."

"Marriage didn't free me," Callie corrected him. "Solomon did."

"Is she talking about me?" Solomon asked as he came for more coffee.

"My sister was just telling me what an awful husband you are," George said, slapping Solomon on the back. "Said she hates like everything that she let old man Chester get away."

Callie laughed and threw a biscuit at him. "Get away from my table!"

George caught the biscuit and took a bite. "I'm going to tell Emmy you're abusing me! Be on the lookout for a *scorching* letter from her."

Solomon laughed as George walked away. But Callie didn't. She was staring after her brother as his words hung in the air, trailing behind him.

"Callie, what is it?" Solomon set his plate down on the table.

At first she couldn't answer. But then the veil lifted and she turned to her husband. "Emmy's handwriting. Remember how we teased her about it at the fish fry when I first met you? She said she looped her *i*'s, and I told you it was the family shame?"

"I remember."

"When I came to myself after I fell, Emmy showed me a note from Lily—a goodbye note. I remember thinking that something about it was off, something I would be able to see if I wasn't so groggy. Now I know what it was. The note was a jumble of printing and cursive writing—the way you might write if you were in a hurry. The cursive *i*'s were looped."

Solomon frowned. "You think Emmy wrote it?"

Callie nodded slowly.

"Maybe she had to," Solomon suggested. "Maybe Lily couldn't read and write."

"Lily worked for a college in Chicago. She was a typist."

"Don't you think you should tell your family what you've remembered?" Solomon asked. "They might know something. They might be able to help you figure out what happened."

Callie shook her head. "They don't know anything. Mama seemed as surprised as I was when Lily left, and if Emmy had shared a secret with anybody besides me, it would've been Mama." She thought about the day she woke up after her fall and heard the news, replaying everything her mother had said. She looked up at Solomon. "Mama said Hepsy took it well."

"What?"

"Hepsy took Lily's disappearance well. That's what Mama said. It surprised her that Hepsy wasn't more upset."

"You think Hepsy knows what happened?"

"I'm not sure."

Solomon leaned across the serving table and kissed her on the cheek. "Might be time to find out."

THIRTY-SIX

Callie looked forward to nighttime at the mill, when the December sky would be sequined with stars. With a day's work done, the field hands would sit around their campfires to laugh and talk or maybe play cards for a few hours after supper. Callie, Solomon, and George would wrap up in heavy blankets, build a fire, and sip warm cider.

Her husband, Callie discovered, brought out a side to her brother that he rarely let anybody see. Emmy always said that George "had the soul and bearing of a poet," with classic features, blue eyes, and blond hair. George's sense of humor and easy charm kept everyone so entertained that they never realized they didn't really know him. Though completely trustworthy, he was, nevertheless, slow to trust.

But Solomon, Callie observed, was so straightforward that he brought her brother's guard down. She often heard them laughing together as they worked, and she loved watching them stop to confer as they solved problems with the machinery. They'd get so excited when they found a solution. She couldn't remember seeing George that way with her other brothers.

Tonight, the three of them had just settled in around the campfire. "Are you still thinking cotton once you get your farm going?" George asked Solomon as he poked at the fire with a long piece of scrap iron.

"To be honest, I'm having second thoughts," Solomon said. "It takes a whole lot of land and workers to do it right."

George took a long sip of his cider. "You could always throw in with us, but I imagine you'd rather stay on your own. I would, anyway."

"What do you think about a horse and cattle farm?" Solomon asked him. "I always thought of cattle as a way to start, but maybe I should stick with livestock for the long haul."

"I never fooled with cows very much, but you married the best horsewoman in Shelby County," George told him. "Callie's a natural."

She was surprised by the compliment. "You really mean that, George?"

"I do."

"I've also been thinking about the huge produce market in St. Louis," Solomon said. "Farmers from all over the place would rent booths and sell their crops there. But I don't know if there's a place like that in Birmingham."

"There isn't," George said, and Callie saw her brother's wheels begin to turn. He knew a good idea when he heard one, and he had a gift for making money. "We could build one, though. Build our own market and sell anything we wanted to raise. Offer booths to other farmers to sell whatever we don't want to grow. Take a percentage. That could open up all kinds of possibilities. They could sell more in one day at a Birmingham market than in a whole week at their own roadside stands or local mercantiles. Especially the colored farmers. Even if they did have a place around here to sell fruits and vegetables to white people, they'd likely get cheated in the process, but we could give them a fair shake and get the best growers to work with us."

Solomon turned to Callie. "What do you think? It's not just for George and me to decide. This is your farm too."

"We already have an apple orchard and muscadines and blackberries," Callie said. "We could grow about anything else we wanted on that land by the creek and still have plenty of pastureland for livestock. Raising horses would be a dream. I have to admit, I'm not as excited about cows."

"Me neither," Solomon said. "Let's forget the cows."

Callie nudged him. "Remember what Ura Prospect said to you at our wedding? Tomatoes by a creek that floods?"

"Ura's prophecy is good enough for me," Solomon said. "We'll raise tomatoes and apples and horses. And anything else that strikes us."

"If I know James," George said, "he'll give you a pristine landscape. Then it'll be a lot easier to see how you want to lay out your farm."

"I still don't feel right about somebody else doing the work for me," Solomon said.

"You're doing work for us, so what's the difference?" George argued.

"Just feels like I'm taking advantage."

"Well, you're not. Nobody else—including me—could run that carriage as well as you do. We couldn't do for Emmy without your help, so it won't kill us to hoe a few weeds—or in your case, a few million weeds." George grinned and winked at his sister. "We can't visit Callie if we can't find her."

THIRTY-SEVEN

George hired local guards to watch the mill over Christmas so the crew could go home to be with their families. Callie would restock the chuck wagon, and they'd all return to the mill right after New Year's Day.

Solomon and Callie came straight to the Bullock house with the rest of the caravan and found it even more somber than before. The Christmas tree occupied its usual spot in the living room, but it appeared to have been decorated minimally—dutifully—not with exuberant joy. No evergreen garlands draped the mantels and stair rails, no wreath offered a greeting at the front door. Callie knew why. It was Emmy who loved Christmas the most and always took charge of the gifts and decorations. Hepsy had likely put up the tree by herself, hanging at least a scattering of ornaments just for Theo's sake.

Solomon and Callie came into the parlor and sat down on either side of her mother, who poured them all cups of mulled cider.

"How's Emmy, Mama?" Callie asked. "Is she getting better?"

"Your sister isn't responding as well to treatment as she did in the beginning." Her mother's hand trembled as she started to raise her cup, thought better of it, and returned it to the saucer in her lap. Those hands had always been so steady before. "Your father thinks it would do Emmy good to come home and be with all of us. But Dr. McKinley is concerned that the long train ride would tax her strength and put a strain on her lungs."

"What do *you* think, Miss Aurelia?" Solomon asked.

She struggled to answer him, her voice breaking as she spoke. "I think—I think I want my daughter home. I just don't know if that's a mother's wisdom or pure selfishness speaking."

"It's not selfish of you to miss Emmy," Solomon said. "Can we do anything to help?"

She laid her hand over his. "No, son. But I won't pretend to be stronger than I am. I'm so glad all of you children are staying with me tonight and tomorrow. I don't know what I would do without you. I miss Emmy and Ira so dreadfully—at Christmastime worst of all."

"We're all happy to be home with you, Mama," Callie said.

Her mother forced a brave smile. "Why don't you and Solomon go upstairs and settle in. And Callie—there's a letter for you on the nightstand."

❧

Solomon set down their suitcase and came to stand behind Callie at one of the tall windows flanking the headboard. "I've always liked this room," she said, looking out at what her father called "nature's sculpture," the bare trees silhouetted against a wintry sky. "It's cozy in here. The room I shared with Emmy is huge."

Solomon slipped his arms around her waist. "Why didn't you just move up here?"

Callie leaned back against him and smiled. "Mama's rule: Boys upstairs, girls downstairs."

Solomon kissed her on the cheek. "I think I'll go have a look at your father's mule barn. George says it might give me some ideas."

"Alright. I'll get my coat."

"No, you stay here, Callie," he said as she turned to face him. He nodded toward the letter on the nightstand. "I think you and Emmy need some time. I'll be back in a little while."

Solomon kissed her again and closed the bedroom door as he left. Callie stared at the envelope. Part of her couldn't wait to open it, yet she was afraid of what Emmy might say.

It does no good to wallow and stew.

She sat down on the bed and ran her hand over the address on the envelope, wishing she could somehow bring Emmy closer just by touching her handwriting. Finally, she took a deep breath and opened the letter.

December 16

Well, hello, dearie—

As always, I was thrilled to receive your letter!

Daddy tells me you have exciting news. He shared Mama's telegram with me. If I know you—and I do—you have worried about telling me, but you needn't. I'm so happy for you and Solomon. My own situation is not your fault, sweet sister. I wish you many, many happy years together.

As much as I want to share nothing but good news, there are some things I need to tell you while there's time. I'm not doing well, Callie. The doctors and nurses try to encourage me—and Daddy—but I know how I feel. I'm getting weaker, not stronger. And the strange thing is, I don't mind. Don't misunderstand—I'm trying my best to get well. But if I don't, that's alright because I'll be with Knox again and I'll be with God.

Think about how you would feel if Solomon, heaven forbid, were on the other side. You wouldn't mind making the crossing to be with him again, would you? It would be a joyful and blessed reunion after a painful parting. That's how I feel about Knox. We were "joined at the soul," Hepsy used to say, and we always will be. But so are you and I, Callie. You're my greatest heartbreak now, for I'll have to leave you to depart this earth and join Knox in heaven.

And now to Hepsy's dropped teacup. I know what you were trying to tell me. You saw something the night you fell—something you don't understand. But I do. So does Hepsy. Now I must plead with you to do something very hard. Don't ask her, Callie. It is grossly unfair of me to put this burden on you, but as your memory returns, you will be tempted to ask her to tell you more, and that could put her in some difficulty. I will find a way to tell you everything. Just trust me as you always have. I promise to be worthy of it.

Take care, precious one, and know that I'll love you forever.

> With all my heart,
> Emmy

Callie lay down on the bed, holding the letter against her chest, and let the tears come. *There's nothing foolish about crying for somebody you love.* That's what Solomon had once told her.

Most devastating of all was her sister's selfless devotion. Emmy, who believed she was dying, had nonetheless taken pains to sound cheerful and happy, to celebrate Callie's joy in the face of her own unfathomable loss. It was too much to bear. And yet somehow she must. Somehow she would.

THIRTY-EIGHT

Anguished over Emmy, Callie's family found at least a fleeting joy in watching Theo open his presents on Christmas morning—a Lionel train set, wooden blocks, picture books, his first pair of "real" work boots, a toy barn with mules and plows, and all the candy canes he could possibly eat.

Callie and Solomon were sitting together on the living room sofa after the noon meal, watching Theo make the train go around its track while Mary Alice rocked her baby by the fireplace. George was catching up with Sam and James, the three of them huddled together in the dining room.

Callie's mother came in and stood before the newlyweds. "It's time for you to go."

"Ma'am?" Callie said as she and Solomon looked at each other in confusion.

"You heard me," her mother said. "I am neither so old nor so selfish as to think a new husband and wife want to spend their entire first Christmas covered up with family. You deserve some time to yourselves."

"Miss Aurelia, you don't have to—" Solomon protested, but Callie's mother put up her hand to silence him.

"You are a kind and giving soul," she said, "but I'll not let you and Callie sacrifice your entire first Christmas together. The horses are already hitched to your buggy, and you'll find supper packed for you in the back seat. Now off you go to your own house."

❧

Callie and Solomon arrived home to find that James and his many workers had begun methodically clearing their farm, starting at the main road and working their way back. The fence line was completely clean and repaired, the driveway wide and clear. All the vines and overgrowth had been removed from around the house, uncovering trees and shrubs that had flowered every spring for decades until they were stifled. Now they would bloom again.

Solomon drove the buggy around the house, where he unhitched the team. Callie helped him bed down both horses before they went back to the house and noticed a wreath of cedar and holly on the front door, whose broken panes had been replaced.

"Mary Alice," Callie said. "That has to be her handiwork."

Solomon swept her up in his arms. "Our first Christmas. I should carry you over the threshold." He carried her into the entryway and kissed her as he set her down. "You have a very . . . *committed* family," he said, looking around.

Walking through the house, they could see that James and his crew had repaired everything while taking care not to change anything. James was thoughtful like that.

In the living room, Callie and Solomon found a small Christmas tree by the fireplace and a magnolia garland on the mantel. Callie went to the tree and gingerly touched the glass ornaments all hanging from red velvet ribbon. "It's beautiful, isn't it?" she said, turning to smile at Solomon.

He came to the hearth and lit the fire already laid there. They sat down together on a velvet settee—the only furniture in the room. It hadn't been there when they left for the sawmill.

Solomon ran his hand along the arm of the settee. "Think your mother's trying to tell us something?"

Callie smiled. "Yes. 'If you don't furnish this house, I will.' Does it drive you crazy?"

He smiled as he took her hand and kissed it. "Just her way of showing she cares. And reminding us who's still the boss."

Callie laughed and laid her head on his shoulder. "Merry Christmas, Solomon."

"Merry Christmas, Callie."

THIRTY-NINE

*S*olomon hitched up the horses, letting Callie enjoy the warmth of the house until the buggy was all set. "Ready to go?" he asked as he came back into the living room.

"Just about." She buttoned her heaviest coat and looked around the room. "We've spent so little time in our own house, Solomon. Part of me wishes we could just stay here until we have to go back to the mill."

He kissed her and put his arms around her. "Me too. But your mother needs some company, and we'll have lots more New Year's Days. Plus you've done nothing but cook all this time at the mill. Enjoy Hepsy's food while you can."

"You're just in it for the fried chicken," Callie said, smiling up at him. "And you're lucky Hepsy's always had a soft spot for George. He never liked the New Year's meal we're all supposed to eat, so she'd fry him some chicken to go with it."

They went outside and climbed into the buggy, where the new mares, Dolly and Honey, were snorting and bobbing their heads, urging the humans to hurry up and get on with it.

"What's the New Year's food we're supposed to eat?" Solomon asked.

"You know—black-eyed peas for good luck in the new year, greens for money, cornbread for . . . I forget what the cornbread means, but it wouldn't make sense to eat peas and greens without it. You never did that?"

"Nope," he said as they set off for the Bullock house in the cold morning air. "What kind of greens do you eat?"

"Some people eat turnip greens, but nobody in our house will touch them except Daddy, so Hepsy fixes collards with salt pork. I could eat a barrelful of them, especially with her fried chicken. Mama always tells her to cook plenty for her family too. When she's ready, George loads all of Hepsy's food and takes her home while the rest of us eat."

"What about George?"

"He has New Year's lunch with Hepsy's whole family."

"Are you serious?"

"He's done it since he was old enough to drive a buggy by himself. Listen to the way Hepsy says his name sometime. The rest of us are 'Miss' and 'Mr.'—Miss Callie, Mr. Solomon—but George is 'M' George.' We all know she means 'my,' not 'Mr.' Hepsy thinks of him as 'my George.'"

"I have so much to learn," Solomon said.

Callie kissed him on the cheek. "Me too. For example, how did you make the leap from 'Mr. and Mrs. Bullock' to 'Mr. Ira and Miss Aurelia'?"

Solomon frowned and rubbed the back of his neck. "I'm not sure. They were both so upset when I found you under the tree and brought you into the house—I think it just slipped out. Now it would seem odd to call them anything else."

"And they call you 'son.'"

"I noticed that."

"Do you mind?"

"No. I kind of like it."

They were nearing the Bullock house when Callie grabbed Solomon's arm. "Look!" She couldn't believe her eyes. Just

ahead, sweeping the front porch of Miss Eva Clark's old house—
the one Knox had arranged to rent before he died—was Lucinda.

"Who's that?" Solomon asked. "She looks familiar."

"Lucinda Montgomery. Ryder's widow. What's she doing at
Miss Eva's house?"

"Should we stop?" he asked her.

Before Callie could answer, Lucinda apparently heard the
buggy and looked up to see them about to pass the house. She
stared for a moment and then timidly put up her hand, perhaps
unsure whether a wave would be welcome.

Callie waved back. "We should stop."

Solomon guided the buggy into Lucinda's driveway.

"Happy New Year," Callie said.

"Happy New Year to you," Lucinda answered, still holding
the broom.

Solomon came around and helped Callie down from the
buggy. "This is my husband, Solomon Beckett," Callie said.
"We were married in November. Solomon, this is Lucinda
Montgomery."

"Pleased to meet you," Solomon said.

"Congratulations," Lucinda said. An awkward silence followed until she put down the broom and added, "Where are my
manners? Can you come up for a minute? I'm sure you must be
on your way to Miss Aurelia's for New Year's dinner."

"Yes, on both counts," Callie said. She and Solomon climbed
the porch steps, and Lucinda propped her broom against the
banister.

"Come in from the cold." She led them into a small parlor,
where a fire was crackling. "Can I get you something to drink?
I have some cider I can warm."

"No, thank you," Callie said as she and Solomon sat down.
"We can't stay long—you know Mama."

"Yes, I remember."

Callie couldn't stifle her curiosity. "Lucinda, why are you here at Miss Eva's house—if you don't mind my asking?"

"I don't mind." Lucinda looked around the parlor and smiled—a real smile, unlike the many artificial ones she'd had to force as Ryder's wife. "It's my house now."

"*What?*"

"Nobody's more surprised than I am," Lucinda said.

"When did you move here?" Callie asked.

"A couple of weeks ago. After Ryder was killed, his parents insisted that I stay with them. They said I owed it to them to take care of them when they get old. I disagreed."

"Well, hallelujah and good riddance."

Lucinda laughed out loud. "I don't remember the last time I heard myself laugh. It's good to know I can still do it after five years in that house."

"Is your mother helping you?" Callie asked.

Lucinda stared down at the empty ring finger on her left hand. "She could never admit her own terrible judgment, so she always blamed Ryder's bad behavior on me."

"Are you managing alright on your own? Do you need help?"

"I'm doing alright." She looked up at Callie. "One advantage to having a husband who liked to drink and cavort is that he never remembered how much money he left the house with. Once Ryder passed out, I'd take some of the money he was carrying and hide it away. And then when Knox died, he left me a small sum. The will said it was a gift from Emmy and him. How is she doing? I heard she was ill—the same as Knox?"

"That's right," Callie said. "Daddy took her to New Mexico. Solomon and George have reopened the sawmill to help pay for her care. She's improving, but . . ." She couldn't bring herself to finish.

"I'm sorry, Callie. I know how close the two of you are. I'll keep Emmy in my prayers."

They were quiet again before Lucinda said, "I'll answer the

question you're too polite to ask. The sheriff has no idea who shot Ryder and probably never will. My in-laws accused everybody they could think of—including me."

"They accused *you*? And then expected you to take care of them?"

Lucinda nodded. "Of course, they tried to find a way to blame Lily and your father's carpenter, but they couldn't locate them or get anybody to talk about them. I don't think any of the colored workers know anything or they would have told it by now, as much pressure as the sheriff put on them. And to tell you the truth, nobody seems to care who did it, except for the Montgomerys."

"Would you like to join us, Lucinda—at Mama's for New Year's dinner?" Callie asked.

"Thank you—truly—but it's a little too soon. I think I'd make everyone uncomfortable, myself included."

"I understand," Callie said. She laid her hand over Solomon's and smiled at him. "I guess we should be going?"

"You two look very happy," Lucinda said as she showed them to the front door.

Callie hugged her goodbye. "I hope this is a good year for you, Lucinda—and a happy one."

FORTY

allie celebrated her nineteenth birthday at the mill. Her mother sent one of the field hands to deliver Hepsy's caramel cake—Callie's favorite—and a pearl necklace with a mother-of-pearl cross hanging from it. The necklace was wrapped in a small box with a note.

To Callie—
So you will always remember—faith, hope, and love abide. Happy birthday, my precious daughter.

Mama

Unable to go shopping for Callie, Solomon and George had built her a rocking chair.

Now, two weeks into February, the crew had almost completed their contract with the railroad when a stranger rode up on horseback. Callie was washing the last of the breakfast dishes in a big washtub. As the rider approached her, she could see that he was young—probably Sam's age.

"Morning, ma'am," he said, tipping the hat of his Western Union uniform. "I have a telegram for Mr. George Bullock."

"He's over there." Callie pointed to the mill. "The sawyer with blond hair and a white shirt."

"Thank you, ma'am." The delivery boy tipped his hat again. Callie watched as he walked quickly to the mill and handed the telegram to George. Her brother reached into his pocket and handed a coin to the boy, who hurried back to his horse and rode away. Solomon stopped the log carriage as George stepped away from the machinery and read the telegram. He stared at the message much longer than it would have taken him to read it. Before Solomon could get to him, George dropped his hands to his sides, let the telegram fall to the ground, and walked away.

Callie ran to Solomon and picked up the telegram lying on the ground. "It's from Daddy," she said before reading it to Solomon.

> Am advising no more mill contracts. Emmy's health failing. Bringing her home. Let family know. I'm sorry, son.

Callie dropped the telegram. Instantly, all the life and energy drained from her body, and she thought she might collapse in a heap of nothingness on the ground. Her legs turned to water, and she couldn't seem to get enough air no matter how fast she breathed.

Solomon grabbed her and held her tight. She didn't cry. Her grief was far beyond tears.

FORTY-ONE

*A*s desperate as they were to comfort Emmy, Dr. Embry urged Callie's family to exercise caution. "Tuberculosis is no respecter of age, race, or anything else," he said. "It could strike Theo as easily as James, or any member of your family. Do not tempt it." He even suggested making Emmy comfortable in Lily's former cabin, but Callie's parents wouldn't hear of it.

"If my daughter is to meet her God, she will pass into the next life from her home in this one," her mother said.

Dr. Embry advised the family to focus on Emmy's contentment and ease at this point. The fresh-air baths practiced at the sanatorium—even in winter—would no longer improve Emmy's health and would only pose additional risks. She was to have whatever she wanted whenever she wanted, including morphine, which he showed Callie, her mother, and Hepsy how to administer.

When the doctor left, Aurelia asked Callie and Hepsy to join her in the kitchen. The three of them sat down at the table.

"I do not want Emeline to suffer, not for an instant," she said calmly, though Callie could see her hands trembling. "But at the same time, I do not want her mind so disturbed that she is unaware of where she is. She should know that we are here and that we will not leave her. I think morphine should be a last resort. Hepsy, would you ask Tirzah to send her elixir and anything else she recommends tomorrow?"

"Yes, Miss 'Relia." Hepsy's voice was barely audible.

"And Callie, you'll learn what to do—what Tirzah recommends—so you can help me?"

"Yes, Mama," Callie said.

Her mother laid her hands flat on the table and took a deep breath. "Alright then. We are prepared. We are ready."

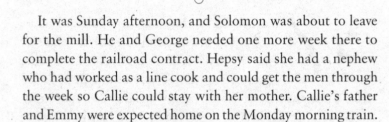

It was Sunday afternoon, and Solomon was about to leave for the mill. He and George needed one more week there to complete the railroad contract. Hepsy said she had a nephew who had worked as a line cook and could get the men through the week so Callie could stay with her mother. Callie's father and Emmy were expected home on the Monday morning train.

"You've got your warm jacket?" Callie asked as she helped Solomon gather his gear for the trip to the mill.

He tugged at his jacket. "Got it on."

"And plenty of blankets? You know it gets so cold at night. You'll need more than one."

"Got plenty."

"But what about—"

Solomon's kiss silenced her anxious questions. "I've got everything I need right here."

She tried to memorize the feel of his arms around her, something she knew she would need in the days ahead. And then he had to go.

FORTY-TWO

As the carriage approached, Callie stood on her parents' front porch with her mother, Hepsy, and Tirzah. The carriage top was raised to keep out the cold. Fate Barbour was driving. He guided the horses as close as he could to the front porch before climbing down to open the door. Callie heard her father say something to him before Fate put the top down on the carriage, took out his handkerchief to cover his nose and mouth, and then stepped a couple of yards away.

Callie's father, carrying Emmy in his arms, climbed down. Both of them were wearing the kind of mask Dr. Embry wore. Hepsy had made a basketful of them and placed them beside Emmy's bedroom door. Callie's father paused and nodded to her mother. The four women covered their faces before he would approach.

Callie's first sight of Emmy hit her with such force that she physically swayed, holding on to one of the columns for fear she might fall. A wave of nausea flooded over her. Emmy looked fragile enough to shatter. Her skin, once an exquisite ivory, was now so pale as to appear translucent, glowing even. Her golden hair hung limply around her shoulders. She wore a nightgown under her winter coat, which hung loosely over her emaciated frame. Callie's father, always a rock, kept his lips pressed tightly together, his eyes straight ahead.

Hepsy opened the front door for him as he carried Emmy to the bedroom she and Callie once shared. Callie's former bed and nightstand had been replaced by two rockers and an easy chair so family members would have a place to sit at a distance as they visited with Emmy or read to her. Hepsy had built a roaring fire in the fireplace.

Emmy wasn't alert. Her eyes were heavy, and she didn't seem aware of where she was.

"Ira, why is she like this?" Callie's mother asked as she sat down at Emmy's bedside and took her hand.

"It's the medicine, Aurelia," he answered, laying a hand on her shoulder. "Dr. McKinley wanted her calm for the trip home so she wouldn't have so many coughing spells. He had me give her a sedative every few hours or so. It'll wear off eventually."

"Tirzah, what do you think?" Callie's mother asked anxiously.

Tirzah walked to Emmy's bedside, bent over her, and looked into her eyes. "She has not yet flown. One foot here. One up yonder. She will not linger, Young Miss. Gird thyself."

⸎

With Solomon gone, Callie decided to stay upstairs at the Bullock house, in the cozy bedroom they had shared over Christmas. Emmy didn't completely shake off the effects of Dr. McKinley's sedatives until two days after her return home. Since then, Callie had stayed with her as much as their mother would allow.

It was Friday morning. Callie had just set Emmy's breakfast tray on a bedside table and helped her sit up, propping pillows against her back. "I hate these things." Callie tugged at the masks on her face as she sat down on the edge of the bed. Emmy couldn't breathe with a mask on, so anyone who entered her room wore two, one on top of the other. "I think I'll see if Hepsy can make me something with a little Irish lace on it."

Emmy spoke with labored breath, her voice soft and raspy, but she was smiling. "*Now* you're concerned with appearances?"

"I take your point." Callie set the tray over Emmy's lap. "Anything look good?"

"You do," Emmy said.

Her voice came and went so that Callie often had to read her lips. It reminded her of happier times when Emmy would sing, skipping words here and there. But Emmy could no longer choose when the words came and went.

"When I . . . was in New Mexico," Emmy said, "I thought I . . . might never see you again."

"Me too," Callie said. She would not insult her sister's intelligence by telling her everything would be fine. Emmy knew better. And she might need somebody, Callie believed, who would let her talk about it—honestly talk about it—which their parents were too heartbroken to do. "How about a biscuit with just a little butter and sugar?" she asked as she prepared one for Emmy.

Emmy took a bite and struggled to swallow. Callie held her teacup for her so she could take a sip. Emmy smiled. "I had forgotten . . . how much I love . . . Tirzah's brew."

"What about just a tiny bite of applesauce?" Callie raised a spoon to Emmy's lips. Her sister tasted it, but just barely.

"Tastes . . . like fall," Emmy said. "I can s-see . . . the apple trees and . . . smell the warm cider. Let's wait a bit . . . and see how that settles."

Callie set the tray aside and tried to take Emmy's hand, but she withdrew it.

"I've been watching . . . people die . . . for months," she said. "I won't . . . take chances with you." She strained to raise her arm and point to the chairs across the room.

"We'll compromise," Callie said. She pulled one of the rockers halfway to Emmy's bed. "If I promise to go douse myself in the Dip afterward, can I stay?"

Emmy tried to smile. "You're hardheaded." They laughed together, but then Emmy started coughing and quickly covered her face with one of the quilts on top of her bed until the heaving subsided.

Callie brought back her tea and held the cup as she sipped it. "Are you hurting, Em?"

Emmy shook her head and took another sip of tea before motioning for Callie to set it on her nightstand. "I can reach it there . . . so you won't have to . . . hop up and down . . . like the Easter bunny." She took a few shallow breaths. "I don't hurt much . . . just my chest from coughing . . . But it's hard to breathe. And . . ." Her voice trailed off as she stopped talking and tried to get her breath. "And I'm weak as water. What was it . . . Granny Carrie used to say . . . when she was sick? 'I don't mind . . . feeling this way . . . but I sure do hate to look like this.'"

Callie laughed at the memory of their paternal grandmother, who had been a stunner and proud of it until the day she died. "Want me to French-braid your hair?" she asked with a grin.

"As if . . . I didn't have . . . enough problems." Emmy's laughter again brought on the cough. She rested and sipped her tea. After a while she asked, "Are you happy, Callie? With Solomon?"

"Yes. I'm very happy with him. But you know I can't be truly happy when you aren't—any more than you were truly happy while I was enduring my pitiful suitors."

Emmy sighed and turned to look past Callie at the window behind her. "I've watched many a storm . . . out that window with you . . . against my better judgment." She looked at Callie. "Do you still need the storms?"

"No. I still love them. But I don't need them anymore."

Emmy closed her eyes and smiled. "That's good."

Callie thought she had fallen asleep, but then she opened her eyes again.

"A women's group visiting the sanatorium . . . gave me a book . . . called *When the End Is Nigh*."

"You have *got* to be joking," Callie said.

"No." Emmy was smiling.

"Well, I wish I could find those old hens and punch them right in their pompadours! Of all the morbid nonsense!"

Emmy grinned at her. "It had . . . a lily on the cover." She pretended to hold a bouquet in her hands, resting it on her torso to mimic a body lying in a casket. Then she turned and winked at Callie. They laughed so hard that Emmy almost never stopped coughing.

Callie brought her a little of Tirzah's elixir to soothe her chest and throat. Then she picked up a clean spoon, poured it full of elixir, and popped it into her own mouth. "I think that might be moonshine," she said, making Emmy giggle the way she did when they were girls.

When they were quiet again, Callie sat down at the foot of her sister's bed. "I don't want so much distance between us, Em. Not now."

Emmy again struggled for breath. "Listen, Callie, before I . . . that is . . . while I can still talk . . . I have answers for you."

Callie moved forward and tried to take Emmy's hands, but once again, her sister pulled them away. "Don't take chances, Callie."

Callie reluctantly moved back to the foot of the bed. "I don't care about my memory anymore, Emmy. If I remember, fine. If I don't, fine."

"No, you need . . . to know the truth. And you will . . . That's my promise . . . Now promise me something."

"Of course."

"Remember . . . my blue and tan? The hat you wore last May?"

"I remember."

"Good." Emmy smiled. "I want you . . . to wear it to my service."

Callie covered her face with her hands. "Please don't make me talk about that."

"We don't have to talk about it. Just promise . . . you'll wear that hat. Mama will make you drape it in black . . . but that's alright." Emmy stopped talking and took a few breaths. Callie lowered her hands to look at her sister. "It will make me happy," Emmy said, "to look down from heaven and know . . . underneath your black veil . . . is a lovely summer hat. Will you . . . will you do that . . . for me?"

Callie couldn't find her voice but nodded.

"Good. I feel better now. I have one more . . . one more favor to ask. Will you stay with me . . . till I fall asleep?"

"Just try to get rid of me," Callie said. She tucked Emmy's covers around her and fluffed her pillow, then sat down in the rocker and watched as her sister fell asleep, occasional coughs disturbing but not waking her.

Callie couldn't say how much time had passed before Emmy opened her eyes. A peace seemed to fall over her, like a dove lighting in the Lookout Tree, and her coughing ceased.

For a few minutes, Emmy lay very still. Then she smiled at the ceiling the way she used to smile at Knox. And she began to carry on a conversation with someone, though Callie couldn't see or hear them. "How I've missed you . . . Of course . . . Right now? . . . I am so happy to hear it!"

With a wistful smile on her face, Callie's sister closed her eyes for the last time. Emmy had taken flight.

❦

Burial was swift for those who succumbed to tuberculosis. Emmy died in the morning, and by noon the undertaker had already come and gone. Callie's sister would be buried immediately at the church cemetery, but her funeral would not be held until Solomon and George could come home.

In the meantime, Dr. Embry recommended that the family

destroy any of Emmy's things that she might've worn or used after she became sick and clean the house from top to bottom. Before they began, Callie went to retrieve the blue and tan hat she had promised to wear to Emmy's service. She knew her sister hadn't worn it since the previous summer, and she didn't want to let anything happen to it.

She found the familiar pink box right where she knew it would be, neatly stacked with Emmy's finer hats in the bottom of her armoire. The lesser ones filled her hat tree in a corner of their bedroom.

Callie set the box on the floor and lifted the lid, just to make sure the hat was in there. She ran her finger around the blue silk ribbon and thought of a sunny day in May when her sister's life was filled with promise. "Shouldn't you two kiss or something?" Callie had teased Emmy and Knox. Now they were both gone.

Every memory was like a raw nerve, stabbing Callie with a unique pain all its own. But she would have to bear those pains. Memories were all she had left.

FORTY-THREE

Callie and Solomon dressed for Emmy's funeral in their upstairs room at her parents' house. She wore a black dress. He had borrowed a dark suit from George. All she had left to do was drape Emmy's hat in a black veil, then pin it to her hair and put on her gloves. But she hesitated. The hat and gloves were all that stood between Callie and a final goodbye. It was a ridiculous notion, but part of her wanted to believe that, as long as she didn't put them on, the funeral couldn't happen and she wouldn't have to say an excruciating farewell to Emmy. She stood staring at the pink hatbox on the bed as Solomon struggled with his tie in front of the mirror.

"Anything I can do to make it easier?" he asked her.

Callie silently went to the mirror and took care of his tie. She let her hands rest on the lapels of his suit coat. Looking up at Solomon, she tried to smile, but her face wouldn't have it. She felt hot tears begin to flow down her cheeks as his arms closed around her and held her tight. Through the window, she heard the sound of horse hooves and carriage wheels. The family was getting ready to leave.

Solomon drew a handkerchief out of his breast pocket and blotted her face. She took a deep breath and slowly let it out. Then she kissed her husband on the cheek and went to the hatbox.

"Solomon!" she cried as she took off the lid and removed the hat. "Come and look!"

He stood behind her, looking over her shoulder. In the bottom of the box was an envelope that said simply, "To Callie." It had been hidden beneath the hat.

"What should I do?" she asked.

He slipped his arms around her waist and pressed his cheek against hers. "You should do your best to get through your sister's funeral. And then when it's all over—when all the neighbors have paid their respects and gone home, when all the to-doing is done and it's finally quiet—you should read her letter. Every single word."

He watched in the mirror as Callie draped Emmy's blue-and-tan in a black veil and pinned it on. She put on black kid gloves. And then Solomon took her by the hand and led her out of their room.

She saw George just beyond the French doors leading to the upper porch. He was standing there in his suit, gripping the banister rail.

Solomon and Callie went to him. Callie took her brother's arm. Solomon laid a hand on his shoulder. Together, the three of them walked down the stairs and prepared to do the unthinkable.

❦

The Bullock family began their solemn journey to the church, one carriage closely following another. Callie could see, lining the roadway, everybody who had ever worked for her parents standing with their families. All the women—and many of the men—were weeping.

Callie's mother had wanted Tirzah and Hepsy to attend the funeral and sit with the family, but Tirzah said no. "That's not the way o' things, Young Miss," she insisted.

Like a little gentleman, Theo had come to Solomon and

asked if he might ride in the buggy next to Callie. Solomon invited his little brother-in-law to help drive the team, which thrilled the youngest Bullock. Now Theo was holding the reins, with Solomon coaching him, the horses keeping a slow but steady pace to the church.

It was a sunny February morning. The forsythia was blooming. Emmy would have liked that—bright flowers to light her path, fountains of yellow beneath the blue.

The church was full when the Bullocks arrived and proceeded down the aisle together. Callie had always thought this practice strange and intrusive—parading a family's grief before the whole community—and was grateful for the black veil that covered Emmy's spring hat and hid her sorrow from all the stares.

The funeral service was lovely. At least, that was what everyone said. It was a blur to Callie. All she remembered was the strength of Solomon's hand as she held fast to it.

At the cemetery, Tirzah and Hepsy joined the outer ring of colored mourners encircling all the white people gathered at Emmy's gravesite. The pastor read her favorite Scripture from Romans: "For I am persuaded, that neither death, nor life, nor angels, nor principalities, nor powers, nor things present, nor things to come, nor height, nor depth, nor any other creature, shall be able to separate us from the love of God, which is in Christ Jesus our Lord."

And then it was over. Just like that. Emmy was gone. As appalled as Callie had once been by the chattering Rosemont hotel guests at the Sacred Harp singing, she was even more bewildered by the cordial conversation that bubbled up all around her after the final "Amen."

Is that your youngest? Why, he's almost grown . . . When did y'all get here? Are you staying at your mother's? . . . So good to see you. Why is it we only get together when a loved one passes? . . . That's our spray right there. I told the florist absolutely no carnations . . .

As the crowd slowly dispersed, Callie and Solomon made their way back to their buggy, where he helped her up. She looked over her shoulder and saw George striding toward a woman standing some distance from the gravesite, her face covered by a veil. George took her hands. He was still holding them when Solomon and Callie drove away.

Emmy would be smiling down from heaven. She had reunited George and Lucinda.

FORTY-FOUR

*D*eath creates a special kind of exhaustion for the living. Callie, like her mother and Hepsy, dealt with an overflow of visitors as neighbors and church members filled their house after the service, paying their respects and continuing to bring food, even though the dining table and buffet were already covered.

Callie had always found it odd that, at a time when people felt the least equipped to be social, a family funeral forced them to entertain everyone they knew. "They mean well," her mother kept reminding her as the house filled, growing louder and louder by the minute and making Callie wish like everything that she was sitting in the Lookout Tree, high above it all. She would have to settle for a brief escape to the upstairs porch.

Callie took the back stairs from the kitchen, which offered more privacy. She was about to reach for the French doors leading onto the porch when she saw George and Lucinda, her black veil gone. They were standing very close. Lucinda reached up and ran her fingers lightly across his lips. They kissed in a passionate embrace. It was beautiful. But it was also heart-wrenching for Callie to see just how much George, with his handsome face and tender heart, had been hurting and longing for Lucinda.

She backed away from the door and left them in peace.

∞

It was early evening before the last guest departed, leaving the women of the house to deal with all the food and dishes. They finished so late that Hepsy stayed in Lily's cabin rather than make the trip home. Solomon and Callie also stayed, so worn out that they abandoned plans to sleep in their own bed and instead went upstairs to what had become their room at the Bullock house.

Marriage had diminished Callie's lifelong struggle with sleep. But tonight, even with the comfort and security of Solomon lying next to her, she couldn't subdue the thoughts spinning through her mind: Emmy holding her hand on Callie's first day of school. The two of them struggling to stifle giggles in their room as they stayed awake well into the night, talking about the teenage boys they met at their first house dances. The way Emmy and Knox looked at each other. The soothing sound of Emmy's voice whenever she listened to Callie's troubles and assured her everything would be alright.

In the wee hours of the morning, Callie grew weary of fighting the urge to toss and turn. She slipped out of bed, trying not to wake Solomon, and tiptoed downstairs, Emmy's letter in hand. In the study, she built a fire and pulled a rocking chair and small table with a lamp up to the hearth. Lighting the lamp, she set the envelope on the table beside it, then quietly went to the kitchen to brew a cup of Tirzah's tea. Her whole body ached from the tension of the day, and her eyes felt scratchy and irritated, like she hadn't slept in a week.

When she returned to the study, the house remained dark and quiet except for the glow of the lamp and the crackling fire. She took a soothing sip of the tea before setting her cup and saucer on the table and opening the envelope.

February 17

Dear Callie,
There is no easy way to say this.

"Can't sleep?"

Callie turned to see Solomon standing at the door of the study. "I didn't mean to wake you," she said as he came in and sat down on the hearth.

"You didn't. I felt lonely all of a sudden and realized you weren't there. I thought Theo might've convinced you to leave me."

"Well, he did try," Callie said with a smile.

Solomon took a fire iron and punched the logs, sending sparks up the chimney and making the warm flames leap higher. "I was pretty sure you were reading Emmy's letter. And I just wanted to make sure you were alright. Want me to leave you alone?"

Callie came and sat next to him on the hearth, the letter in one hand, her teacup in the other. "Now that you're here, I think I need you to be with me for this if you're willing."

"Always."

"I'll share my tea if you'll read it to me," she said.

Solomon took a sip as she handed him the letter. Then he began reading aloud.

February 17

Dear Callie,
There is no easy way to say this. I fear the memory you cannot retrieve is a secret I thought I had managed to keep from you. Somehow you must've discovered it. Please believe my intent was always to shield you, never to deceive you. I'm going to make it right with a little help from Hepsy.

She'll put this letter in a safe place until it's time for you to read it.

Solomon frowned, running his hand through his hair. "Emmy knew what happened to you?"

"Not exactly," Callie said. "She's been figuring it out from the letters I wrote to her."

Solomon continued.

Two things have come to light. First, Hepsy brought me a message from Tirzah: "Baby Girl's shoe got river mud on it." And then it wasn't long after that when I received your letter about Ura Prospect and Hepsy's dropped teacup. If your shoe was by the river, then you must've followed me there. And if you found it underneath James's pine tree, then you saw what I did. What you need to know, if you are to heal, is why I did it.

The night you followed me to the river, Fisher had made a very dangerous decision. He got word that Ryder intended to pass himself off as Knox and come after Lily. Fisher decided to start watching the Montgomery house at night—with a loaded shotgun. Early in the evening, he saw Ryder come out of the house wearing the same light blue suit he had seen Knox wear to visit Lily. Ryder stopped on the front porch and combed his hair smooth like Knox. But he climbed onto his own horse, which Fisher recognized. It's the only Thoroughbred around here.

After Ryder mounted his horse, Fisher ran to hide by the river road, intending to shoot. But someone beat him to it. Fisher heard gunshots and saw Ryder fall off his horse. It startled him so badly that he dropped his own shotgun, and it went off. He heard horse hooves coming toward him, so he ran into the woods. A man's voice he didn't recognize called out, "Get back here—I see you!" But Fisher kept running and hid.

Solomon paused. "Heavenly days, Callie. Fisher's life wouldn't be worth two cents if he got blamed for this."

"No, it wouldn't," she said.

Fisher and Lily were already talking about moving to a freedmen's community in Houston, and Lemuel had given Fisher the name of a colored riverboat pilot who might help them get there. Lily had plenty of money, thanks to the railroad settlement. They just needed a way to get downriver to meet the pilot. Hepsy's cousin had a boat and was willing to take them, but he was too terrified to come ashore once they told him what happened. They would have to swim out to his boat in the middle of the river.

"Lily couldn't swim," Callie said. "Fisher probably could, but Lily couldn't. I'm sorry I keep interrupting—go ahead."

We didn't know who shot Ryder—or if they meant to kill Knox instead. We also didn't know if the voice that called out to Fisher belonged to someone who really did see him and recognize him. So we had to get him out of here. Hepsy didn't want to involve the family any more than she had to, but she knew how well I could swim and asked me to help. She said Fisher "wasn't home in the water." He could probably get himself across but might not be able to get Lily and Josie to the boat too.

Everything was so frantic. I didn't even notice that you weren't in your bed when I slipped into our room and threw on my swim dress and coat. Hepsy told us to wrap Josie in a blanket and put her in one of Tirzah's baskets, along with the railroad money. She wanted everyone to think Lily and Fisher just decided to leave on their own, but Lily's hands were shaking too much to write a goodbye note. So Hepsy asked me to write it.

Callie rubbed her forehead. "Lily was scared, but Emmy was too. That's why the note looked so chaotic."

"Does your head hurt?" Solomon asked, concern on his face.

Callie squeezed his hand. "I'm alright. Let's keep reading."

Fisher navigated us to the Dip, thank goodness—I'm not sure I could've remembered how you did it, as anxious as I was. From there, we just followed the river south to James's pine. Hepsy had told her cousin to meet us there because it's the tallest tree on the riverbank, and she knew he would be able to spot it in the dark, especially since there was a decent enough moon out. He signaled us with a lantern from the water, and I signaled back from the bank.

"The flash of light you remembered," Solomon said.

Fisher went first. Then I swam across with Lily. You can't imagine how cold the river was, Callie. Once Lily was on board, I came back to the bank for Josie's basket and the railroad money. When I finally returned to the bank for a second time, I was so exhausted—and freezing—that all I could do was fall to my knees and cry. Then I put on my coat, walked home, and slipped back into the house—back into our room.

Callie, I think you must've been sleeping on the porch when all the commotion woke you up, and you followed me to the riverbank. I don't know how much you saw. Or why you didn't let me know you were there. But if you saw me go into the river with Josie and come back empty-handed, I can only imagine what you must've thought. Then again, I trust you to trust me. And I imagine it's that very trust that has been the source of your confusion—you remembered what you saw but couldn't believe I would do such a thing. And you were right—both times, sweet Callie.

*Please forgive me for causing you pain. Forgive me for
leaving you. And never forget that I'll love you forever.*

> *Your devoted sister,
> always—
> Emmy*

Callie and Solomon sat silently together, listening to the fire
crackle. The grandfather clock in the study struck five.

At last, Callie said, "I remember why I didn't show myself
that night. It was something I heard Emmy tell Hepsy when I
was on the upper porch and they were scrambling down below.
She said, 'I wish Callie were the best swimmer because she's
the brave one.'"

"She was right," Solomon said.

"I was afraid she'd get lost in the woods." Callie laughed
softly. "Emmy always had the *worst* sense of direction. I knew
Fisher could get them *to* the Dip. I just wasn't sure Emmy could
get back by herself. I wanted to be there if she got into trouble, but I wanted Emmy to feel brave that night. I thought she
needed to. And I believed seeing Lily free herself from Ryder
would somehow free Emmy from him too. So I hid in the reeds
on the bank."

"Why would Emmy need freeing from Ryder?"

Callie stared into her teacup before looking up at Solomon.
"Because he hurt her. He hurt her in a way she never got over."
She told Solomon something she had never revealed even to her
own family—Emmy's secret.

Solomon put his arms around her. They were quiet together,
listening to the fire crackle. After a while, he said, "Everything
you've been through—your fall, your struggles to remember—
that all happened because you wanted to give your sister courage and protect her at the same time." He kissed the top of
Callie's head. "Did you follow her home?"

She thought about it. "Yes. After I saw her come out of the water without Josie and then fall down and cry, I couldn't imagine what had just happened. Emmy finally got up and started walking home. I let her get far enough ahead so she wouldn't see me, but then I got worried that I had waited too long and she might get lost. My foot slipped in the mud as I was scrambling up the bank, and I was so worried about losing Emmy that I just left it there. I must've fallen and hit my head under the Lookout Tree."

He ran his hand lightly across her forehead where the bandage had been. "What do you want to do now, Callie?"

She was silent for a moment, listening to the fire pop and hiss, before she said, "I want to go home."

FORTY-FIVE

George and Lucinda married in the spring, in a quiet family ceremony at the Bullock house. He rented space for the Birmingham market until a permanent location could be built.

Solomon and Callie had their first successful summer crop of tomatoes and a fall harvest of apples and pecans. He had given up on continually repairing the old woodstove and bought Callie a brand-new one for her kitchen. And her mother had just about furnished their entire house, sending wagonload after wagonload—everything from beds and chifforobes to a dining table and chairs to a gun cabinet and a grandfather clock—all with notes in her finely scripted handwriting:

Just a small gift on the occasion of your marriage.

Love,
Mama and Daddy

Now it was two weeks before Thanksgiving, and Lemuel was pulling into the driveway with yet another delivery from her mother. Callie grabbed a shawl and called out, "Solomon, Lemuel's here! Mama's at it again."

On the front porch, she saw that her mother, Hepsy, and Tirzah had followed Lemuel in a buggy.

Solomon helped the women down and kissed his mother-in-law on the cheek. "What have you done this time?" he asked her with a grin.

"Hush up and don't spoil it for me," she said.

Callie couldn't believe her good fortune. Her mother not only liked Solomon but adored him. And he felt the same way about her. As different as they were, it made no sense, but Callie was grateful for it. She greeted Hepsy and Tirzah as Solomon shook hands with Lemuel and helped him unload a mahogany cradle.

Callie gasped when she saw it. "Oh, Mama!"

"It's beautiful, Miss Aurelia," Solomon said as he and Lemuel set the cradle on the porch.

Callie ran her hand over the fine carving on what soon would be her baby's bed. "I thought I'd be using one of the old ones from the attic."

Her mother linked arms with her. "You and Solomon deserve a fresh start."

The men carried the cradle to the bedroom while the women went into the kitchen and gathered around the table. Callie brewed them a pot of Tirzah's tea. "One day, Tirzah," she said as she returned to the kitchen table, "I'm going to talk you or Hepsy into teaching me how to blend your tea."

Tirzah closed her eyes and held up her hand. "The time is not come for you to learn. I will say when." Then she opened her eyes and motioned for Callie to come closer. "Let me see to you."

Callie sat down in a chair next to Tirzah and did as the midwife directed. Tirzah moved her hands all around Callie's belly, then pressed her ear against it and listened. She looked into Callie's eyes, held her hand against Callie's forehead to gauge her temperature, and wrapped her hands around Callie's ankles to see if they were more swollen than the last time.

"Three weeks from today," Tirzah said, turning away from Callie to sip her tea.

"Three more?" Callie was disappointed. "But I'm so *big*."

Tirzah put a dollop of honey in her tea and stirred it, then took a long sip. "The bed for you now. No more work till you deliver."

Callie groaned. "You want me to stay in *bed*, Tirzah? But I have so much to do to get ready . . ."

Tirzah took another sip of her tea. "Must be bed for you."

Callie's mother was staring down at her teacup. Her smile had left her.

Looking at her, Callie began anxiously running her hand back and forth across her stomach. "There's something wrong, isn't there, Tirzah?"

In a rare hint of affection, Tirzah laid her hand over Callie's. "No call for fear. All is well. Bed keep it so."

Callie's mother moved her chair so that she sat very close to her daughter. She put her arms around Callie, who rested her head on her mother's shoulder. "If Tirzah says there's no cause for alarm, then you can be assured there isn't. And if she says you must go to bed, then you must go. We will help you. And in the end, you and Solomon will have a healthy child to love. Your very first."

Callie raised up and looked at her mother, who gave her an encouraging smile. Then she turned to Tirzah and took her hand. "Thank you."

Tirzah shuddered and pulled her hand away. Apparently, all this emotional to-doing offended her sensibilities.

Callie laughed. "I'll be forever grateful, Tirzah, whether you like it or not."

There was a knock at the back door. Hepsy answered it and showed in Mary Alice and Lucinda.

"Y'all come on in," Callie said, "and have some tea with us."

Everybody settled in around the table as Hepsy poured more tea. Callie knew Lucinda had never laid eyes on Tirzah before and was relatively certain she had never sat at the kitchen table with any of the colored help, at her parents' house or the Montgomerys'. Lucinda kept looking from Tirzah to Hepsy to Callie's mother, trying to piece the scene together.

"Lucinda," Callie's mother said, "this is Tirzah, Hepsy's mother. Tirzah has saved more than one life in our family. And I know I don't have to tell you what Hepsy means to us—George most especially."

"I'm—pleased to—to meet you," Lucinda stammered.

Tirzah stared at Lucinda, her eyes narrowing. Slowly, she raised her arm and pointed at Lucinda. "You have felt the sickness this very mornin'. Not first time either."

Lucinda looked around the table at the other women. Her mouth opened to offer an answer, but she couldn't seem to find one.

"Yo' food won't stay?" Tirzah asked.

Lucinda stared at Tirzah and silently shook her head.

"How long have you felt unwell, Lucinda?" Mary Alice asked her.

"At least two weeks," Lucinda said, her lower lip trembling. "I can't keep anything down till late afternoon. And I'm weak and tired all the time." With tears in her eyes, she looked at Mary Alice. "I'm so afraid I've got something awful."

Mary Alice put her arm around Lucinda and gave her a napkin to dry her eyes. Lucinda collected herself, taking a sip of the tea her sister-in-law handed her.

"Wipe yo' weepin' eyes," Tirzah said. "You not facin' death. You carryin' life. You carryin' hope."

The teacup made a loud clank as Lucinda almost dropped it into the saucer. Her eyes wide, she could only stare at Tirzah until she finally spoke, almost in a whisper. "The doctor—the one they sent me to—he said I couldn't. That's what Ryder told me he said."

Tirzah raised her arm above her head like a preacher offering up the benediction. "Lies been chainin' you, George-Miss," she said to Lucinda. "New baby gonna break them chains. Almighty bring truth. Almighty let you see. Shout hallelujah to kingdom come. Almighty set you free."

Epilogue

May 1927

"Why can't we take the car, Mama?"

"Because, Emmy, Mr. Ford did not consider a family this size when he built his automobiles," Callie said to her sixteen-year-old daughter. "Also, your grandmother despises them. You and Janey need to start herding your brothers to the carriage." She sighed as Solomon came into the kitchen. "Where on earth did all these children come from?"

He raised an eyebrow and grinned at her. "Well, Callie . . ."

"Stop!" she said, laughing with him.

He put his arms around her and kissed her.

"Sometimes I forget how many we have until we're all together," she said, looking up at him. "I remember it started with twin girls, and then there was a blur of boys. How are we going to raise six?"

He frowned, pretending to think it over. "I guess we should probably feed them every now and then. You teach them to ride. I'll teach them to fish. After that, they're on their own."

Callie laughed again and kissed him on the cheek.

"Is everybody in the carriage?" he asked.

"I have no idea. I put Emmy and Janey in charge. Let's go count heads."

She heard a knock on the kitchen door. Solomon opened it and then froze. Callie heard Hepsy say, "Don't worry, Mr. Solomon, this ain't no ghost."

Callie joined him at the door and saw Hepsy standing there with Lily. But it couldn't be Lily. This girl was a teenager, and Lily would be in her thirties by now, just like Callie.

"This is Josephine," Hepsy said. "Baby Josie."

Callie's hands flew to her mouth. "*Josie?*"

The girl smiled and nodded.

"You look *exactly* like your beautiful mama," Callie said. "I mean *exactly*."

"Thank you," Josie said.

"Callie, don't you think . . ." Solomon nodded to the door they were blocking.

She slapped her forehead. "Oh, good gracious, I've lost my mind and my manners! Y'all come on in."

"We're not gon' stay," Hepsy said. "I know y'all headed to Decoration Day like ev'body else. I just wanted you to see Josie while she's here—and I wanted to give you our news."

"Can I get you some coffee?" Solomon asked.

"Naw, we got to go. Josie's here visitin' with her mama and daddy—with Lily and Fisher."

"They're here?" Callie exclaimed. "After all this time?"

"Just for a little while, then they goin' back to Texas," Hepsy said. "This is the first time they been to Alabama since—you know—since they left."

"What brought them back?" Callie asked.

"You ain't gon' believe this, but the sheriff."

"The new one?" Solomon asked.

"That's right," Hepsy said. "He come to see me last week. Said he got a letter from the wife o' that factory owner—the one Mr. Knox won his big case over right 'fore he passed. The factory man's dead now and his wife's real sick. Said she wanted to die with a clear conscience. So she wrote the sheriff a letter and told him it was her husband that shot Mr. Knox. Sent him the gun and evah-thang. She didn't even know her husband shot the wrong man—well, the wrong man far as he was concerned. Your mama let me use her telephone and helped me call Lily to tell her."

"So now she and Fisher can come home?" Callie asked.

Hepsy sighed. "Alabama wasn't never home to Lily. Her and Fisher was always meant to leave. Just ended up goin' quicker than they planned on. They happy in Texas. But it makes me glad to know they can visit now without any trouble." She smiled and put her arm around her great-granddaughter. "And I can see my Josie again."

"I'm happy for you, Hepsy." Callie hugged her. "And I'm so glad to see you again, Josie."

"I'm very pleased to meet you, ma'am," Josie said. She turned to Solomon. "You too, sir."

"Well, we best go," Hepsy said. "And y'all need to get on out to that carriage. Looked to me like two o' your boys was tryin' to turn the horses a-loose."

❦

At the cemetery, Solomon and Martin, the oldest of the Beckett boys, unloaded picks and hoes that were tied to the back of the carriage. "Come on, fellas," Solomon said to his sons. "The ladies get the flowers, and we get the weeds."

Callie and her twin daughters joined her parents and Mary Alice at the spacious family plot outlined with a black iron fence. Besides the imposing headstone made for Ira and Aurelia Bullock, four others dotted the freshly mown grass. Three small white ones, each topped with a lamb, honored the babies Callie's parents had lost, while a tall obelisk underneath a cedar tree marked Emmy's grave. Until Callie had children of her own, she couldn't begin to imagine the pain those stones represented for her parents.

"Is my sister still working you to death?" George clapped Solomon on the back as he and Lucinda arrived with their family.

Solomon tossed him a hoe. "This is for you, my friend." The two of them, along with James, worked to clear weeds, vines, and wild violets from the fence line, with Solomon and Callie's boys helping as much as they could. When it was time to clean the graves themselves, they put down their hoes and cleared them by hand.

Callie was holding Lucinda's newborn, her first boy after three girls. "He's so handsome," she said to her sister-in-law. "But prepare yourself. Boys are different. They want to take everything apart and put it back together again. My house is covered up with pieces of things that used to work."

Lucinda laughed and tickled her son under his chin. "Let's hope he starts with my washing machine. It's worn out. Sam and Theo couldn't come?"

"No," Callie said. "Theo has exams at API—says he's going to bring modern science to the family farm. Sam and his boat, according to his latest letter, are somewhere in the Florida Keys."

Callie looked around the cemetery at all the families coming together to tend their gravesites and place flowers on the headstones. Their chatter was loud—joyful almost. But she knew what was about to happen. As the graves were cleared, the distraction of labor finished, the cemetery would grow ever quieter until a solemn silence fell.

Solomon and George put away the tools and called their children together. Callie handed George his son. She, Lucinda, and Mary Alice carried wreaths of roses inside the fence and passed them one by one to Callie's parents. When they came to Emmy's, Callie handed the wreath to her mother, who lightly ran her hand over the inscription on Emmy's tombstone. Callie knew it by heart.

Dear, you are not dead to us,
but an affectionate one unseen.

Callie's children, normally so rambunctious, were instinctively still and silent, sensing a loss they couldn't yet understand. Only when they were all back in the carriage, bound for a family dinner at the Bullock house, did normalcy return and one of Callie's twins began to sing.

"Hm-hm-hm-hm-hm of the earth,
La-ti-da-ti of the skies.
For the love which hm-hm-hm,
La-ti-da around us lies."

Janey giggled. "Emmy! Learn the words, for heaven's sake!"

"Janey! I can sing without words, for heaven's sake!" Emmy said, laughing. "Mama says Aunt Emmy used to skip words all the time. I'm carrying on a family tradition."

"You'll never be a famous chanteuse if you don't learn the words," Janey teased.

"I don't want to be a famous singer anymore. I want to train horses like Mama."

"You should probably learn to saddle one first," Janey said, making her brothers laugh.

"That's what boys are for!" Emmy shot back, and more laughter erupted from the carriage.

Callie looked at Solomon and smiled. Their children were happy. The sun was shining. The sky was brilliant blue. Callie couldn't help wondering if Emmy had petitioned God above to grant them, on this day of remembrance, the extraordinary solace that was His alone to give—the beauty of the earth and the glory of the skies.

Author Note

More than any other book I've written, *Letters from My Sister* was inspired by my own family. Most especially, it's inspired by my maternal grandmother, Icie Wyatt McCranie, and her only sister, Effie Jane Wyatt, for whom my mother is named. The protagonist, Callie Bullock, is named for Callie Mitchell, a teacher and artist who knew her way around livestock. (We weren't related by blood, but she let me call her "Aunt Callie" anyway.)

My grandmother—we called her "Grandme" because an older cousin tried for "Grandma" and misfired—lived for almost a century. Near the end of her life, my mother asked her if she had any regrets, and she said, "I wish I'd been more like Effie."

I never knew my great-aunt. She died before I was born. But by all accounts, she was very feminine and refined, a schoolteacher and faithful churchgoer. My grandmother, on the other hand, thought most women were boring! She much preferred talking with local farmers about their crops and the cotton prices. Though a devout Christian, she had a spotty attendance record at our local Baptist church and would defend her absences thusly: "I am *not* a Baptist. I am a member of the Christian church."

This book is not the story of Grandme and Aunt Effie. It's a work of fiction. But the relationships they had with each other and the rest of their family—as well as their closeness to a Black woman named Bama McCoy, who ran the family home—lie at the heart of the book.

Bama not only helped deliver many (if not most) of my grandmother's eight children but also taught her all the skills she would need to run a household. My grandmother's respect wasn't easily won, but she revered Bama.

While the bonds between two Southern families—one White, one Black—at the turn of the twentieth century might seem unusual, I know that they were possible. And I believe our innate humanity, a gift from God, will always have the power to overcome hatred and injustice.

As a writer and a human being, I don't think we should ever settle for what's likely. We should always reach for—and celebrate—what's possible.

ACKNOWLEDGMENTS

As always, I owe a great debt to my husband, Dave, for his love and support and to my parents, who are always there with words of encouragement, assuring me that my editors "don't need to change a word." If only I had their confidence!

Love and gratitude to my extended family, church family, and dear friends for all their encouragement, support, and prayer.

Thank you, Leslie Stoker, my agent and good friend, for your wisdom and unfailing support. I value your many contributions to my work more than I can say.

From the start, Kelsey Bowen has championed my writing and guided each manuscript from the seed of an idea to a story I can be proud of. Thank you, Kelsey.

I'm blessed with another terrific and insightful editor in Jessica English, who has saved me from myself too many times to count. I so appreciate you, Jessica!

Thank you, thank you to every writer's safety net, the proofreaders. I so appreciate you, Christy Distler and Carrie Krause.

To Laura Klynstra and her creative team—thank you for a gorgeous cover that captures the spirit of my book so beautifully and will make my heart skip a beat every time I see it in bookstores.

To Michele Misiak, Karen Steele, Brianne Dekker, and the marketing and publicity teams at Revell—my unending gratitude for your tireless and creative efforts on my behalf. I value your support and your friendship so very much.

I'd like to say a special thanks to those who kindly reviewed advance copies of *Letters from My Sister*: the Honorable Theoangelo Perkins, mayor of my hometown, Harpersville, Alabama; and two fine novelists willing to share their valuable time, Patricia Bradley and Sarah Sundin.

Many thanks also to Chris Jager of Baker Book House for all her encouragement and support.

Some of the details from *Letters from My Sister* wouldn't have been possible without the help of my cousin (and family historian) Jimmy Wyatt. Thank you so much, Jimmy, for your generosity with images, news clippings, and other research materials. Thanks also to Dan Lavender for sharing information about Clairmont Springs, Alabama, which inspired the resort in my story.

To my dear friend, photographer Mark Sandlin, thank you so much for the gift of your author portraits, your sense of humor, and your kindness.

As always, my heartfelt thanks to Sid Evans, Krissy Tiglias, Caroline Rogers, Nellah McGough, and the *Southern Living* staff for your continued support.

Finally, I want to thank all the readers, booksellers, and media who have supported my writing, as well as the book club and writers' club members who have invited me to join them in person or on video. I'm honored to share my stories with you.

Turn the page for a preview of
another immersive historical novel from
VALERIE FRASER LUESSE!

Prologue

1947

Raphe Broussard was just a boy when he first saw it—glimpsed it, at least. Mostly hidden in the saw grass and canes, it had temporarily left the tip of its long alabaster tail exposed in the sunlight—a rare mistake. The streak of white offered only a hint of what lay hidden, the promise of what might be revealed. Raphe had watched silently, reverently almost, as the tail thrashed back and forth just once before disappearing into the green, leaving him to wonder if he had truly seen it at all. He told no one.

Over the years, Raphe would return to that secluded spot whenever his mind was troubled, as it was now. He had a choice to make, and it was weighing on him that day as he paddled deep into the bayou, gliding across remote but familiar waters where the pines and cypress trees towered above. They cast this solitary pool in perpetual shade as if a veil had been tossed over the sun, not blocking its hot rays entirely but reducing them to a warm softness. The water was glassy, carpeted around the edges with water hyacinth and duckweed. Floating here on still waters, in a pirogue carved out of a cypress tree by his grandfather, Raphe could quiet his mind and think. He could come to a decision about a thing.

Should he give up his freedom and become a father to his orphaned nephew, or listen to that preacher? Most of the evangelicals who had come into the Atchafalaya Basin seemed well-meaning enough, but there was a particularly strident one, Brother Lester, who had somehow gotten wind of Raphe's plight and urged him to give Remy, his blood kin, to a "good Christian family"—strangers. The child needed a mother and father, the preacher said. A single young man like Raphe— Cajun, Catholic, and therefore prone to drink—would surely be a bad influence.

Raphe imagined himself as a young father with no wife, limiting his own possibilities while praying he didn't make some horrible mistake that ruined his nephew's life. And then he pictured a choice he found completely unbearable—trying to live with the expression on Remy's face, the one that would haunt Raphe forever if he let strangers take the boy away.

That heartbreaking image—of a child realizing he had been abandoned by the one person he trusted most—was burning Raphe's brain when the alligator appeared. It came out of the cattails at the water's edge and silently glided in. What a sight! The alligator had to be twelve feet long and pure white except for a single swirl of pigment trailing down its back like curled ribbon. It passed so fearlessly close to Raphe that he could see the piercing sparkle of its blue eyes. On the far bank, it climbed onto a fallen tree in dappled light, taking in as much sun as its pale skin could tolerate.

Raphe had never put much stock in the swamp legends that the old-timers recounted again and again around campfires. He loved the tales about the white alligator, but they were just entertainment, nothing more. Still, he was comforted by the notion that this enigmatic denizen of the bayou was keeping watch while he wrestled with Remy's fate and his own conscience.

As he sat silently in his pirogue, the massive white head slowly turned, almost in his direction but not quite. In the filtered light, Raphe could see one side of the alligator's face, one of those sapphire eyes. Only a few seconds passed before it turned back, gliding slowly across the tree and silently disappearing into the canes.

Fishermen and hunters along the river called the alligator *L'esprit Blanc*, French for what the Indians had named it—"The White Spirit." It was strange—all of them knew about L'esprit Blanc, repeating stories they had heard for years, but all those who claimed to have actually seen it were taken by the storm. All except Raphe. While his neighbors speculated about the high price such a rare hide would fetch—if it truly existed— Raphe found it impossible to believe that anyone who laid eyes on something so extraordinary could bring himself to kill it. Still, he kept his sightings to himself.

Raphe looked up at a darkening sky. Rain was coming. He sat in his boat, listening to the wind stir the trees overhead and watching ripples begin to roll across the mirrored surface of the water. His choice was clear.

He would never tell a soul where to hunt the white alligator. And he would never send Remy away. Some things belonged right where they were.

ONE

FALL 1949

Ellie Fields sat in a bustling marina café in Bay St. Louis, Mississippi, watching a train make its crossing and wondering what it would be like to ride two rails suspended in air, the water below, the sky above.

"That be all for you, hon?"

Ellie smiled up at the waitress standing next to her table, holding a pot of coffee. She was wearing a pink uniform with a white apron and a name tag shaped like a dolphin. Her hair was strawberry blond, teased and pinned into a French twist in the back. She looked about forty.

"That's all, thanks," Ellie said. "Hey, I like your name. I don't think I've ever met a woman named Geri before."

The waitress rolled her eyes. "It's short for Gertrude! Can you believe my mama hung that on me? It was her grandmother's name."

"You're definitely more of a Geri. I'm Ellie—short for Juliet. My little brother couldn't pronounce the *j* or the *l*, so he renamed me. I was 'Eh-we' till he got the hang of the *l*."

Geri put her hand on her hip. "It's not fair that your family gets to label you for life, is it?"

"No, it's not."

"I'll be right back with your ticket, hon," Geri said, pointing another customer to a booth on her way back to the counter.

Ellie looked out the window next to her table. The engine of the train had long since passed the trestle over the bay, while the caboose was still some distance away—one had yet to see what was already a memory for the other, yet they were part of the same machine.

She reached into her purse and pulled out a letter she had folded and unfolded, read and reread countless times since it arrived in her parents' mailbox in March. She spread it out on the table in front of her. Something about the letter gave her courage, which she needed right now. One more read couldn't hurt.

March 1, 1949

Dear Miss Fields,

We have never met, but I am the town physician in Bernadette, Louisiana, where it is my understanding that you have been offered a teaching position. While I have little influence with the school board, I do have one friend remaining among its members. He was struck by your application and thought I might be as well, so he forwarded a copy to my office. I was especially drawn to the way you answered, "Why do you want this position?" I believe I heard great sincerity in your answer: "I want to serve where I am most needed and to use whatever gifts God has given me to make the world a better place, especially for children."

Miss Fields, you will find no children in greater need of a gifted teacher than those in Bernadette, nor will you ever find another place where your efforts will be more appreciated. Should you decide to accept the position and join our little community, my wife and I will offer you our wholehearted support and will be happy to provide housing, free of charge. It might not be luxurious, but it will be safe and comfortable.

Sincerely,
Arthur Talbert, MD

"Here ya go, hon," Geri said as she laid a ticket on the table, drawing Ellie's attention away from the letter and back to the journey at hand.

"Could you tell me how far I am from New Orleans, Geri?"

"Gonna do a little partyin'?" Geri gave her a smile and a wink.

Ellie pictured herself embracing with abandon the revelry on Bourbon Street and shook her head. "I'm afraid a Birmingham ballroom on New Year's Eve is about as wild as I get. I just took a teaching job in a little town called Bernadette, Louisiana. It's supposed to be about eighty miles or so from New Orleans. Thought I'd stop over and see the city on my way."

"Well, congrats on the new job, hon! You're not too far. Just keep followin' 90 and you'll be there in about an hour. Some people call Bay St. Louis 'Little New Orleans' on accounta we get so many summer people from over there. You from here in Mississippi?"

"No, I'm from a tiny little town you never heard of—Maribelle, Alabama."

"And here I thought you was headed to the backwoods, but Bernadette might be a step up for you." Geri laughed and winked at her again.

Ellie remembered how a couple of Atlanta girls who lived down the hall at her college dorm always gave her grief about coming from a town that "didn't even get a dot" on the state map. "If Bernadette has more than one traffic light," she told Geri, "it'll be a step up, alright."

"Ain't nothin' wrong with that," the waitress assured her. "No shame in bein' a small-town girl. But now, you watch yourself on the road—'specially in New Orleans. All them one-ways in the Quarter's just murder to figure out your first time around. And you're gonna wind your way through some bayou country before you get there. I know we're supposed to be all modern and everything now that the war's over and done with, but there's some deserted drivin' between here and there. Make sure you fill up before you leave, okay?"

"I will—thanks, Geri."

The waitress stared down at Ellie and shook her head. "You got a face like an angel, you know that? You any kin to that woman in *Casablanca*?"

"No." Ellie smiled. "But thank you."

"You need to get you one of them hats that dips down over your eye like she wore. I bet that'd look real good on you."

"Maybe I'll find one in the French Quarter."

"You be *careful* in the Quarter, you hear?"

"I will," Ellie said, holding up her right hand. "Word of honor. Thanks for looking out for me."

Geri gave her another wink and a wave before hurrying to grab a water pitcher from the counter and greet a new customer. Ellie left a tip and then paid her check at the register.

She filled up at a local Pan-Am and got back on the highway, relieved to know she would make it to New Orleans in plenty of time to find her hotel before dark. Even though she had only a week to get settled before school started, Ellie had decided to allow herself one night in the fabled city, which she had never seen.

She had spent her first night on the road with her mother's sister in Ocean Springs, a pretty little town with cottagey storefronts and shady streets sheltered from the coastal sun by the craggy, arched branches of live oak trees. Her parents had insisted that she make a stop there and let her uncle give the old Ford a good going-over before she went on to Louisiana. She had bought the used 1939 Deluxe, which she named Mabel, with the salary from her first year of teaching. The old girl had been rolling for ten years now and was showing her age, but she still had some miles left in her. Ellie's aunt insisted on introducing her to just about everybody in town before she left, so she and Mabel had gotten a late start.

Her whole family thought she was crazy for accepting a teaching job in rural Louisiana when there were, as her mother put it, "perfectly good schools from Mobile to Muscle Shoals and enough bachelor vets in Alabama to marry every girl in ten states." But Ellie could no longer bear the burden of invisibility. That's how she felt—as if her truest self were invisible to everyone around her and had been for so long that it was now banging on her chest from the inside out, demanding to be seen and heard. If she could just go through the motions, everything would be so much easier, but that would be a lie of a life. And what Ellie yearned for—what she had come to demand for herself—was authenticity.

She had shown, more to herself than anyone else, that she was willing to walk away from anything, including marriage, if it demanded that she be satisfied with anything less than what she was meant for—whatever that might be. And now she felt it would be unkind to continue dating war vets who had been so homesick overseas that they never wanted to leave Alabama again. When they looked at her on a dance floor or took her hand in a movie theater, she couldn't shake the feeling that they were picturing her hanging diapers on the line or sliding a pan of biscuits into the oven before she poured their morning coffee and kissed them off to work. Even the one she had believed to be different turned out not to be.

All those soldiers had seen horrible things, Ellie knew, and she was ashamed to admit, even to herself, that she was jealous of them. They had left as boys and come home as men. They had *done* something. Ellie had gone from high school to college and back home again. Was that it—her circle complete, her story told?

Her mother insisted that Ellie just needed a little change of scenery and would "come home lickety-split" as soon as she got the wanderlust out of her system. But Ellie knew that wasn't true. What she longed for was not change but transformation. Just like the tall stands of pine trees and oaks that dissolved into water and sky as she crossed the Pearl River into Louisiana, Ellie hoped her old self would dissipate, releasing something new and interesting, something with purpose.

The highway sounded different as she drove onto the bridge that would carry her across Lake Pontchartrain and into New Orleans. Though Highway 90 spanned a narrow channel between marshlands, she could look to the northwest and see the vast, unknowable waters that stretched far beyond the tenuous safety of the bridge. Mabel's tires bumped along as they made it across, only to thread more water, with Pontchartrain on one side of the highway and Lake Saint Catherine on the other.

Ellie found herself surrounded by simple wooden houses on stilts—most with some kind of boat on a trailer parked in the yard—separated by the occasional bait-and-tackle shop or small grocery store. The landscape was flat and stark, the sky a brilliant sunny blue. Now and again, Ellie would glimpse a woman watering her flower beds or a man loading fishing rods into his boat.

As Mabel carried them through a string of small towns, they passed lakes and crossed bayous, sometimes on bridges so rickety that Ellie held her breath from one side to the other. She imagined Mabel doing the same. Though she had seen the bayous around Mobile and Biloxi, Louisiana was a different kettle of fish. Bayous here were boundless and dense, lit with shades of green—from deep ivy to bright chartreuse—as algae, lily pads, and water hyacinth spread over them. They were dotted with ancient cypress trees, their Spanish moss hanging like the lace-gloved fingers of a Louisiana debutante, reaching down to stir ripples on the water.

Ellie began to encounter more traffic and bigger houses as she drew nearer to New Orleans, guiding the old Ford along a now busy Highway 90 until she made it into the city and caught her first glimpse of the road sign she had been waiting for: Vieux Carré—the French Quarter. She followed Esplanade to Royal Street and almost wrecked Mabel as she marveled at the plaster walls in shades of yellow, burnt orange, red, and forest green, with weathered old shutters hanging just enough askew to show they'd lived a life. Scrolled black wrought iron framed upper balconies where hanging baskets bursting with ferns, begonias, and periwinkle spilled sweet potato vine all the way down to the sidewalk. Mysterious garden gates, tucked into alleyways, conjured notions of romantic assignations in the hidden court-yards that lay beyond. Ellie wondered what the gas streetlamps would look like once they began to flicker in the darkness. New Orleans was everything she had imagined and then some.

Careful to dodge bicycles, taxicabs, and street vendors, she slowly made her way to a hotel she had heard about from a fellow schoolteacher who moved to rural Alabama from Bir-mingham. Adele had grown up in New Orleans and gave Ellie a well-marked street map, circling all the things she "absolutely *must* see." Ellie had memorized every street name, landmark, and critical turn as best she could but still kept the map spread out on the seat next to her, stealing a glance whenever she came to a stop sign or traffic light.

At last she spotted it—the Hotel Monteleone—and sighed with relief. After parking Mabel, she made her way to the main entrance, a blue overnight case in hand, and tried not to look like a hayseed as she took in the palatial lobby with its grand pillars and gorgeous chandeliers. The Monteleone looked like something out of a movie, and Ellie imagined herself not in the cotton dress she wore but decked out in a sequined evening gown, an air of mystery about her. The thought of it made her giggle out loud—Ellie Fields gussied up like Ingrid Bergman.

"Now that's what we like to see at the Monteleone—a happy

guest," said a voice behind her. She turned to see a smiling bellman in a crisp gray jacket and black pants. He tipped his hat to her.

"Between you and me, I'm not a guest yet," Ellie confessed. "I'm hoping they'll rent a room to an Alabama girl who has no idea what she's doing."

The bellman raised his eyebrows. "First time in New Orleans?"

"First time ever," Ellie said.

"Aw, you're in for a *treat!*" the bellman said. "My name's Theodore. I've lived here all my life. You have any trouble, you send for me." He gestured toward a long, ornate front desk. "It would be my pleasure to escort you to reception."

"Thank you so much." Ellie fell into step with him. "I'm Ellie—Ellie Fields."

"I'm honored to meet you, Miss Fields." Theodore led Ellie to the front desk and introduced her to a hotel clerk, who looked to be about her father's age. Then he took the overnight case from her. "This'll be waitin' for you in your room."

"Thank you again." Ellie was about to turn back to the clerk when she remembered Adele's instructions: *Don't forget to tip in New Orleans!* "Oh, wait, Theodore!" She caught up with him, slipped a quarter into his palm, and whispered, "Did I do that right?"

Theodore gave her a slight bow. "Perfect. And I thank you, Miss Fields."

Ellie hurried back to the front desk and checked in, then caught the elevator to her floor and wandered several long corridors until she found her room. There, on a luggage stand just inside the door, was her overnight case as Theodore promised. She kicked off her shoes, removed her hat and gloves, and carried her friend's map over to the tall windows, where she set about getting her bearings.

The Monteleone faced Royal Street. With an upper-level room on the front of the hotel, Ellie could look across the block and see what had to be Bourbon Street, already lit up like a carnival even in the afternoon sun. She had heard tales of its debauchery but also of its music, which she intended to hear. With any luck, the serious sin wouldn't start until later in the evening. She could hear some jazz and retreat to the safety of the Monteleone before then.

The hotel bathroom was the fanciest Ellie had ever seen, all white tile and marble, with a gilded mirror, plush towels, and hand soaps that smelled like gardenias. She stared at her reflection in the mirror. Geri said she had a face like an angel, but Ellie couldn't see it. Her maternal grandmother, Mama Jean, would often say to her with great pride, "Your name might be Fields, but *you* are a Galloway!" Then she would trace Ellie's cheekbones with her fingertip. "You did not get those doe eyes and these fine Scottish features from *their* side!" she would proclaim.

Ellie splashed a little cool water on her face and patted it dry with a fluffy hand towel. She ran a brush through her hair, which she had always considered an indecisive brown. It looked like it couldn't make up its mind whether to be dark or light, so it had settled on deep brown streaked with a lighter shade here and there. Once, she had driven to the salon at Loveman's in Birmingham to get it colored, but the stylist flatly refused, saying, "Do you have any idea how much women in this city would pay to get what you're asking me to cover up?" Ellie had reluctantly agreed to a shoulder-length cut, which the stylist promised would still be long enough for her comfort yet short enough to ensure that she didn't look juvenile. It had a natural wave to it, so at least it was easy to curl. That was something, she guessed.

Her overnight case had room for only one outfit, and she would need that tomorrow. New Orleans would have to take her as she came—wearing a deep-rose cotton dress with a full skirt, cap sleeves, and a sweetheart neckline. She would wear her wide-brimmed hat to keep the sun off her face but forgo the formality of gloves. On this, her first trip to New Orleans, Ellie would embrace the storied city bare-handed.

Valerie Fraser Luesse is the bestselling author of *Missing Isaac*, *Almost Home*, *The Key to Everything*, and *Under the Bayou Moon*. She is an award-winning magazine writer best known for her feature stories and essays in *Southern Living*, where she recently retired as senior travel editor. Specializing in stories about unique pockets of Southern culture, Luesse received the 2009 Writer of the Year award from the Southeast Tourism Society for her editorial section on Hurricane Katrina recovery in Mississippi and Louisiana. A graduate of Auburn University and Baylor University, she lives in Birmingham, Alabama, with her husband, Dave.

"A **heartwarming** story of the power of relationships
and how the most inopportune circumstances can yield
unexpectedly **rewarding** results."

—*Publishers Weekly*

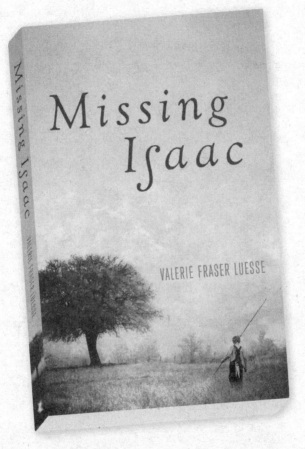

When a Black field hand disappears, a wealthy
white boy he has befriended sets out to find him.
But Pete McLean discovers more than he bargained
for—including unexpected love and difficult truths
about race and class in 1960s Alabama.

Revell
a division of Baker Publishing Group
www.RevellBooks.com

"Luesse, an award-winning writer and editor for *Southern Living*, demonstrates her **love** for Alabama in this inspirational romance. . . . Luesse's uplifting tale will **delight** fans."

—*Publishers Weekly*

As America enters World War II, a melting pot of the displaced and disenfranchised enters Dolly Chandler's boardinghouse in Blackberry Springs, Alabama. When tragedy strikes, the only hope of salvation lies with the circle of women under Dolly's roof and their ability to discover what happened to a young bride who lived there a hundred years before.

Revell
a division of Baker Publishing Group
www.RevellBooks.com

Available wherever books and ebooks are sold.

"Valerie Fraser Luesse once again directs a symphony of characters, charming readers with her storytelling expertise and captivating dialogue."

—*BookPage*

Through poignant prose and characters so real you'll be sure you know them, Valerie Fraser Luesse transports you to the storied Atlantic coast for a unique coming-of-age story you won't soon forget.

ℛ Revell
a division of Baker Publishing Group
www.RevellBooks.com

Meet Valerie

FOLLOW ALONG AT

ValerieFraserLuesse.com

and sign up for Valerie's newsletter to stay up to date on
news, upcoming releases, and more!